SUMMER
AT THE
OLD BOATHOUSE

(HOPE COVE BOOK 3)

HANNAH ELLIS

To Anth
with love

Prologue

It was Valentine's Day. Josie should have been getting ready to go out for a meal with Sam. Instead she'd made the mistake of flopping onto the couch when she got home from work and couldn't muster any motivation to move. Sam would be home any minute, reminding her he'd made dinner reservations and telling her to hurry up. Maybe she could persuade him to stay in and get a takeaway. It had been a busy week, and she'd be more than happy to spend the evening curled up with Sam in their cosy little house.

A blanket lay draped across the back of the couch, and she pulled it over herself. That was a bad idea. Her eyelids were already heavy. She told herself she'd have two minutes to relax and then get in the shower.

Her phone vibrated in her pocket moments after she'd nodded off. It was probably Sam saying he was on his way home. Discarding the blanket, she fumbled for the phone. It wasn't Sam after all.

Emily's name was on the screen. For a moment, Josie considered ignoring it. Except she'd ignored her best friend's previous three calls too. Or was it four? She was always too busy to chat.

"I'm sorry," she said quickly when she answered. "Sam's taking me out for dinner and I'm in a rush to get ready. Can I call you back tomorrow?"

"No." Josie was surprised by Emily's voice.

Something was wrong. "I'm not doing this any more."
A lump automatically formed in Josie's throat when
she heard that Emily was crying. "I understand that
you're angry, but I don't think I deserve it and I'm
sick of waiting for you to be my friend again."

"What?" Josie sat up quickly. Things had been
strained between her and Emily in the six months
since she'd moved to Devon, but she had no idea
Emily was so upset by it. "I've just been busy with the
kennels and my classes, I barely have time for anyone
…"

"Well, you don't have to worry about making
time for *me* any more. I'll save you the trouble of
making excuses for why I can't visit you or why you
don't want to meet up."

"They weren't excuses—"

"They were! It's all excuses. You're selfish and
stubborn and I'm sick of being the one who tries to fix
our friendship when you're clearly not interested."

"Of course I'm interested. You're my best
friend."

"Best friends don't treat each other the way
you've treated me. I might have done some stupid
things, but I apologised. I never wanted to hurt you.
But I think you want to hurt me."

"Please, just calm down and we can talk about it
properly …"

"I can't calm down," Emily shouted. "I hurt Jack.
I did it on purpose and he'll probably never speak to
me again. But you don't even care."

Josie felt the colour drain from her face. Why
wouldn't Jack speak to Emily? It didn't make sense.
"I don't understand …"

"You and Jack were my best friends." Emily choked through a sob. "And I lost you both."

"That's not true," Josie said, desperately trying to keep up with the conversation. "Of course we're still friends."

"No." The sadness in Emily's voice turned to anger. "We're not. I won't call you again. I don't want anything to do with you."

The line went dead and Josie sat staring at the phone. She'd been so close to Emily and Jack when she was living in Oxford. They might have had their issues, but they'd always be friends. Wouldn't they? Her heart raced as she scrolled to Jack's number. Jack was her ex-boyfriend as well as her friend. She'd barely spoken to him since she moved to Devon. Only once, in fact, and that hadn't been a particularly friendly conversation. They were still friends, though. She was sure of it.

As the ring tone echoed in her ear, she knew he wasn't going to answer. Her chest tightened as she imagined him looking at his phone and choosing not to answer, just as Josie had done to Emily so many times in the past months.

"I thought you'd be all dressed up and ready to go." Sam's tone was light and cheery. She hadn't even heard the door, but he was suddenly in front of her. "Are you okay?"

She held out her phone as though it held all the answers. "Emily just called."

Sam shot her a quizzical look as he sat beside her. "Who's Emily?"

That's when the tears came. Deep down, Josie knew Emily was right: they weren't friends any more.

For a long time she'd blamed Emily, but truthfully it was just as much her fault.

It was Josie who'd ruined everything.

Chapter 1

Two years earlier…

Being envious of Josie was nothing new for Emily. This felt different, though. Josie was at the first day of her first acting job. It was an important milestone. The first step on the path to Josie becoming a successful actress. The dream which she'd talked so much about was suddenly within reach. Emily was happy for her best friend, of course. But she couldn't help but reflect on her own dreams.

It had been two months since she'd got up the courage to send off her manuscript to literary agents and publishing houses. She'd actually written a novel. That was the first step on the path to *her* dreams. Step two was the querying process: approaching publishers and agents. It felt like that might also be the final step. Maybe she wasn't good enough. She hadn't heard back from anyone. She'd been expecting a rejection letter or two at least. The silence was killing her. She knew she needed to be patient, but it was so hard when she'd put so much into her first novel.

Now Josie was off following her dreams, and Emily was daydreaming behind the counter at the gift shop at Oxford Castle and Prison. It was actually quite a nice job; it just wasn't her dream. She wanted to be writing, not working in a shop. At least it gave her time to daydream about her next book. The characters came alive in her head, and at the end of the day she'd go straight home to her laptop and get as much down as possible.

"Sorry." She smiled as she looked up. How long had the middle-aged couple been grinning and waving their hands in front of her?

"You were miles away," the man said.

"I was. I'm sorry." She took the notebook from the woman and turned it over to check the price. It was more reflexive than anything since she knew the price of everything in the shop.

"Did you do the tour?" she asked.

"Yes." The woman beamed. "It was fascinating. And the tour guide was great. Really charismatic. He obviously loves his job."

That would be Bernie. Everyone loved him. "I'm glad you liked it." Emily pressed buttons on the till and took the money. "Enjoy the rest of your day," she said as they left.

Her mobile was tucked away under the counter and she glanced at it discreetly. There was a message from Josie, which she opened and skimmed over. Then she sat heavily on the stool behind her.

Great. Not only was Josie having an amazing time on the TV set, but apparently she'd met a gorgeous guy who was taking her on a date after they'd finished filming for the day. That was bloody typical of Josie.

***

Emily had a constant stream of messages from Josie over the course of the week, gushing about how amazing the job was and how wonderful the new guy was. It was Saturday when they caught up properly. Emily arrived at Josie's apartment late in the afternoon.

"I think I'm in love," Josie said dreamily.

Emily dropped onto the couch in the cosy living room. "With the job or the guy?"

"Both!" She sat cross-legged in the oversized armchair and scraped her glossy brown hair into a ponytail. "But I actually meant the guy. He's so amazing."

"I can't believe you started a new job and met a guy on the first day."

"I know! I can't believe it either. I have the best luck."

She could say that again. "So he's an actor?"

"He's an extra, like me. He's playing a soldier, and he's so hot in his uniform." Josie's words came fast, and her eyes danced with excitement. "I have to wear these awful shoes with crazy high heels. I was trying to get used to walking in them on Monday, and I tripped." She put a hand to her forehead and fake swooned. "He reached out and caught me. It was like something from a film. He saved me!"

They both laughed.

"Saved you from the mild embarrassment of falling over in a room full of strangers?"

"Exactly! Then we got chatting. He's so funny. He's constantly cracking jokes. And he lives near here so we've been travelling in to work together. I've been out with him every evening this week." Her eyes sparkled mischievously. "I stayed at his place the last two nights."

"So you got the job of your dreams and the man of your dreams all at once?"

"I think so! He's perfect. And the job is great. It doesn't even feel like being at work."

"What do you have to do? Do you have to talk at all?"

"Not yet. But my agent, Michaela, said they're thinking of developing the character. So I might get my own storyline later. At the moment I stand in the background, polishing glasses and pouring drinks. And I'm surrounded by guys dressed as soldiers. Talk about a dream job."

"Really?" Emily asked seriously. "Even though you're only in the background? You don't think you'll get bored of it?" She didn't want to dull Josie's enthusiasm, but she struggled to see what was so great about it. And Josie did have a short attention span. She got tired of things quickly.

Fortunately, Josie didn't take offence. "There's something about being on set," she said dreamily. "It's such a buzz. I can't explain it. It's all so exciting. I've never had a job that I enjoyed so much." She raised her eyebrows. "And you know I've had a lot of jobs."

"I'm glad it's going well," Emily said. "But I guess if your new man lives in Oxford, you won't be so keen to move to London?" That had been their dream: to share an apartment in London while they built up their careers. As soon as Josie got the part in the soap opera, she'd started talking more seriously about it.

"Oh, I didn't even think about that. Maybe he'll move too. Commuting to London is a nightmare."

Emily smiled. "I know that. Remember when you got me the job at the magazine and I complained for three months about all the travelling?"

"I remember. And now I understand."

"I suppose it's much more bearable if you've got a hot guy to keep you company."

"Definitely. It would be terrible if I was on my own every day."

"So what does he do?" Emily tried to choose her words carefully. *Does he have a proper job?* might be an offensive question seeing as acting was Josie's chosen career path. "I mean, what was he doing before this? Does he do the acting full-time?"

"No," Josie said. "This is his first acting job. He was working in a phone shop in Oxford before."

"And he decided he'd like to do some acting instead? That's an odd career change."

"I don't actually know how he got into acting." A smile broke over Josie's face. "All I know is he's amazing."

"I can't believe how quickly you fall in love," Emily said. Actually, this was nothing – she'd known Josie fall in love across a crowded room, only to fall out of love again when she didn't like his shoes. "What else do you know about him?"

Josie looked thoughtful. "He plays football. And hangs out with the lads in his team a lot. They go drinking every week in the Fox and Greyhound. How many times have we been in there? I bet we've been in there at the same time loads of times."

Emily inwardly sighed. She'd been wanting to

hear something a bit more meaningful, but as far as Josie was concerned, which pub a guy drinks in was important information.

"I can't wait for you to meet him," Josie said.

Emily shot her a quizzical look. "What's his name again?"

"Jack." Josie exhaled a dramatic sigh. "His name's Jack. You're going to love him."

Chapter 2

Josie insisted Emily come out for a pub lunch with her and Jack that Sunday. There had been a suggestion that Jack could invite a friend along too, but Emily insisted that if she was being set up with someone she wouldn't come. As it was, she agreed to have one drink with them and then leave them to have lunch alone. Playing third wheel to Josie's new relationship wasn't overly appealing. Knowing Josie, it would be a tactile relationship, and public displays of affection made Emily uncomfortable.

The pub sat beside the River Cherwell in the northern part of the city. It wasn't one of their regular haunts; Emily had never been there or even known it existed, so she assumed it was Jack's choice. The building was very pretty with ivy creeping up the white walls around the entrance.

She arrived a little later than arranged. Walking into bars and restaurants on her own always made her nervous, and she wanted to make sure she didn't end up waiting alone.

As soon as she walked in she spotted Josie, sitting by the window at the far side of the light and airy pub. She was leaning into Jack with her elbows on the table. They were chatting animatedly until Josie reached for his hand and kissed it. Emily's lip curled up automatically. That cemented her decision to only stay for one drink.

She caught Jack's eye before Josie saw her. He smiled up at her while gently elbowing Josie. Jumping up, Josie wrapped her in a hug. "This is Jack," she said when she stepped back.

"I'm Emily." She extended her hand when he stood.

He took her hand but leaned in and kissed her cheek as well. "I've heard all about you."

"Don't worry." Josie aimed a wink in her direction. "I only told him the good bits!"

"I hear you're a writer," he said as they sat.

The blush crept up her neck and landed on her cheeks. "Not published or anything." She glared at Josie. Why had she told him that?

"Not yet," Josie said. "But you will be." She turned to Jack. "We have this plan – Emily is going to be a famous author and I'll be a famous actress. We're halfway there now that I've got an acting job."

"Oh, you're famous, are you?" Amusement made Jack's eyes sparkle. "Sorry. I didn't realise."

"Well, I'm acting!" Josie said, indignantly.

"You call that acting? It looked more like polishing glasses to me, and I don't think you were even doing that very well."

She slapped his arm playfully. "I'm a very convincing barmaid."

"I was only teasing," he said lightly. "I'm sure you'll both end up very successful, and one day I'll tell everyone about the day I had lunch with you both." He smiled warmly at Emily. "I'll go to the bar. What do you want to drink?"

"I can get my own," she said.

He shook his head and glanced at Josie's almost empty wine glass. "Same again?"

Josie nodded and Emily asked for the same.

"What do you think?" Josie whispered as he walked away from them.

"He seems nice." It shouldn't really have been a surprise, but he wasn't quite what Emily was expecting. He was good-looking, of course, with his smooth brown hair and sparkly eyes. And he seemed funny, just like Josie had said.

For some reason, she'd expected him to be a bit aloof. Maybe it was the acting thing. She expected people in that business to be a bit above themselves. But he wasn't at all. He seemed warm, and genuine and entirely down-to-earth. So far he'd made a good impression.

"He's great," Josie said. "Wait until you get to know him better. He's so lovely. You should have come out with us last night. He's got some really fit friends."

"I didn't feel like it. I thought you'd be off with Jack all night and I'd be left alone." She wasn't overly keen on nights out with Josie at the best of times. Drinking copious amounts of alcohol, talking to strangers and dancing the night away wasn't Emily's idea of fun.

"Of course I wouldn't leave you alone," Josie said adamantly. Apparently she'd forgotten all the nights where she'd done exactly that.

"I had some work to do anyway." All Emily's spare time was spent working on her next book. "It's good that you met his friends."

Josie's eyes strayed to Jack, and then quickly whipped away again when he turned to come back over.

"Quick, change the subject so he doesn't know we were talking about him."

"What else would we talk about when he goes to the bar?"

"I don't know," Josie said with a cheeky smile. "Literature, current affairs … something that makes us seem intelligent."

"We are intelligent!"

"Say something clever then," she hissed.

Too late. They were silent and stifling smiles when Jack arrived with the drinks.

"What do you write about?" he asked.

"Don't ask her that," Josie said. "She can write a whole book, but if you ask her what it's about she gets this look as though her head might explode."

Emily felt herself blush. It was true.

"Sorry," Jack said. "I guess I'll have to wait until it's in the shops and read it for myself."

Emily forced a smile. "You might be waiting a while."

"But the book's finished and you're trying to get it published?"

"She also doesn't like to talk about that," Josie said, frowning comically. "She's still waiting to hear back from agents and publishers."

"Sorry," Jack said. "It's interesting, though. I think it's amazing that you wrote a book."

"Thanks." Emily glanced nervously out of the window. The slow-moving river was wide, and a weathered-looking boat was moored on the far riverbank. The trees were dark and foreboding, with crows dotted on the bare branches. Spring was fast approaching, and in a few weeks the view would no doubt be wholly different, but even the eerie winter scene was breath-taking. A pair of ducks flew from the bank, making a splash as they broke the water surface. "The view is amazing."

Jack grinned at her. "Smooth subject change." He glanced at Josie. "You could've warned me not to talk about the book."

"It's fine," Emily said. "It's sweet of you to ask. I'm just a bit ..." She sought for the right word. How was it she could write a whole book but struggled to speak a full sentence?

"She's a bit shy about it," Josie said. "That's all."

Jack's smile was reassuring. His gaze followed Emily's to the window. "It really is a great view. I love this place. Great food, great view, what more could you want?" He reached for the menus propped in the centre of the table. "Speaking of food, I'm starving. Shall we order?"

"I'm not going to eat," Emily said. "I only called in for a quick drink, then I'll leave you to it. You order, though."

"You should stay for lunch." Jack handed her a menu. "This place does the second-best shepherd's pie in Oxford."

"Where's the best?" she asked.

His eyes twinkled. "My mum's."

Automatically, Emily scanned the menu. She'd anticipated wanting to run away almost as soon as she arrived, but she was surprisingly relaxed. "The chicken pie's hard to resist ..."

After a few moments of listening to Josie deliberate between most items on the menu, Jack went to the bar to give the order.

"I really wasn't going to stay for lunch," Emily said. "I'm not in the way, am I?"

"Of course not. I invited you for lunch. I knew you'd get on with Jack. He's very easy-going."

He arrived back a few minutes later and directed his attention to Emily. "If you like this view, my uncle has a café by the river near Folly Bridge: The Old Boathouse. It's stunning in the summer."

"I know that place," Josie said. "It gets really busy on hot days."

He nodded. "I work there on weekends. It's closed over the winter but we'll open again next weekend if the weather's decent."

Josie's eyes lit up. "I've probably seen you there. Isn't it weird? We must have crossed paths loads of times."

Emily knew the place too. It was a lovely spot with a wonderfully peaceful atmosphere. There was a long stretch of grass beside the café where people would laze in the shade of the huge trees.

She was intrigued by Jack's job situation. "So you have acting jobs in the week and work at the Boathouse at the weekends?"

Jack looked amused. "No. This acting thing is a one-off. It's only temporary. I'm just filming the pilot for two weeks."

"So what were you doing before?" she asked.

"I work at a mobile phone shop. I took two weeks' holiday for the acting job. It all came about by accident, but it seemed like a bit of fun so I thought why not?"

"And I'm so glad you did." Josie rested her head on his shoulder and squeezed his arm.

"How on earth did you accidentally get an acting job?" Emily asked. Josie had been trying to get a job for ages, and he got one by accident?

He chuckled. "They were doing open auditions and my mum's friend wanted to give it a go. I got roped into driving her to the audition and they thought I was auditioning too. They offered me a job there and then."

"Oh, wow!" Emily couldn't help but laugh.

"I know," he said. "I wasn't going to do it, but I thought it might be a nice change."

"It sounds like it's fun."

"We have a laugh." He patted Josie's leg affectionately. "The job itself is pretty boring. Lots of waiting around."

"It's so exciting being on set." Josie beamed. "Watching the actors and hearing the director shout 'action' and 'cut'. I love it."

"But you're only doing it for two weeks?" Emily glanced quizzically at Jack.

He nodded. "They're just filming the pilot at the moment."

Emily was confused. "So you're only working for two weeks as well?" she asked Josie.

"It's the two weeks for now. Then there'll be a break before they film the first series."

"If it gets commissioned," Jack said.

"It will, though." Josie crinkled her nose. "Michaela said it's almost certain."

"Fingers crossed," Emily said diplomatically. She

was fairly sure Josie's agent was prone to telling her clients whatever they wanted to hear. At least judging by the things she'd heard of her before. But if Josie wasn't worried, she supposed she shouldn't be either.

When the food arrived it was every bit as good as Jack had said. Conversation flowed easily as they ate, and Emily was amazed at how fast the time went and how comfortable the atmosphere was. Almost three hours had passed before they finally wandered outside.

"I can give you a lift home, if you want," Jack said as they stood in the car park and Josie hugged her goodbye. She was going back to his place so they could go into work together in the morning.

"No, it's fine. I can hop on the bus. It doesn't take long."

"I'm happy to drop you off."

"Thanks, but it's out of your way." She'd already discovered he lived south of the city centre, on the Iffley Road. It wasn't too far from her place but she didn't like to put him out. Plus she felt like some fresh air. It was cold but the sun was shining and she felt like making the most of it. "I'll probably walk some of it too. Burn off some of that food."

"Okay." He leaned and kissed her cheek. "It was great to meet you."

"You too." Amazingly, it was true. She'd been pleasantly surprised by him.

Chapter 3

The next time Emily saw Josie, she had finished filming the pilot for the soap opera. It was a Monday morning and Josie came into the shop at the castle. It was quiet. Monday mornings usually were. There was a school group due to take a tour, and they'd no doubt stream through the shop afterwards, disturbing Emily's peace while buying nothing.

She was psyching herself up to vigilantly watch for shoplifters. Not that she didn't trust teenagers but … well, no, she didn't. The tour hadn't started yet so she still had at least an hour of calm before they disturbed her.

"So you're unemployed again?" Emily asked Josie. She hadn't quite figured out the exact situation with this acting job.

"Technically, yes," Josie said flippantly. "But Michaela says it'll only be a few weeks before they start filming more episodes. So I don't need to start job hunting or anything."

"That's good," Emily mused.

"Yeah it's more like a little holiday for me."

"Hmm." Emily busied herself straightening out a display of little knight figures. It seemed as though Josie was on holiday more than she worked. And from what Josie had told her about the filming, it didn't sound particularly taxing. "It's a shame you don't know when they'll need you for filming again. I imagine it would be good for you to find a temporary job to tide you over for now." But she knew Josie wouldn't worry about money.

They'd always had a different outlook when it came to money. Emily constantly worried, whereas Josie probably hadn't worried about money once in her life.

It was actually slightly ironic that Emily was the one who made sure she always had a regular income, but it was Josie who had her own apartment while Emily still lived with her mum. That was her choice, though. She could afford to rent somewhere and had considered it from time to time. At twenty-six it was probably about time she moved out. But it seemed pointless when she got on so well with her mum.

Josie hopped onto the stool behind the counter and swivelled. "I'm okay. Mum and Dad are happy to help me out with my rent. And there really isn't any point in looking for another job now," she added. "Not when the acting will start up again in a few weeks."

Emily mumbled her agreement. Returning to the counter, she straightened up the flyers next to the till. She was mostly just jealous, she told herself. How lovely would it be if someone told her there was no point in her working because her writing career would take off anytime now? But she knew she'd refuse financial help even if her mum was in a position to give it. And what did Josie do all day if she wasn't working? It baffled Emily.

"So have you got any plans for the next few

weeks?" she asked. Another pang of jealousy hit. It would be lovely to have a few weeks off work. She could completely immerse herself in her writing.

"Not really," Josie said. "I'll probably hang out here a bit."

Emily smiled tightly as Josie went on.

"I said I'd go and visit Lizzie next weekend, so that should be fun. I can't believe I haven't seen her new house yet."

Josie's sister, Lizzie, had recently moved to a little seaside town in Devon. It was a fairly drastic move from Oxford to Hope Cove, and Emily had been surprised when she'd heard about it. She knew Lizzie fairly well. She'd been an intern at the magazine where Lizzie had worked as an editor. Lizzie had edited Emily's book for her before she sent it off to the publisher. It was quite inspiring how Lizzie had packed up and started a new life at the coast.

"It'll be great to have a few days at the seaside," Emily said. Being envious was a bad trait, wasn't it? She must be a horrible person. "I hope Lizzie's doing okay."

"I can't wait to see her," Josie said. "I feel a bit guilty that I haven't been sooner."

The door to the shop opened abruptly. It was Doug, one of Emily's colleagues. He oversaw the day-to-day running of the place. He was in his early sixties and usually very relaxed and jolly. Today he appeared stressed. He looked momentarily confused at the sight of Josie. She quietly slipped off the stool and moved out from behind the counter.

"Hi, Doug." Emily waved to draw his attention. "Everything okay?"

"It's going to be one of those days," he grumbled. "Bernie just called. He fell off his bike on the way in and he needs to go to the hospital for an X-ray."

"Oh no," Emily said. "He's okay, though?"

Doug took an exasperated breath. "He's fine. But I've got a group of school kids waiting for a tour, and no tour guide."

It was only then that Emily noticed what Doug had in his hand. The fabric was similar to a hessian sack, but she knew it was actually one of the costumes for the female tour guides. The tour guides each took on a different role and played the part of a character from history to give the tour of the castle and prison.

Emily began slowly shaking her head as Doug held out the drab grey dress.

"Any chance you could be Emily the prisoner from the 1900s for the next hour?" His eyebrows were raised as he looked at her hopefully.

"No." More head-shaking as she walked behind the counter. "I'm afraid I'm very busy being Emily the shop girl."

"I'm really stuck, Emily. They're waiting outside and I don't want to have to send them away."

"*You* could show them around," she suggested.

"I can't," he said. "I'm expecting a delivery for the café any minute. And I've got about twenty phone calls I need to make. Plus I have to find someone to cover for Bernie for the rest of the day."

"Well, I could do all that stuff," Emily said eagerly. "That would free you up to take the tour group."

"You know I can't manage all those steps with my bad knees."

Panic started to set in. There was no way she could be a tour guide. She worked in the gift shop and it was comfortable and stress-free. "I've never taken a tour," she said. "I wouldn't know how."

Doug leaned on the counter, scanning the bookshelf over Emily's shoulder. "How many of those books about the history of this place have you read?"

She glanced back but knew the answer immediately. She'd read all of them, most of them multiple times. It saved her from getting bored during quiet times at work. Not knowing the information wasn't going to be a plausible excuse.

"And you've been on the tours before. You know how it works. Just pretend you're a prisoner from a hundred years ago and show the group around."

"I can't," she said, as forcefully as she could. "I'm no good at that sort of thing. I can't act."

"I can!" Josie said. "If I knew anything about this place I'd do it. It sounds like fun."

Doug eyed her quizzically, clearly wondering who she was. He didn't have time to ask, though.

"You should do it," Josie urged Emily. "You'll be great."

"I'm not good with kids," Emily said.

"They're not really kids," Doug said. "They're fourteen and fifteen-year-olds."

"That's even worse." Emily walked to the window and peered out. There they were, the group of teenagers waiting to be shown around. A couple of them were fighting – hopefully just a play fight. "I don't want to," she said.

"You'll be fine." Doug's tone had changed. He

didn't seem to be asking any more. "Come on. Get this on." He held out the dress. Josie helpfully took it from him and pulled it over Emily's head.

"No," Emily whined. "What about the shop?"

Doug flipped the sign on the door to closed, then smiled brightly at her.

Before she knew it, she was being pushed out of the door and across the courtyard to the waiting group.

"I feel sick," she whispered to Josie.

"Check out the teacher," Josie replied in an excited whisper. "He's cute!"

Emily glared at her, disbelieving. "What?"

"Well, he is. You should give him your number after the tour. Tell him he can call you if he has any follow-up questions." Josie elbowed Emily as they walked. "Wink at him as you say it."

"Josie! I'm about to have a nervous breakdown and you're thinking about men!"

They fell quiet as they reached the group. Emily finally noticed the teacher. Josie was right; he was easy on the eye. He was tall and blonde with a wide smile.

As he stepped forwards, he held his hand out to Emily. "I'm guessing you're our tour guide," he said. "This rabble call me Mr Proctor, but you can call me Stuart." His smile was warm. Emily's heart rate, which was already soaring, increased further at the feel of his hand in hers.

"Hi," she said weakly.

"This is Emily," Doug said. "She's one of our most knowledgeable guides. You'll be in great hands."

Stuart turned and shouted at the rowdy teenagers, getting their attention and telling them to quiet down. Meanwhile, Emily glared at Doug. Why on earth had he said she was their most knowledgeable guide? She wasn't even a guide, and she suddenly felt sorry for the group. They should have Bernie showing them around. He was full of energy, and funny and great with people – a real showman who thrived on being a tour guide. This poor group were stuck with her, and she had no clue what she was doing. Maybe if it had been a group of old people she'd have been okay, but she was certain she couldn't engage a group of teenagers.

The group fell silent and all eyes were on her. Oh, God what was she supposed to say? She waved awkwardly. "Hi ... I'm Emily ..." She didn't even know how to start. Should she jump straight into character or give them an overview of the tour first? Her cheeks were getting redder, she could feel it. Maybe she should turn and run ...

Doug cleared his throat and spoke loudly to the group. "I'm sure you're all aware what year it is, but just in case ... it's 1913! This is Emily. Emily is twenty-seven years old and has been a prisoner here for the last two years." Doug glared at her. "Haven't you, Emily?"

She nodded. "That's right." Her voice was croaky and she swallowed hard. "Today I'm going to show you around the castle and the prison and tell you exactly what it's like living here. If you could follow me ..." She set off across the courtyard in the direction of the tower. At least climbing the steps to the top would give her a bit of time to collect her thoughts. She reminded herself that she knew everything there was to know about the place. If she could control her nerves, she could definitely give an interesting tour.

Glancing back, she saw the group following her. Josie and Doug hung back and Josie gave her an enthusiastic wave and thumbs up.

"If you have any questions as we go," she called to the group, "please don't be shy …"

"Why were you in prison?" a girl beside her asked. Emily smiled. Having some eager kids throw questions at her would make it far easier.

"Stealing," she said, trying to throw her voice so the whole group could hear. "I stole two loaves of bread. My husband lost his job and we didn't have any money. The kids were starving so I stole bread. I got caught and sentenced to five years here." The kids at the front of the group nodded, and she felt herself relax slightly. "There are a hundred and one steps to the top of the tower." She stopped for a moment at the entrance. "Feel free to count them if you don't believe me."

They followed her inside and she set off up the narrow stone steps. Maybe it wouldn't be so bad after all.

Chapter 4

The tour went surprisingly well. Emily found herself enjoying it once she got into it. The kids were easily engaged with stories of the awful conditions in the prison and the poor treatment of the inmates. Most of the kids, anyway. There were a group of four boys who seemed to have no interest whatsoever. They stayed at the back, occasionally shouting what they seemed to think were hilarious comments. Emily ignored them.

Stuart came over to her as the group explored the nine-hundred-year-old crypt beneath the castle. "Sorry about my group of jokers."

"It's fine," she said. The kids roamed in small groups. It was the last part of the tour, and even though it had gone far better than Emily had expected, she was still looking forward to getting back to the comfort of the shop.

"It's an interesting job you've got. How long have you been doing this?"

Her mouth twitched upwards at the corners. "Not long."

"Well, you'd never know. I'm very impressed. It's a fascinating tour."

"I usually work in the gift shop," she admitted. "But they were short of a tour guide today."

He looked at her intensely. "I'm doubly impressed then. It's not easy to keep the attention of teenagers."

"I was surprised by how interested they were." Emily scanned the room until her gaze landed on the group of troublesome boys. "Most of them, anyway."

The four boys were taking it in turns to punch each other on the arm.

"Teenagers," Stuart said. "Blame it on the hormones." He chuckled, then leaned into her, lowering his voice. "Some of them are also just little pricks."

She couldn't help but laugh.

"I better split them up," Stuart said, walking away as one of the boys put another in a headlock. "Billy! Let go of Josh …"

After another few minutes, Emily rounded the group up and wrapped up the tour. She felt a sense of achievement as she led them back up the steps and into the courtyard.

Scanning the group, she looked for Stuart to say goodbye. She remembered Josie telling her to give him her number. It was tempting. He did seem lovely. If only she had Josie's confidence. Never mind, he was probably taken anyway.

She was vaguely aware of the small group of troublemakers somewhere over her left shoulder. They were talking and laughing loudly. Catching Stuart's eye, she smiled and was about to move in his direction.

Then she felt a hand on her bum, squeezing. She jerked away, glancing over her shoulder. It was Billy – a name that had registered with her due to the amount of times Stuart had told him to stop messing around. His face was red with acne and he was grinning. Behind him, his friends laughed and jeered.

Instinctively, she snatched at his hand. In a moment she had him pinned against the castle wall. His arm was twisted behind his back and his cheek was squashed into the rough stone. While silence fell around them, he let out a faint whimper. She wasn't sure who was more surprised – him or her. Apparently the self-defence classes Josie had insisted they take a couple of years ago had been useful after all.

Her fingers were wrapped tightly around his wrist and his arm was at an odd angle.

"Get her off me," Billy hissed.

Stuart had arrived beside her but didn't seem to be in any rush to help the kid out.

Billy's voice was high-pitched as he squirmed. "I was only mucking about. Let go."

When Stuart reached out to her, she released her grip.

"He touched me," she said quickly. Billy flexed his arm and rubbed his elbow. She hadn't meant to hurt him.

"I was only joking around," Billy spat. "Bloody psycho. I could get you done for assault."

Emily looked at Stuart with wide eyes. Surely she wouldn't get into trouble. "He touched me," she said again.

Stuart laid a hand heavily on Billy's shoulder and swung him back to face Emily. "Do the words sexual harassment mean anything to you, Billy?"

"But I was only—"

Stuart cut him off. "You should probably

apologise quickly and hope Emily doesn't report this to the police or make a formal complaint to the school …"

Billy looked suddenly nervous. "Sorry," he mumbled without conviction before walking sheepishly back to his friends.

The school group remained quiet, and Emily was self-conscious and embarrassed. Quickly, she turned and stalked away across the courtyard.

"How was it?" Doug appeared from the café and handed her the keys for the shop.

"It was okay, I suppose." Up until the part when she assaulted a fifteen-year-old anyway.

"Great." He grinned. "You can be our standby tour guide from now on."

"No chance. It was definitely a one-off."

"Thank you," he called as she retreated to the shop. Hopefully her tour group needed to get back to school and wouldn't come in to browse souvenirs.

She'd reached the counter when the door opened and Stuart walked in.

"I just wanted to apologise." He stopped halfway between the door and the counter.

Emily was suddenly angry. "Do you ever think it might be useful to put off teaching the history of Oxford Castle and focus on something basic like how to act appropriately in a civilised modern society?"

One of his eyebrows twitched, and he seemed taken aback by her outburst.

She should have stopped there but her mouth was out of control. "You're a teacher, aren't you? Teach them! Teach them how to behave in public. This is the problem with our society. You don't even teach

34

adolescent boys to keep their hands to themselves …" She stopped talking and took a deep breath.

Stuart's mouth twitched ever so slightly at the corners. "I think it's safe to say you taught him that lesson."

A sliver of a laugh escaped her. Realising she was still in costume, she gathered up the bottom of the dress to pull it over her head.

Stuart looked at her intently, then glanced through the window. His class were waiting at the other side of the courtyard.

"He couldn't really press charges for assault or anything, could he?" As Emily's anger subsided, she was bothered by her own behaviour.

"No. If anyone has grounds for complaint it's you, and you have a lot of witnesses to that."

"I don't know what came over me. I just saw red."

He smiled and the intensity came back to his eyes. "You were amazing."

She blushed and looked away.

"I should get that rabble back to school. I'm sorry again. And thank you. It really was a great tour."

"You're welcome."

His hand was on the door, but he paused, turning back. "Would you like to go for dinner with me sometime?"

Her eyes widened. Was he asking her on a date? After she'd shouted at him and questioned his teaching abilities? She opened and closed her mouth as she tried to form a response. It was a long time since anyone had asked her on a date. He seemed sweet, though. If she could get her brain and mouth to communicate she'd agree to dinner.

"Sorry," he said. "I'm sure you're already spoken for and this is probably inappropriate …"

She pushed her hair off her face. "I-I don't think it's inappropriate," she stammered. "But I'm not sure I'm thinking straight at the moment so I don't know …"

"Okay." He approached the counter quickly. "How about I leave my number, and you can call me sometime, if you want to?"

"Okay." She pulled a notepad and pen from under the counter and passed it to him.

He smiled warmly when he said goodbye. Finally alone, Emily leaned on the counter. What a morning! Needing to talk to someone, she sent a message to Josie asking her to meet her for a drink after work.

It was only Monday, but she'd definitely earned a drink.

Chapter 5

The Head of the River was a large, charming pub situated beside Folly Bridge. A little further down the river was the café that they'd talked about with Jack – his uncle's place. It was a lovely part of Oxford, and walking distance from the castle, so Emily was happy when Josie suggested they meet there.

When Emily arrived, there was no sign of Josie. She hoped her friend wouldn't be long. At the bar, she ordered a glass of white wine and had just taken a sip when she spotted a familiar face. Jack was sitting at a table by the window, smiling at her.

He stood and kissed her cheek when she went over.

"Why are you here?" She bit her lip and frowned as her cheeks flushed. Why couldn't she be cool and confident instead of saying stupid things all the time? "Sorry, that sounded rude. I didn't know you were coming, that's all."

He chuckled as they sat down. "Don't worry about it. I didn't know you were coming either. I got a message from Josie telling me to meet her here after work." A boyish smile played on his lips. "I'm learning it's best to do as I'm told and not ask questions."

"That's probably a good idea when it comes to

Josie."

"I can always disappear," he said quickly. "I don't want to be one of those boyfriends who's always around."

"No, it's fine. I only wanted to vent about my ridiculous day at work. As long as you don't mind listening to that …"

"Not at all. What happened?"

She looked at him seriously. "I almost broke a kid's arm."

"You did what?" Josie asked, appearing behind her.

"I went all crazy and put my self-defence lessons to use on some spotty kid."

"Oh my God!" Josie said. "I wondered what could have happened for you to suggest drinks on a Monday night. I thought maybe you'd listened to me for once and got the hot teacher's number." She gave Jack a quick kiss and set her wine down before shrugging off her coat and taking the seat beside him.

Emily's mouth twitched to a smile as she remembered Stuart asking her out for dinner. She glanced out of the window as a little motor boat puttered past. Tree branches blew wildly on the opposite riverbank. It was very picturesque.

"Don't keep us in suspense then," Jack said. "I'm imagining you going all ninja on some poor child."

"He wasn't exactly a child," Emily said, refocusing on the conversation. "He was a teenager and taller than me."

"I thought playing tour guide would be a good change for you," Josie said. "I was expecting you to be brilliant at it and decide the gift shop was far too boring for you in the future."

"Do you even know me at all?" Emily said jokily. She sighed. "The tour went pretty well, actually. Up until the class clown grabbed my arse."

Josie almost spat her wine out, and Jack barely stifled a laugh.

"Seriously?" Josie asked. "Cheeky little sod."

"I'm not sure what happened after that. I could hear him laughing with his friends, and I just whipped round and grabbed hold of him. Next thing I knew I had him against the wall with his arm twisted at a funny angle."

"Go you!" Josie said proudly.

"I can't believe I did it." She shook her head. "If that wasn't bad enough, I then shouted at the teacher when he came to apologise for the kid's behaviour."

Josie frowned. "I thought he seemed nice."

"He is."

"But you shouted at him instead of giving him your number?"

Emily took a sip of wine and eyed Josie over the rim of the glass. "I got his number, actually."

"No you didn't." Josie laughed.

Jack nudged her and looked at her accusingly.

"I'm sorry," Josie said, amused. "But there's no way she got his number. I know my best friend and she doesn't ask guys for their numbers. Ever."

"Well, maybe he just gave her his number and begged her to call," Jack suggested.

Emily liked the fact that he didn't even seem to be mocking her. "That's pretty much what happened." She pulled the scrap of paper with Stuart's number out of her bag as proof.

Josie's shocked expression quickly turned to an encouraging grin. "You had an interesting day, didn't you?"

Emily nodded her agreement. It definitely hadn't been dull.

"So what happens now?" Jack asked, tipping his head in the direction of the phone number. "Do you stick with the three-day rule or what?"

"Haha! It'll be more like a three-year rule with Emily."

Jack looked puzzled.

"Emily's not going to call a random guy," Josie said.

"Did anyone tell you you're a terrible best friend?" Jack said, squeezing her knee affectionately.

"I'm not being awful," Josie insisted. "I know how shy Emily is about this stuff."

"It's true," Emily said. "I'll never have the nerve to call him."

"But I thought you liked him?" Jack seemed to be struggling to get his head around things.

"Yeah. I do. I just hate the idea of calling when I barely know him … and then having to go on awkward dates and all that stuff."

"So you don't date?" Jack asked. "Ever?"

"I do. But usually people I already know somehow."

"Graham!" Josie said excitedly. "We met him at drama club, so she already knew him a bit. Ooh and the guy you worked with at the cinema … what was his name?"

"Ben," Emily said. "Although it turns out it's not a good idea to date someone you're working with."

"Okay," Jack mused. "I get it. I suppose that makes some sense. I kind of feel sorry for this guy, though ..." He leaned in to read the name on the slip of paper. "Poor Stuart will be waiting for your call."

"There was something that bothered me about Stuart anyway." Emily stared out of the window, replaying the eventful day in her head. "He seemed way more interested in me after the incident with the kid. I think he quite enjoyed watching me defend myself. So what does that say about him, if he gets a kick out of watching a woman beat someone up? Not that I really beat him up, but you know what I mean ..."

"Sounds like a normal guy to me," Jack said. "I know what I'll be imagining when I go to bed tonight anyway ..." He stopped with his beer bottle in front of his lips. The grimace was comical. "Did I say that out loud?"

Emily laughed so hard she blew a raspberry, then punched Jack playfully on the arm. He spilled his beer as Josie hit his other arm at the same time. His smirk was adorable.

Josie glared at him. "Did you really just say you're gonna be fantasising about my best friend?"

He chuckled as Josie pouted dramatically. "That's definitely not what I said ..." Leaning back in his chair, he draped an arm around Josie's shoulders and pulled her closer to plant a kiss on her cheek. "It was a joke!"

"We've been dating for two weeks! I think it's a bit early for those kinds of jokes." She smiled nonetheless and rolled her eyes at Emily.

"I might get myself another drink," Jack said,

draining his beer.

The girls watched as he walked to the bar.

"He's funny," Emily remarked.

"Yep." Josie had a look of contentment as her gaze followed him.

Chapter 6

The scrap of paper with the dishy teacher's number on it ended up propped against a pot of pens on Emily's desk. For a week or so she looked at it daily, sometimes even picking it up and contemplating calling. Josie was right, though; she didn't have the guts. What would she say? He'd probably already forgotten her, and it would be a few moments of her awkwardly explaining who she was before giving up and ending the call.

After a while she stopped even noticing the piece of paper with the jagged edge. Her encounter with Stuart was all but forgotten.

She spent a lot of hours sitting at her desk under the window in her bedroom. The sun streamed in on one of the first nice days of spring, and she pulled the curtain across to block it out.

For an hour she'd been staring at the laptop screen, waiting for inspiration to hit her. She'd plotted out the whole of her second novel, but she had the feeling she hadn't plotted it very well. It didn't feel right, and she was tempted to start all over again.

When her phone rang she was glad of the distraction.

"I hope you're taking advantage of this weather?" Josie said. Her cheerful tone was surprising, given that the last time Emily had spoken to her, a couple of days before, she was in floods of tears over an argument with Jack.

"I've been trying to get some writing done but it's not going well."

"So you can come out and sit in the sunshine with me?"

Emily stared at the laptop. Realistically she wasn't going to get much done. Her mind was blank. "Yeah. Where shall we meet?"

"Jack's working at his uncle's café. The Old Boathouse. I said we'd go down and annoy him at work."

Emily propped her head on her hand, her elbow on the desk. It was really hard to keep up with Josie's life sometimes. "I thought you'd had a huge argument with Jack? I got the impression you were splitting up …"

"Oh, we sorted all that out," Josie said flippantly.

"I thought you'd gone to Hope Cove to stay with Lizzie? Why haven't you been answering my calls? I was worried about you."

"Sorry. It was a crazy weekend. I went down to Hope Cove for a night and then came back to sort things out with Jack. Plus, I needed to get out of Lizzie's way. That guy Max turned up."

"The guy she met on holiday? I thought he was married?"

"Long story! I have loads to fill you in on. I'm leaving the house now. Meet me at the Boathouse and I'll explain everything."

"Fine." Emily puffed her cheeks out. "I'm a bit annoyed with you, though. I get a phone call from you all upset and then you ignore my calls for two days."

"I'm sorry. I was going to call you yesterday, but …"

"But what?"

"I was busy making up with Jack," Josie said cheekily.

***

The Old Boathouse was busy when Emily arrived. It was only a small, self-service café, but the folding doors opened up fully and an array of tables and chairs were set up on the patio in front. Thankfully, Josie had already arrived and grabbed them a table.

"I haven't been down here in so long." Emily looked around as she sat on the plastic patio chair. There was nothing fancy about the Boathouse, but the quaint little building had a certain charm. Once upon a time it had been used for storing rental boats in the winter, but had been renovated to a café. Inside, pictures hung on the wall, showing how it used to look.

Sitting on the patio, she felt like she was in the middle of nowhere. They were so close to the city, though. Behind the café was Christ Church Meadow – a huge expanse of green – and beyond that the cathedral and university buildings created a magnificent skyline.

"It's gorgeous here, isn't it?" Josie handed Emily the menu, a laminated A4 sheet of paper. "I love the houseboats."

Emily turned to the river. The sun was glistening off the water on the shallow stretch of the Thames, and a row of houseboats bobbed on the opposite bank. A huge weeping willow stood a little further downstream with its long branches sweeping over onto the water.

A dusty path ran parallel to the river, and joggers and cyclists went past at intervals. Beside the café was a stretch of grass dotted with huge, sturdy oaks and sycamores.

"I don't even know which way to look," Emily said. "There are perfect views from every angle."

"I know," Josie said. "But look at the menu for a minute, please. I'm hungry. Tell me what you want to eat and I'll message Jack with the order so we don't have to stand in the queue."

"That's a bit lazy, isn't it?" She scanned the selection of cold sandwiches and salads on the menu.

"We're VIPs here." Josie grinned. "We're allowed to be lazy. What do you want?"

Emily chose a sandwich and Josie relayed it to Jack via text message. Through the queue of people at the counter, Emily caught sight of Jack. He smiled and waved, then pulled his phone out of his pocket and glanced down. He gave them a thumbs up and got back to work.

"So what happened with you two?" Emily asked. "You sounded so upset on the phone."

"It was awful," Josie said dramatically. "We had this huge argument. Jack said he thought our relationship was moving too fast, and then I got all upset and shouted at him. And when I suggested we split up, he didn't really argue with me so I got more upset and stormed out. I really thought things were over between us. I didn't know what to do with myself so I got in the car and drove to Hope Cove to see Lizzie." She paused and took a sip of her Coke. "He didn't even reply to my messages that day so I was convinced it was over, but he finally replied the next morning and agreed we should talk."

Emily glanced in Jack's direction. He didn't seem like someone who would mess people around like that.

"Why did he think things were moving too fast?"

The way Josie screwed up her face made it clear there was more to the story than she wanted to let on.

"You know what men are like," she said vaguely. "You say the wrong thing and they freak out …"

Emily narrowed her eyes. "What did you say?"

"Not much. He overreacted."

"Josie! What on earth did you say?"

After a brief pause she leaned forwards to whisper. "I suggested that we move in together."

"Oh my God! You've only been together a few weeks. I'm not surprised he flipped out."

"We've been together six weeks," Josie protested. "And for me that's long enough to know I want to live with him. I don't know why he was so dramatic about it."

"To be honest, I'd be worried if he'd agreed to it. It's far too soon."

Josie pouted. "Whose side are you on?"

"Honestly? Jack's! Why did you suddenly decide you wanted to move in with him?"

There was that look on Josie's face again. Like she was getting caught out with all the questions.

"Did I tell you that the TV show isn't being commissioned?"

Emily shook her head.

"So I don't have a job."

Emily wanted to point out that this shift to unemployment wasn't particularly unusual. Having a job never seemed to be high on Josie's list of priorities. And surely Josie had known there was a good chance the TV show wouldn't go ahead?

"I'm sorry it didn't work out," Emily said. "But you can get another job. Just get a waitressing job or something until you find something else."

"I really want to get another acting job. And Michaela said she's going to find more auditions for me. It doesn't make sense to get another job if I'm going to be auditioning for parts. But Dad's already dropping hints about the rent. And since I stay at Jack's place so often anyway, I thought it would make sense for me to move in with him."

Emily put a hand to her mouth to make sure she didn't blurt out what was in her head. Josie probably didn't want to hear that she was completely spoilt and that it was utterly ridiculous that she had asked Jack if she could move in with him. Poor guy.

"It's not a very romantic reason to move in together," she said, surprised by the calmness of her voice.

"That's what Jack said. He thinks we should wait until we're really ready to move in together and not rush into it because it's financially convenient."

"And you realise that if you lived with Jack you'd have to pay him rent?"

"I know." She waved her hand. "But it wouldn't be so much."

The conversation was paused as Jack came

towards them with sandwiches. He slid the plates onto the table and smiled warmly as he greeted Emily.

"You look busy," she said, glancing at the counter and the long queue.

"Everyone's out enjoying the sunshine," he said.

"I feel guilty that you have to work while we just sit here."

He flashed a cheeky grin. "You should."

"Can you have a break and come and sit with us?" Josie asked.

"Maybe in a little while, if things calm down. Enjoy your sandwiches!"

He went back to the counter and the girls tucked into their food. It was basic but there was nothing to complain about.

"So does Jack work every day?" Emily asked, as she swallowed a mouthful of her cheese and pickle sandwich.

"Pretty much." Josie wiped mayonnaise from her mouth. "He works in the phone shop all week and most Saturday mornings. Then he works here every Sunday. Sometimes Saturday afternoons too."

"Wow! He doesn't get much time off at all."

Josie rolled her eyes. "Usually he's off on Sunday mornings, but he plays football then. I think we'll need to spend our weekends hanging around here or I'll never get to see him."

"That doesn't sound so bad." Emily smiled at her surroundings. Nearby a goose pecked at long grass. "Next time I'm going to bring a blanket and we can set up camp over on the grass. These chairs aren't particularly comfy."

Josie beamed. "That's the summer planned out

then."

Chapter 7

A week later they were back at the Boathouse. This time Emily brought a blanket and they lay on it, happily chatting. It wasn't quite shorts and T-shirt weather, but it was surprisingly warm for so early in spring.

They'd been there about an hour when Jack took a break from work and joined them. "You really are completely opposite personalities," he remarked, sitting between them. "One likes sun and the other shade."

Emily laughed. They'd set up the blanket to suit them both, at the edge of the shade of the large oak tree. They'd had to move once when Emily's shade had gradually disappeared. "I'm too pale to sit in the sun all day."

"And I can't let the good weather go to waste." Josie stretched out her arms. "I need to soak up every ray I can." They'd already discussed the likelihood of Emily getting burnt in April, but she knew from experience not to risk it. She could go from milky white to bright red in no time.

Jack shuffled over to Emily's side of the blanket and lay down in the shade. "It's really warm in the sun today. And I'm hot enough from running around at work."

"Well, I'm glad Emily gets you at her side of the blanket if you're all sweaty and smelly!"

"I don't smell." He grinned as he lifted an arm to sniff his armpit. "Do I smell?" he asked Emily.

"Not from here," she said lightly. "But I won't get any closer just in case."

"It is a lovely day," Josie said. "Shall I get us ice creams?"

Jack sat up. "I'll go. What do you want?"

"You only just sat down," she said.

"I don't mind." He looked at them questioningly as he stood up.

"Strawberry Cornetto, please," Josie said.

Emily asked for the same and Jack headed back to the café.

"He's so lovely." Emily flashed Josie a soppy smile as they watched him go. "He treats you like a princess."

"I know. I think I've done quite well for myself there."

"You have. It even makes me think about dating. Maybe it would be worth it if I found myself a lovely guy like Jack."

"I don't know why you won't go on dates. Why don't you call that teacher who gave you his number?"

Because the thought terrified her, that was why. "I'll think about it."

Josie gave her a look as though to say she wouldn't hold her breath.

"Did you have any more thoughts about getting a job?" Emily asked in a bid to change the subject. Even the idea of dating made her uncomfortable.

"Michaela's got a couple of possible auditions for me. I'll call her on Monday and get her to firm them up."

"Maybe you could get a part-time job while you're waiting for auditions."

"Maybe," Josie agreed. "I suppose it would keep my dad happy."

Jack arrived back and handed out ice creams. "Do you ever work weekends?" he asked Emily.

"Yeah. I'm supposed to work alternate Saturdays but it's usually more like every Saturday. It's busier at the weekend so I prefer it. I take a day off in the week instead."

"That means we can come and visit you at work one Saturday," he said.

She shook her head. "It's pretty boring."

"You could give us a tour of the castle." Jack had a look of mischief. "I promise not to grab your bum, so you won't need to go all kung fu on me!"

Emily gave him a friendly shove as the three of them chuckled.

"We *should* visit you," Josie agreed. "It's hardly fair if we come here to visit Jack and never honour you with our presence."

"It's really okay with me if you don't visit …"

Jack raised an eyebrow. "It almost sounds like you don't want us to."

"Which just guarantees that we will," Josie said with a wicked laugh.

***

It was the following Saturday when Josie and Jack

turned up at the castle. A tour group had just come into the shop and she was rushed off her feet.

"You chose the worst time to visit." Emily flashed them a smile as they loitered beside the counter. A queue of people were waiting to pay and there was no way she could take a break. "Four pounds ninety-nine," she said to the woman in front of her as she handed the postcards and pens to Amanda to bag up while she took the money. She always worked with Amanda on Saturdays. She was a jolly, middle-aged woman, and the two of them rubbed along nicely.

"I didn't expect it to be so busy," Jack said.

"It comes in waves as the tour groups finish. It'll be dead again in five minutes."

He nodded. "We'll grab a coffee next door and come back later."

Glancing outside, Emily saw Bernie walking sombrely across the courtyard to a waiting tour group.

"Can you take over for a minute," she said to Amanda, then turned to Jack and Josie. "Quick, follow me."

She rushed across the courtyard and managed to get Bernie's attention before he reached his tour group.

"What have I told you about disturbing me when I'm already in character?" he said through tight lips.

"Sorry." She was out of puff after her quick dash. "But my friends are visiting. Can they join your tour?"

He looked over her shoulder at Jack and Josie. "Yeah, of course they can," he said jovially.

"Thanks so much." Emily turned to make introductions. "This is Bernie …"

"It's Bernard," he said theatrically. "Now follow me and try to keep up."

"You'll have a great time," she said, squeezing Josie's arm. "Bernie's great. I'll arrange my lunch break for after the tour and we can hang out for a bit."

"Thanks!" Josie said excitedly. She pulled on Jack's arm. "Come on."

Emily rushed back to Amanda. As expected, the shop quietened down again quickly. Doug came out of the office to cover for her on her lunch break, and she was waiting for Jack and Josie when they finished their tour.

"I got us sandwiches," she said, holding up the paper bag from the café. "We can go up on the castle mound to eat." She led the way to the grassy hill.

"You know we already walked about a thousand steps up the tower," Josie complained as they walked up the steep incline to the top of the mound.

"It's actually only a hundred and one steps up the tower," Emily corrected her. "And look at the view . . . " She turned, looking out over the city. "It's a lovely picnic spot."

Josie sat down heavily on the grass. "It's a great view," she admitted.

"So how was the tour?" Emily asked. "Bernie's amazing, isn't he?"

"It was surprisingly interesting," Josie said. "I can't believe I've never done a tour of this place before."

"I came with school," Jack said. "But I didn't remember much of it."

"Did Bernie tell you the story of Oliver Butler?" Emily didn't wait for an answer. "He was hanged here in 1952. I'm always fascinated by his story. I don't know why. Maybe because he was buried here in the courtyard. I often wonder about him. He was younger than me when he was hanged, you know …"

At some point Josie lay down on the grass and listened in silence as Jack peppered Emily with questions about the history of the place. It was half an hour later when Josie sat up, grinning widely. "You realise we already did a tour of the castle, Emily? Your friend Bernie told us all this already."

Emily's ears and cheeks felt suddenly hot. She'd been prattling away for ages. "Why didn't you tell me to shut up if I was boring you?" She shot Jack an accusing look.

"You weren't. It's more interesting the way you tell it."

"Yeah right," Emily scoffed. "Bernie's so passionate about the place and he makes everything so fascinating."

"I hate to break it to you," Josie said, "but you and Bernie are like two peas in a pod when it comes to this place."

"You definitely have the same level of enthusiasm," Jack agreed. "I think you'd make a brilliant tour guide."

"No way. I'm quite happy in the shop." Emily gasped as she checked the time on her phone. "I've got to get back to work. Thanks for coming."

"Do you want to come out with us tonight?" Josie asked. "We're meeting some of Jack's friends for a pub crawl."

Emily was already moving away from them. She spoke without inflection. "No, thanks."

Josie's eyebrows twitched in amusement. "You're supposed to make up an excuse so you don't offend us!"

Emily thought for a moment. "I don't want to go on a pub crawl," she said bluntly. "Don't be offended, though!"

"Fine!" Josie laughed. "Meet me at the Boathouse tomorrow afternoon?"

Emily smiled. "I'll bring a blanket."

Summer at the Old Boathouse

Chapter 8

Josie wasn't at the Boathouse when Emily arrived the next day. She waved a quick hello to Jack and then found a spot to sit in the shade of a huge oak tree. The air was pleasantly warm and a couple of bees hovered over the grass nearby. Birdsong floated around her, mixed with the sounds of children playing. The gentle flow of the river made everything so peaceful. Emily took out her notebook and began to scribble an idea for a chapter of her book.

An hour passed without her noticing. She was still writing furiously when Jack flopped down beside her.

"Where's Josie?" he asked.

"I don't know. I spoke to her earlier and she said she'd have a shower and see me here. I messaged her a while ago but she didn't reply."

"She'll have gone back to sleep." Jack lay on his front with his head resting on his arms. He looked like he might fall asleep himself. "She was so drunk last night. She kept ordering more shots, and when I finally convinced her to go home, she invited a bunch of the lads back to play poker."

Emily grimaced. "Oh dear."

"I had to open this place this morning so I gave up and went to bed at 4 a.m. They were still drinking."

"You must be exhausted. What time did you get

up?"

"About eight. I might have to stop going out on Saturday nights."

"Or maybe just go home earlier."

"I don't like to leave Josie." He smiled wanly. "And she doesn't like to go home early."

Emily smiled at him and then looked out over the water. She felt suddenly self-conscious.

"Can you do me a favour?" he asked. "I've got half an hour's break. Will you wake me up in half an hour?"

"Okay." She wasn't quite sure if he was serious, but he turned his face away from her and fell quiet. Emily went back to writing in her notebook. When she looked over a few minutes later, she was drawn to the steady rise and fall of his back. His breathing was shallow and even, and he definitely seemed to be asleep. Emily envied people who could fall asleep on demand. It always took her hours to get to sleep, no matter how tired she was.

Her eyes stayed on Jack. He looked so peaceful. Her stomach felt light and fluttery. It was so long since she'd had butterflies in her stomach. Heat rose in her cheeks. What was wrong with her?

Her previous chat with Josie about finding herself a boyfriend came back to her. Maybe she should make the effort. Seeing Josie in a stable relationship really did make her envious.

She lost her flow with the writing, and her mind refused to focus on it. Instead, she stared ahead, watching the bustle of people around the Boathouse and the activity on the water: a variety of small boats manned by people who mostly seemed to have no clue what they were doing.

"Jack," she whispered after half an hour. She hated to wake him. "Jack!" she said again, louder but still no response. She should give him a nudge, but she felt strangely uncomfortable at the thought of touching him. Instead, she leaned closer and said his name louder still. It had no effect.

When she touched his shoulder she could feel the warmth through his T-shirt. With a little shake, she said his name again. Finally he stirred.

He rolled onto his back and groaned. "That can't have been half an hour."

"It was a bit longer actually."

"It's not much fun for you today, is it? First Josie doesn't turn up, then all I do is sleep. I could probably have been better company."

"It's fine." Her heart rate increased. She wished he'd go back to work; it was uncomfortable being alone with him. Why was she always so awkward with people? She never knew what to say and always got herself into a state trying to think of things. Surely it would be easier if she just relaxed. If only she knew how to do that. She shifted her weight. "I always have a notebook with me. I've been getting some work done."

"The next book?"

She nodded and automatically reached for her pen. Maybe he'd get the hint and leave her to it.

"What's this one about?" He propped himself up on an arm.

Emily didn't look up. Her mouth opened and closed and she felt her cheeks getting redder. She swallowed hard and fought for something to say.

"Sorry." He sat up and patted her leg. She caught the teasing in his eyes. "Josie's right. The look on your face! It's exactly how I'd look if someone asked me to multiply 384 by a million."

She frowned. "But—" A smile washed over her face. "That was another joke, wasn't it?"

"Couldn't resist," he said cheekily.

"Don't you need to get back to work?" Her smile slipped and she sounded slightly colder than she'd intended.

Thankfully he didn't take offence. "I probably should." His features turned serious as his gaze landed on her notebook. "What happened with the first book? You sent it off to publishers?"

She shrugged. "I never heard anything back."

"Maybe it just takes some time," he said. She'd heard that several times before and couldn't muster anything more than a half-hearted smile. "Or maybe you didn't send it to the right people," he suggested. "There must be other places you could send it. It seems like such a waste that you write a whole book and no one gets to read it."

"Well, maybe I didn't hear back because the publishers didn't think anyone would ever want to read it."

"I don't believe that. Keep sending it until someone sees how brilliant it is. All the best authors got rejections to start with, didn't they? I'm sure JK Rowling sent Harry Potter to like twenty different publishers before she got a book deal."

"She must have had a thicker skin than me."

"But if you're not even hearing back from people, maybe it's just sitting in a pile on someone's desk. It doesn't mean they don't like it. Get a thicker skin and keep sending it out."

"That's easier said than done." She looked quietly out over the water again. "There's a smaller publishing house I found that's taking open submissions. I was thinking about sending it to them."

"Do it," he said enthusiastically.

"I don't know."

"What's the worst that can happen?"

"They hate it and post all over social media about the worst manuscript they ever received."

He laughed. "That seems unlikely. I'm going to keep nagging you about this so you may as well send it."

"I'll think about it."

"Good." He stood to go back to work. "I'll be back in a bit if it's not too busy."

"I'm probably going to go home."

"Don't. Josie will be here soon. I'll bring you something to eat."

"You don't need to."

He ignored her. "Write a book while I'm gone, okay?"

"Okay!"

He walked away and she was staring at a blank page of her notebook when he shouted her name. Her head shot up and she saw him just reaching the café.

"It's 384 million, right?!"

She couldn't help but laugh. When he grinned back, her insides went all jelly-like again.

She really needed to find herself a date.

***

As promised, Jack arrived back with a sandwich and drink for her. She felt bad; she could easily have gone in and got herself something. The trouble was, there was generally a queue, and she genuinely had intended to go home. The sandwich sustained her, and she got back into the flow of writing. It was two hours later and she was about to go home when Josie finally turned up.

"I'm so sorry." Josie looked rough, even with the cover of her dark sunglasses. "I fell back asleep."

"Fun night, was it?"

She groaned and lay on her side. "I'm never drinking again."

"Until next week."

"Probably! Have you seen Jack?"

"He came over for a nap earlier."

"Was he angry with me?"

She shrugged. "I don't think so. Why?"

"He wanted to go home last night and I invited everyone back for a party at his place. I don't think he was very happy about it."

"He seemed fine. Just tired."

"Good. Sorry I left you alone all day."

"It's fine." Nearby, a little boy was standing by the water with his dad, throwing stones in the river and laughing when he got splashed. "I like it here."

"Me too." Josie closed her eyes and went quiet.

Jack joined them a little while later. He sat beside Josie, and when she didn't stir he put a hand on her thigh and shook roughly.

She batted him away. "Get off me."

"What's wrong?" he asked mockingly. "Aren't you feeling great? It's a good job you didn't have to work today. Imagine how unbearable that would be."

"I know," she whined. "I'm sorry. Why didn't you stop me drinking so much?"

Jack laughed loudly and Emily's mouth twitched into a smile. She knew exactly what Josie was like on a night out. There was no stopping her.

Jack turned his attention to Emily. "How come you never come out with us?"

"Because I don't want to end up like that." She nodded in Josie's direction.

"She used to come out," Josie mumbled. "But since I've got you to go out with she's been let off the hook."

"Now I feel bad." Jack nudged Josie. "You're not supposed to ditch your friends because you start seeing someone."

"It's not like that," Josie grumbled, irritated.

"It's really not," Emily said. "You're doing me a favour."

"Maybe we could alternate weekends," Jack said with a cheeky grin.

Emily shook her head. "No! You're stuck with her."

"Hey!" Josie said, her eyes still closed. "I'm right here, you know."

"Well, next weekend is my birthday," Jack said. "So we'll all have to go out."

Josie sat up. "I didn't know it was your birthday. I suppose this means I have to buy you something."

He draped an arm around her shoulders. "It does indeed." He looked at Emily. "And you have to come for a night out with us!"

She frowned and opened her mouth to protest, but

Josie spoke over her. "You have to. It's the birthday boy's request. It would be rude to say no."

"Very rude," Jack echoed. "I'd be completely offended."

Emily sighed. A night out wouldn't be so bad. It actually might do her good to get out more.

"Jack's got some cute friends," Josie said, smirking at Emily.

"Have I?" Jack's eyebrows shot up. "I thought you only had eyes for me?"

She grinned and leaned into him. "Of course I only have eyes for you. But I'd be a terrible friend if I didn't keep an eye out for someone for Emily."

Jack laughed. "Yeah, yeah."

"You will come out with us, won't you?" Josie asked seriously. "I worry you work too much."

She and Jack looked at her pleadingly until she finally agreed.

Chapter 9

Jack's friends weren't quite what Emily was expecting. She'd imagined a rowdy bunch, loud and obnoxious. But they were actually pretty calm, chatting in small groups as they moved between bars and pubs.

Emily was sitting at a round table with Josie and Jack in the third bar of the evening. It was busy and seemed very popular with students. A couple of Jack's friends stood nearby chatting.

"Who wants to dance?" Josie asked, jumping out of her seat. There was a small dance floor at one side of the dimly lit room.

Emily and Jack shook their heads in unison.

She reached for Jack's hand. "Well, it's not really optional for you," she said. "Come on."

Wearily, he followed her to the dance floor. After a moment, Jack's best friend, Lee, slipped into the chair opposite Emily. They'd been introduced earlier in the evening.

"I hear you're a writer?" he said.

Emily tensed and forced a smile. "I wish Josie wouldn't tell people that."

"It was Jack, actually." Lee had a kind face. His features were warm and friendly. If only she were better at conversation. He smiled. "He also said you're a bit shy about it."

"There's just not much to say."

The silence that followed was uncomfortable, and they both scanned the room. When it came to killing conversation she was a highly skilled marksman.

"They make a good couple, don't they?" Lee said. Emily followed his gaze to Jack and Josie, laughing and swaying on the dance floor nearby. "Jack's seemed much happier since Josie came along."

She nodded vaguely. "Josie too."

"Can I get you another drink?" he asked.

"No." She swilled the ice in the bottom of her empty glass. "I'm fine, thanks."

More silence. Lee glanced at her and smiled. Then more silence. Horrible awkward silence.

Thankfully it wasn't long before Jack and Josie arrived back. Josie was swinging on Jack's arm, asking him to come back and dance some more.

"No." He laughed. "You know I hate dancing. And it's my birthday, leave me alone."

She looked hopefully at Emily.

"No way."

Josie took a sip of her bright red cocktail and pouted.

"Do you want another drink?" Jack asked, looking at Emily's empty glass.

"No," she said. "I've had enough."

"Emily can't handle her alcohol," Josie said lightly. "If she drinks too much she'll either be in the bathroom, puking all night, or crying in a corner somewhere." Her smirk was full of mischief. "And she doesn't get upset about the usual stuff like boys and bad hair." She shook her head for emphasis. "She cries about starving kids in Africa and melting ice caps … serious stuff!"

"Well, come on," Emily said. "If I'm going to get drunk and emotional there are better things to be upset about than my love life." Though come to think of it, her love life was pretty upsetting too.

She looked at the amused faces around her. "I know!" she said. "I'm weird. But I get enough teasing from Josie, I'm immune to it by now."

Jack chuckled and shook his head. "I can't argue with your logic. It sounds very sane to me."

"Come on." Josie looked at Lee. "You'll dance with me, won't you?"

Lee seemed to be considering it when Josie took his hand and pulled him up. "See you in a bit," he called behind him.

"Lee's a good guy," Jack said.

"He seems nice."

Jack eyed her intently. "Josie thought you might like him."

"I didn't have much to talk to him about. I get so uncomfortable around people," she said bluntly. "Josie can talk to anyone about anything. I'm so awkward."

"I don't think you're as awkward as you think you are."

She frowned. "I am."

"Nope," he said firmly. "I guarantee you, you're not. At least not when you remember to talk."

She turned to him animatedly. "That's the problem! And it's not that I forget. I don't know what to say. I can't do small talk."

"You worry about it too much. That's the

problem."

She chuckled. "Thanks very much, Doctor Jack! What's the cure for this then?"

"It's very easy." He grinned. "Just stop worrying."

"Ah! Is that all? Where have you been all my life?"

They beamed at each other and then Jack nodded at the dance floor. "So you don't like to dance?"

"No. I don't dance. I hardly drink. I don't do small talk … you can see why I don't particularly enjoy nights out with Josie."

"You are quite the opposites, aren't you?"

"We are." It was one of those friendships that had grown over the years. They'd gone to school together, but didn't really become close until after they left school. It was funny, really; of all the people they'd gone to school with, Emily would never have expected for her and Josie to keep in touch. Josie had made all the effort – dragging Emily along to drama club, and self-defence classes, then getting Emily a job at the magazine where her sister worked. It was an unlikely friendship, but they seemed to balance each other pretty well. It was definitely good for Emily to have someone who nudged her out of her comfort zone now and then.

She glanced over to the dance floor, thinking that she'd spent enough time out of her comfort zone for one evening. "I think I might sneak away while Josie isn't looking. I'm about ready for bed."

"You can't do that," Jack said. He reached over and swapped Emily's empty glass with Josie's full one. "Not after I've just got you a drink."

"It's Josie's," she said, laughing.

"I don't think Josie needs another drink."

"That's true. But neither do I."

"Leave it there, though. It'll be fun convincing Josie that she already finished her drink."

"She's not that drunk!"

"Maybe not, but she's easily confused."

"You're mean."

He rolled his eyes. "Okay. Fine. Put the drink back where it was and get off home to bed."

Emily paused for a moment. Then took a sip of Josie's drink.

"I knew you couldn't resist staying around for some fun!"

"I just don't think you'll be able to convince her," Emily said.

"You underestimate me."

It was only a few minutes later when Josie arrived back at the table.

"Where's my drink?" she asked, confused.

Jack dipped his eyebrows and nodded towards the empty glass. "There."

"That one's empty."

"You finished it before you went to dance." He frowned and gave the most over-the-top look of confusion Emily had ever seen. Josie would never fall for it.

"I could've sworn it was almost full." She shook her head. "Guess I'm going to the bar. Have you got money, Jack?"

"Josie!" Emily shot back. "It's Jack's birthday. You should be buying his drinks."

"I know but I'm skint," she said happily.

Emily rooted in her handbag and gave Josie twenty pounds. "I'll get it."

"You're the best!" She waltzed away.

"So it's the Royal Bank of Emily today?" Jack raised an eyebrow. "That's a change."

Emily watched Josie squeeze in beside a guy at the bar, grazing his arm with her chest as she went. "Knowing Josie she'll get that guy to pay and bring me the money back."

Emily couldn't take her eyes off Josie. The guy at the bar said something to her and a smile lit her face. A hand gesture made it obvious he told her to order first. She turned and laughed at something he said. Then the drink arrived on the bar, but Josie chatted to the guy for a couple more minutes before walking away without paying.

"See." Emily turned to Jack. "It's a skill of hers!" She bit her lip as she remembered who she was talking to. "Sorry," she said quickly.

"Don't worry," he said, unconcerned.

"It's not even intentional," she said.

"I know."

"She was brought up being given everything." Emily had a sudden urge to defend Josie. "It's just what she's used to. And you know when she's got money she's more than happy to buy the drinks. But she's not working at the moment ..." She trailed off.

Jack smiled, his eyes firmly on Josie as she stood and chatted with his friends. "She's not working because everyone around her pays for her."

"I don't think you can really comment," Emily said after a short silence. "I've noticed she doesn't pay for much when you're around. You're an enabler!"

He turned back to Emily. His eyes were warm and caring. "I know. I'm not complaining really. She's not working because she's adamant she wants to get more acting work. She auditions for every part she can." He paused and took a sip of his drink. "I like that she's so determined to follow her dreams. She absolutely believes she'll get a job if she keeps at it." An eyebrow twitched. "Which reminds me, did you send your book off to more publishers?"

"Yes," she said shyly.

"Really? Or are you just saying that to shut me up?"

"I did," she said, smiling. "I'm quite sure that nothing will come of it but—"

"But when it does, you can thank me." He grinned.

"Yes."

Josie arrived and draped herself around Jack.

"Here …" She handed the money back to Emily. "There was some guy at the bar buying drinks."

Summer at the Old Boathouse

Chapter 10

Just a few weeks later, at the beginning of May, Emily dropped an A4 envelope into the postbox on the corner of her street. Her hands were shaking and she was overwhelmed with so many emotions. That morning she'd signed a contract with NewBridge Publishing. Now it was in the post and there was no going back.

Traffic rumbled down the main road, and people and bikes passed Emily by. It felt so momentous. Tears formed in her eyes, and when she pulled her phone out of her pocket she had an overwhelming desire to talk to Jack. It was him who'd encouraged her to keep trying. She may never have sent her manuscript off to NewBridge if it wasn't for him.

When she'd seen him and Josie at the Boathouse the previous week, she'd told them about the publishers requesting to see the full manuscript and then calling to say they were interested. Jack and Josie had been over the moon, but Emily hadn't let herself get too excited before things were definite. It had all happened so quickly. She still couldn't quite believe it.

Scrolling through her phone, she found Josie's number.

"I did it!" she said. "I actually did it. I signed the

contract and put it in the post."

Josie squealed so loudly that Emily moved the phone from her ear, laughing.

"This is so amazing," Josie said. "I'm so happy for you. Let's go down to the Boathouse. Jack's working but he'll want to congratulate you."

"It's Saturday," Emily said automatically. "We always go to the Boathouse on Sundays."

Josie laughed. "I think we can make an exception for a special occasion. Jack said we had to go down as soon as you'd signed the contract. I think he might be more excited than you."

"Mum wants to buy me lunch first."

"Okay. Let's go late afternoon and then we can go straight out after."

"Out where?"

"Bars, clubs, wherever. We need to celebrate."

Emily was unenthusiastic. "I suppose."

"See you later." Josie hung up.

***

Emily's mum took her to a local Italian restaurant for lunch, and after a celebratory glass of wine, she felt even more giddy.

She was brimming with excitement when she arrived at the Boathouse. Josie and Jack were standing on the grass at the side of the café, chatting. They both cheered when they saw her, drawing the attention of everyone nearby. Emily flushed bright red.

Josie wrapped her in a big hug. "Congratulations!"

"You're amazing." Jack put his arms around her and squeezed her tightly. Before she knew it, her feet were off the ground and she was being swung around in circles. She laughed loudly and clung to him, hoping they wouldn't land in a heap on the ground.

"Put me down," she protested when he slowed. With her cheek against his, she whispered "Thank you" just as her feet touched the ground again.

He beamed at her. "I'm so proud of you."

"I still can't believe it. Two books! They want two books." When Emily had got over the shock of the publishers being interested in her book, she was completely bowled over when they asked about any other projects she was working on. She outlined her work in progress and then sent them the first rough chapters. The contract they offered was for both books. It was more than she'd ever dared hope for.

"Of course they want them both," Josie said. "They'd be crazy not to."

"I'll be back in a minute," Jack said, walking in the direction of the café. Josie and Emily moved to sit on the blanket nearby.

"I'm so happy for you," Josie said. "We need to celebrate properly."

"You're going to drag me around a load of pubs aren't you?"

Josie chuckled. "Jack and I were trying to think of what we should do to celebrate." She had a mischievous glint in her eye. "Something you'd really enjoy …"

"You know I'd be perfectly happy to sit here and enjoy the sunshine."

"Funny you should say that …"

Emily followed her gaze. Jack was wandering over with a bottle of champagne in one hand and a small platter in the other.

"Cheese and biscuits." He placed the food in the middle of the blanket. "And some bubbly for a proper celebration."

Emily felt suddenly emotional and put a hand to her mouth as tears welled in her eyes.

"We were trying to think of your favourite place," Josie said, grinning. "And we came up with here."

Jack cocked an eyebrow. "Of course if you'd rather go on a pub crawl we can still arrange that."

"No." Emily beamed. "This is amazing. You guys are the best."

She laughed as Jack popped the champagne cork and filled three plastic cups.

As they toasted her writing career, she was overcome with happiness. The sun shone brightly. Kids played. People laughed. And in the middle of it all, Emily drank champagne with her two wonderful friends and felt that life was absolutely perfect.

When the bottle of bubbly was gone, Josie thought it would be a great idea to rent a rowing boat. They walked along the river until they reached the rental place and climbed into a lovely little boat made of dark wood. The boat rocked, making them all laugh.

It was a fun half hour. They took it in turns to row and had a whale of a time. The afternoon was idyllic, and Emily was disappointed when they headed back to the Boathouse after the fun of splashing around on the river.

The sun was almost at the horizon and the orange

and red streaks across the sky were wonderful.

"Shall we hit some bars?" Josie said, clearly not wanting the evening to end either.

Emily would head home, she decided. She'd had a great time celebrating but really wasn't keen to move to rowdy pubs.

"I've got another bottle of fizz inside," Jack said. "I presumed one wouldn't be enough."

Emily looked to Josie. "If you want to go into town, it's fine. I've probably had enough to drink anyway. I'll head home."

"No." Josie slung an arm around Emily's shoulder as they reached the blanket. "We're celebrating your amazing news." She rolled her eyes as she flopped onto the blanket. "Obviously sitting around drinking champagne is really awful for me, but if it makes you happy that's what we'll do!"

"I really have had enough to drink," Emily said, but Jack was already on his way to get the champagne.

She'd definitely had enough to drink, but she didn't care. When her head started to spin after the next cup of champagne, she lay back on the blanket and giggled.

"I love you guys," she said, staring up at the darkening sky.

Jack and Josie laughed in unison.

"Yay!" Jack cheered. "I finally get to see Emily drunk."

"I'm only tipsy. Maybe a little drunk. But I'm happy drunk so it's okay." She rolled onto her side and looked up at her friends. "If it weren't for you two, I'd never have got published. You're the best friends ever."

"I like to think you're friends with us because of our sparkling personalities," Josie said. "Not just because of how we help your career."

"Especially since we didn't have much to do with the book deal," Jack added.

"You did." Emily grinned at them. "If Josie hadn't got me the job at the magazine, Lizzie would never have edited my book, and I'd never have had the confidence to show anyone."

"So you've forgiven me for the job?" Josie said.

"Yes!" She glanced at Jack. "Did you hear about that? Josie got me a job at the magazine with her sister and I hated it! Anyway, it all worked out well in the end." She paused. "And if Jack hadn't encouraged me, I may never have sent the manuscript to NewBridge. See, you had a lot to do with it."

"You'd have got there without help too," Jack insisted.

"Whatever." Emily was so relaxed. "I still love you."

Josie patted her shoulder. "We love you too, Emily."

"I think I have to go home before I fall asleep," she said, dragging herself up.

"I'd offer to drive you," Jack said. "But I've had far too much champagne."

"I can get the bus. It's still early."

"Are you sure you're okay alone?" Josie said. "You're not too drunk?"

She insisted she was fine and hugged them both goodbye before leaving them to finish the champagne.

Emily walked happily in the direction of the bus

stop. After a few minutes she glanced back. Josie and Jack were still on the picnic blanket, their bodies tangled together as they kissed, completely oblivious to anything around them.

Emily tensed and her smile disappeared. An hour ago, life seemed perfect, but suddenly her life felt utterly terrible.

If only she had someone as wonderful and devoted as Jack.

Summer at the Old Boathouse

Chapter 11

Alcohol was evil. This was the reason Emily didn't generally drink much. Her mind whirred as she sat on the bus on the way home. It had been such a great day. She'd signed a publishing contract, for goodness sake. Her dream had literally come true. But all she could think about was how happy Josie looked with Jack. And instead of being happy for her best friend, all she felt was lonely.

Afternoon drinking really wasn't good. It was only nine o'clock, but it felt way later. At home, her mum was in the living room watching TV. She muted it when Emily dropped heavily onto the couch.

"Did you have a nice time with Josie?" her mum asked.

"Not really." She felt like she had the weight of the world on her shoulders. Stupid alcohol.

Her mum's face fell in concern. "What happened?"

"Nothing." Emily put her head in her hands, then rubbed at her eyes. "I'm just an idiot. It was a lovely afternoon. Everything is great. But I feel miserable."

"How much did you have to drink?"

"Too much!"

Her mum laughed. "You know what you're like. You can't handle your alcohol. I'm not sure where you got that trait from!"

"I know. And I know I'm being irrational. But I was looking at Josie with Jack and I got so jealous. Jack is perfect, and Josie's so lucky."

"Emily." Her mum's voice was suddenly stern. "He's your best friend's boyfriend."

"I didn't mean it like that," she said quickly. "It's not Jack specifically. I'm jealous that she's in a relationship. I want someone to look at me the way Jack looks at her. I'm sick of being on my own."

Her mum moved to sit beside her on the couch, putting an arm around her shoulders and giving her a quick squeeze. "You need to get out and find someone then. You spend too much time shut away in your room. Get on Tinder or whatever people use these days. Go on some dates."

"I just hate the thought of it. Meeting someone I don't know and trying to make conversation with them."

"But you'll never meet anyone sitting in your room."

Emily rolled her eyes. "I realise that, Mum!" She sighed. "Why can't I be more confident like Josie? She's not scared of anything. She doesn't even wait for guys to ask her out. She could be in a bar and see a guy she likes the look of and she'd just give them her number or ask them out …"

"Comparing yourself to Josie isn't going to do you any good," her mum said.

"I know but I'm so nervous that even when a cute guy gives me his number I'm too scared to call." She remembered the teacher whose class she'd taken on a tour of the castle. Her features crinkled as a thought occurred to her. "What if I call him?"

Her mum was completely confused. "Who?"

"The teacher."

"What teacher?"

"Stuart. Remember I told you about the day I had to take a tour group around the castle. A school group? The teacher asked me out for dinner. He gave me his number."

"I remember you taking the tour. I don't remember you mentioning the teacher asking you out."

"I didn't bother mentioning it because I knew I wouldn't have the guts to call him." She stood abruptly. "I'm going to call him."

"Now?" Her mum looked sceptical.

Emily checked the time on her phone. "It's not late."

"I didn't mean it was too late. I only wonder whether you're in the right frame of mind. Maybe it'd be better to call tomorrow when you haven't been drinking."

"It would definitely be better to call tomorrow," Emily agreed. "Except for the fact that tomorrow I'll be too scared to call. I'll realise what a stupid idea it is. It's now or never."

"Okay." Her mum frowned. "Good luck then."

Emily made it to the living room door, then turned back. "It's two months since I met him. He probably won't even remember me. This is a crazy idea, isn't it?"

"Just call him." Her mum chuckled. "Quick!"

"But—"

"The worst case is he doesn't remember you and

you have a slightly awkward phone conversation and then get on with your life. The best case is you fall madly in love and marry a teacher!"

"Ooh, I like that option. I can definitely imagine myself ending up with a teacher."

"Me too. Go! Call him."

"Okay." Emily dashed away and was halfway up the stairs when her mum shouted after her.

"Don't mention marriage on the phone, Em!"

She laughed loudly. "I won't!"

It took a few minutes of madly searching her desk before she finally found the piece of paper with Stuart's number on. It had fallen under the desk and was lying propped against the skirting board.

Quickly, she tapped the numbers on her phone and then paused with her finger over the dial button. Maybe she should send a message. That would be less scary. She took a deep breath. It was only a phone call. She could do it.

Panic hit her as it rang. Her heart rate went haywire. Maybe he wouldn't answer. It was Saturday night after all. He'd probably be out somewhere. Or he was dating someone else since Emily had taken so long to call. Or he wouldn't answer because it's an unknown number....

"Hello?" His voice was surprisingly familiar. He sounded relaxed.

"Hi." She faltered. It was so tempting to hang up. "Sorry. This is a bit weird. We met a while back. At Oxford Castle. I'm Emily?"

There was a brief pause and she was terrified he wouldn't remember her.

"Emily the thief?" he asked.

"Erm?" *What?*

"Emily who stole a couple of loaves of bread and ended up in Oxford Castle Prison?"

She laughed and her shoulders relaxed. "No. You're thinking of 1913 Emily. I'm the modern-day Emily who works in the castle gift shop ..."

"I remember," he said lightly. "What can I do for you, Emily?"

"You invited me out for dinner," she said quickly. "I'd like to take you up on it."

"Really?" There was a hint of amusement to his voice.

"If you still want to?"

Another pause. "You don't know much about dating, do you? Ever heard of the three-day rule?"

"Yes," she said confidently. "You're supposed to wait three days to call. That's the minimum you have to wait so you don't seem too keen. I'm not aware of a time limit, though. Did I miss the cut-off date?" She smiled. Alcohol was amazing!

"Well, there's no danger of you seeming too keen."

"So? Are you still up for dinner?"

"Yeah. I am."

"Okay." The grin took over her face. "Good."

"Are you free tomorrow evening?"

"That's soon," she blurted.

"I know. Do I seem too keen? You might need to give me some lessons in playing it cool ..."

"Oh, I'm the master at that," she said.

"So, tomorrow?"

"Yes. I'm free tomorrow. Where shall we meet?"

"Let me have a think and I'll message you in the

morning."

"Okay. See you tomorrow then."

She was absolutely beaming when she ended the call. Her mum appeared at the bottom of the stairs when she shouted down to her from the landing.

"Looks like I'm going to marry a teacher!"

Her mum laughed. "I hope you're going to go on a few dates with him first."

"First date is tomorrow."

"Shall we have a celebratory drink?"

"I've celebrated enough today. I'm going to bed."

They shouted goodnight to each other and Emily wandered happily back to her room.

It had been quite an eventful day.

Chapter 12

"Of all the restaurants in Oxford, he chose the one that's a two-minute walk from the Boathouse." Emily smirked as she filled Josie in. She checked the time yet again. There were still a few hours before she was meeting Stuart, but she needed to go home and get ready first. She was already nervous.

"I can't believe he's taking you to The Folly. That place is classy."

Emily had never been to The Folly before, but she always thought it looked lovely. It was just a little farther along the river, up by the bridge. They had tables on a deck, right over the water. It looked very pretty in the evening, when it was illuminated with fairy lights.

"I also can't believe you called him." Josie lay back on the blanket. "We should make you drink champagne more often."

"I'm glad I called him," Emily mused. "Maybe it was because of the alcohol, but he was very easy to talk to on the phone. I thought it would be weird because I left it so long to call, but it wasn't at all."

"You did leave it a long time. But he obviously didn't care about that. What are you going to wear?"

"I was thinking about my blue skirt and—"

"Wear a dress."

"I thought about a dress but I'm more comfortable in a skirt or trousers."

"You made the guy wait two months for a date." Josie pulled her sunglasses down and gave Emily a mock serious look. "Wear a dress … And a push-up bra."

"I don't even own a push-up bra."

Jack loomed over them. "Seems like I chose a great time for my break …"

The girls laughed.

"Emily's got a date tonight," Josie said. "We're discussing what she should wear."

Jack sat between them on the blanket. "Who's the guy?"

"The teacher I met at work. When I was giving the tour to the schoolkids."

"Really?" Jack chuckled. "You finally called after all this time?"

Emily gave him a friendly shove. "It's all your fault."

"Why is it my fault?"

"You made me drink all that champagne yesterday and then I called him when I was drunk."

Jack raised an eyebrow. "I don't have any recollection of pinning you down and pouring champagne down your throat." He paused. "But a date's a good thing, isn't it?"

"I don't know yet. I'll tell you afterwards."

"Wear your blue wraparound dress," Josie said thoughtfully. "That's still fairly casual. It plunges nicely at the neckline."

Emily grinned. "I was hoping to win him over with my personality rather than my cleavage."

"Can't hurt to have a backup," Josie said, mischievously.

"Where's he taking you?" Jack asked.

"The Folly." Emily looked in that direction. There was a bend in the river so you couldn't see it, but it really was very close.

Jack looked at her seriously. "What time?"

"8 p.m."

"Okay." He closed his eyes into the sun.

"Why do you want to know what time?"

"So I can stand on the bridge and pull faces at you."

"You better not!" She gave him a playful kick.

Josie glanced at Emily and shrugged. "We don't have anything else planned for the evening."

"I wouldn't put it past you," Emily said. "That's the worrying thing."

Josie smiled. "Well, since I don't even remember the last time you went on a date, I suppose we'll leave you in peace."

"Spoilsport!" Jack said, before turning to Emily. "If you get bored, send a message and we'll come and do a dance on the bridge."

"Fingers crossed I won't get bored!"

***

Stuart was waiting on the bridge when Emily arrived at a couple of minutes past eight. He was leaning casually against the wall, wearing a pair of chinos and a blue checked shirt. Emily felt self-conscious as she walked towards him. It was hard to resist the urge to tug the front of her dress up over her cleavage. She kept telling herself the dress was completely acceptable. It just looked revealing from her angle. But no one else would be looking from that vantage point. Although, Stuart *was* pretty tall. If he was standing close and looking down … wow, she did like to overthink things.

He straightened up as she got nearer. His warm smile put her a little more at ease. "Hi!" He kissed her cheek. "You look great."

"Thanks." She automatically pulled at the top of her dress and then chastised herself.

"Hungry?" he asked, glancing down at the restaurant below the bridge. Tables were set with white cloths and tall candles, while strings of fairy lights glowed overhead.

She was far too nervous to have any appetite. "A bit."

"Come on then." He led the way down the steep stone steps beside the building and told the maître de he had a reservation. They were seated immediately on the deck right over the water. Heaters were scattered around, keeping the air on the deck perfectly warm.

"So what made you call, after all this time?" Stuart asked as they perused the menu.

"Alcohol," she said flatly, making him laugh.

They ordered wine and chatted easily while they waited for the food. The main course had just arrived when Emily happened to glance up to the bridge. She snapped her attention back to Stuart, vowing to kill her friends next time she saw them. When she looked up again, Josie broke into dance and Jack mimed walking down stairs until he disappeared below the wall of the bridge. He jumped up again and grinned at her. She blurted out a laugh, then covered her mouth with her napkin.

"What's so funny?" Stuart began to turn, and she put a hand on his arm to stop him.

"Don't look," she whispered in a panic. "The woman behind you spilled red wine down her top."

"You laughed really loud."

"I couldn't help it. She's glaring at me now. Don't look!"

She braved a look over Stuart's shoulder. Jack and Josie waved madly and then began to walk away. Pair of idiots. She couldn't help but smile.

"Sorry. What were you saying?"

"I was saying the food looks amazing."

"It does." She tucked into the sea bass. It tasted as good as it looked. Thankfully, Stuart was a better conversationalist than she was. Just as she began to feel uncomfortable, searching for something to say, he asked her about her job, then where she went to school, and her family. He kept the conversation flowing seamlessly. It was a skill she envied. She was surprised how much she enjoyed his company, and when he asked her if she wanted to go for another drink somewhere, she didn't hesitate to say yes.

After he paid the bill, Emily started towards the exit, but he took her elbow and pulled her in the other direction.

"How do you feel about boats?"

A small motorboat pulled up beside the deck and several people stepped out. Throughout dinner they'd watched people taking the little trip up and down the river to enjoy a drink on the water.

She glanced at Stuart. "I thought you had to book in advance."

"I did," he said with a smile.

They stepped on board and the waiter handed them a glass of champagne. They took a seat at the back of the boat, tucked in the corner with their legs touching. The driver was in the middle of the boat, and the waiter hovered beside him.

Stuart clinked his glass against Emily's and they took a sip of the bubbly.

"I'm really glad you called me."

"Me too," she whispered.

He was so close. When he leaned towards her, she met him halfway. It was just a quick kiss, but it felt wonderfully natural.

Another couple stepped into the boat and they exchanged smiles. Stuart put an arm around her as the boat puttered down the river. She relaxed into him and enjoyed the motion of the boat on the water as she sipped her champagne.

It was very romantic, and she was impressed by the effort Stuart had gone to. He took her hand as she stepped out of the boat and didn't let go of it as they walked through the restaurant and back out to the road. They automatically wandered in the direction of the city centre. A few people sat outside The Head of The River, enjoying the mild weather.

"Do you want to get another drink?" Stuart offered.

"I should get home." She'd had enough to drink, and it seemed like a good point to bring the evening to an end. Besides, there was a chance Josie and Jack were in the pub, and she didn't like the thought of introducing Stuart to them on their first date.

The taxi rank was only a couple of minutes' walk.

Stuart smiled as they stood beside the car. "I'm slightly nervous you're going to say you'll call me and I'll hear from you again in a few months."

"To be fair, I never said I was going to call you."

"That's true. And I suppose I've got your number now so I can call you."

"You should probably wait three days," she suggested. "So you don't seem too keen."

They stood close together. She should get in the taxi, but she was enjoying the banter and was hoping he'd kiss her again before she left. He leaned in as though reading her mind. His lips brushed gently against hers.

"Thanks for the tip." He opened the door to the taxi and she climbed in.

It was only a few minutes into the drive when her phone rang. She was happily reflecting on the evening, and her smile widened as she answered.

"That definitely wasn't three days!"

"There was no way I could wait until Wednesday to call you. How about we go out again on Wednesday instead?"

"Where to?"

"Your turn to choose."

"Okay then. I'll think of something."

She wished him goodnight and ended the call. The grin didn't leave her face the whole way home.

Summer at the Old Boathouse

Chapter 13

"You've been on three dates with him already?" Josie asked. The weather that Sunday was overcast and chilly so they sat inside at the Boathouse. They had the place almost to themselves.

"Yes." Emily smiled into her coffee. "On Wednesday we went to the rooftop restaurant at the Ashmolean museum, and yesterday we walked around the botanical gardens."

Josie propped her head on her hand. "Wow." She rolled her eyes. "You're like a tourist or something."

"I'm not!" Emily laughed.

"A museum and the botanical gardens. I'm guessing they were your choices?"

"Yes! They're two of my favourite places. You know Lewis Carroll used to hang out at the botanical gardens? It's where he got the inspiration for *Alice in Wonderland.*"

"I know." Josie rolled her eyes again. "You've told me once or twice."

"Sorry!"

Emily caught Jack's eye as he served someone at the counter. He'd been in the back when she arrived. He flashed her a smile and walked over to them a couple of minutes later.

"You look tired," she said automatically.

He sat down and slouched in the chair. "I am."

"How was football?" Josie dragged her chair closer to him and rested a hand on his shoulder.

"I didn't make it. I forgot to set my alarm and didn't wake up until late."

Josie's brow creased. "The only reason I didn't stay at yours was because I didn't want to get woken up by your annoying alarm."

He shrugged and took a gulp of Josie's coffee.

"I suppose I'll have to get used to your annoying alarm." Her eyes lit up when she looked at Emily. "I'm moving in with Jack!"

"Oh!" Her brain struggled to form a response. It wasn't long ago that they'd almost split up because Jack thought it was too soon to move in together. She glanced quickly at Jack. He was staring absently out of the window.

"Wow!" Emily said as Josie grinned at her expectantly. "That's great."

"I'm moving my stuff this week."

Jack kissed Josie's cheek and stood up as an elderly couple walked in. He left to go and serve them.

"I thought you'd decided against moving in so soon," Emily said quietly.

"Yeah, but that was a while ago. Jack's fine with it now. It makes sense financially. I don't want to keep on the way things are, with my parents paying my rent."

"So there's no news about a job?"

"Oh, there is." She sighed. "I didn't get the audition I went for last week, but I've found a part-time office job." Her mouth twitched to a frown. She clearly wasn't thrilled by the idea. "My dad set it up for me. It's a PA position at an advertising firm. It's just to cover maternity leave. So I'm going to do that for a while. It's only twenty hours a week so I'll still have time to go to auditions."

"But it's not enough money to cover your rent?"

"Not really. Dad said they'd still help me out, but I think it makes more sense that I move in with Jack."

"And he doesn't think it's too soon any more?"

"He's fine with it," she said cheerfully.

Emily glanced over to him. He really did look exhausted. "Maybe he won't need to work so much if you're paying half the rent. He looks like he needs a day off."

"You know what the problem is?" Josie leaned in and whispered. "His mum. I'm fairly sure he gives her money. That's why he works so much."

Emily squinted, not quite sure they should be gossiping about Jack, especially when he was on the other side of the room. On the other hand, she was intrigued.

"I thought you liked his mum when you met her?"

"She was nice enough. But she's very demanding. Jack has to go over to her place at least once a week for dinner … and now I'm fairly sure he gives her money too. Only because I overheard something on the phone. He's very cagey when I ask."

"It's just his mum? His dad's not around?" She felt uncomfortable asking. She should change the subject …

"His dad died a few years ago," Josie said.

"In that case, I think it's good of him," Emily mused. "If he helps his mum out."

"I think she guilt trips him into it." She shook her head. "But like I say, he clams up when I try to talk to him about his family so I've stopped asking."

They fell quiet as Jack walked over to them again. He had a coffee in his hand. "I prefer it when it's busy," he said. "I'm bored. What were you talking about?"

Emily peered into her coffee mug, feeling guilty.

"Emily's love life," Josie said casually.

Jack's eyes twinkled. "How was the date? It looked like it was going well …"

"Oh my God!" Emily had almost forgotten about the two of them on the bridge. She swatted at Jack's arm. "I can't believe you did that! Thank goodness he didn't see you."

"She's been out with him twice since then," Josie said. "To the museum and the botanical gardens!"

"Tolkien used to hang out in the botanical gardens," Jack said.

"And Lewis Carroll," Emily said excitedly.

"It's where he got the idea for *Alice in Wonderland*," Jack added. "And I bet one day people will say 'Emily Winters used to spend time in the botanical gardens. That's where she wrote her very famous international bestseller that made her filthy rich'."

"I might start taking my notebook and find myself a quiet corner to write in."

Jack's uncle, Clive, was clearing the table next to hers. "You should come in here to write," he said. "Then when you're famous, I can put your picture on the wall and tell everyone my claim to fame."

She grinned widely. It was a nice thought. Not

that she wanted the fame, but the idea of her books being successful was a dream that she generally didn't let herself dwell on. First, she needed to see her book published. She still couldn't believe it was actually happening. She'd had a couple of nice phone conversations with a lovely editor at NewBridge Publishing. They wanted her to make some small changes to the manuscript but nothing major. There was no publication date yet, but they seemed to think it could all progress pretty quickly.

Clive finished wiping down the table and straightened up. "You may as well get off, Jack. It doesn't seem like it's going to get any busier."

"Thanks." Jack yawned and turned to the girls. "Shall we grab an early dinner somewhere? Then I'm off home to bed."

"I'll leave you to it," Emily said as they stood. "Three's a crowd and all that …"

"Don't be daft." Josie collected up the coffee mugs to return them to the counter. "Of course you're coming to dinner with us."

Emily didn't bother protesting again until they reached the road and Jack's car.

"I'm going to hop on the bus home." She began walking slowly away. "I've got some stuff to do."

Jack went after her and slung an arm around her shoulders as he redirected her to his car. "Three's not a crowd," he insisted. "I'm buying you dinner, then I'll drop you home."

"But—"

"I'm too tired to argue." He opened the door for her. "Just do as you're told."

"Please come with us." Josie eyed her over the

roof of the car. "Jack's in one of his moods. He'll have a tantrum if he doesn't get his own way."

"I will." His eyes sparkled with amusement, and Emily sighed as she stepped into the car.

"You should bring Stuart out with us sometime." Josie clicked her seatbelt into place and turned back to Emily. "We can double date."

Emily frowned. "Maybe."

Chapter 14

It was a few weeks later when Emily introduced Stuart to Josie and Jack. She hadn't intended to. It was Sunday, and she and Stuart were having a stroll around the university buildings after a quiet lunch in a quaint little café.

"I once applied for a job here." Emily contemplated the beautiful buildings. She loved Oxford with its stunning architecture. "I thought it would be amazing to come here every day. Since I missed out on university, I thought it would be the next best thing. It was only an admin job. I didn't get it anyway."

"Don't you ever think of going to university now? You could still go."

They walked hand in hand through the pristine gardens. Stuart gently stroked her hand with his thumb.

"No. I should have gone straight after school, but I was too worried about money. I intended to save up a bit and then go. Then I just got comfortable working I guess."

"You wanted to study journalism?"

"Yes." She laughed. "I had a job as an intern at a magazine once, but I hated it. I decided I probably wasn't cut out for journalism even if I do love writing."

"It's a shame that you can't make a career out of what you love."

"Maybe I will one day," she mused. "I live in hope!"

"What I really don't understand is why you work in the gift shop at the castle instead of giving tours. You're a great tour guide, and your knowledge of the place is amazing."

"You sound like Jack," she said. "He says the same." She paused. "Jack's my best friend's boyfriend."

"I know." He chuckled. "You've mentioned him before."

"Have I?"

"A few times," he said lightly.

"Sorry. Do I talk about them a lot?"

He nodded. "Maybe I should meet them. Put faces to the names."

Hesitating, she wondered whether she wanted him to meet them or not. She couldn't think of a reason why not. Things seemed to be going well with Stuart, and she was spending a lot of time with him. Meeting friends seemed like a milestone. If they met each other's friends, next he'd be wanting to meet each other's families. It seemed too soon for that.

"Josie keeps asking when she'll get to meet you too," she finally said. "I'm seeing them this afternoon – I'll find out when they're free."

"I thought when you said you had plans this afternoon it was something important, not just ditching me because you'd rather hang out with your friends!"

A hint of a smirk played on her lips. "No, it was only that I'd rather see my friends. But it seemed rude to say that."

She squeezed his hand when he went quiet. Was he actually annoyed about it? "I thought you had marking to do anyway?"

"I do." They walked in silence for a few minutes. "Why don't I come with you to meet your friends now? Are you going straight from here?"

"Yeah I was going to have a walk through the botanical gardens and round the edge of the meadow. I'm meeting them by the river."

"So I could join you?"

"Erm …" Again, she couldn't think of a reason why not. "We just hang out by the Boathouse. It's a café. Jack works there."

"I know. You've mentioned it before."

"Oh." She swallowed. "Of course you can come. It might be a bit boring, that's all. We'll only sit by the river and chat. Jack joins us when he gets a break."

"Don't you want me to meet them?"

"I do," she said quickly. Actually, she didn't, but she couldn't put her finger on why. "You can definitely come. Josie will be happy to finally meet you."

"Okay. Good."

They chatted as they walked. Emily couldn't quite fathom why, but the closer they got to the Boathouse, the more nervous she felt. It was ridiculous – she was introducing Stuart to her friends. It wasn't a big deal. He was lovely, they were lovely. It would be fine.

Emily had taken to leaving her blanket at the

Boathouse and Josie was lying face down on it when they arrived. The straps of her vest top were pushed off her shoulder, presumably to ensure an even tan. She didn't bother adjusting them when she jumped up to greet them.

"I kept asking when we'd meet you," she said as Emily introduced her to Stuart.

"I've been wanting to meet you too," Stuart said. "Given how much Emily talks about you."

The girls smiled, then automatically reached to take hold of opposite corners of the blanket. Stuart got a shock when he went to sit down, and they both shouted at him. They laughed at his bemused expression.

"We have to move over a bit," Josie explained as they dragged the blanket. "Didn't Emily tell you she's descended from vampires?"

"I'll burn in the sun." Emily pulled a face at Josie and they stopped when they were half in the shade of the sycamore tree.

"Now you can sit," Josie told Stuart.

He lowered himself onto the edge of the blanket close to Emily. "So Emily was saying you want to be an actress …"

"Yeah. It's difficult to get into." Josie looked at him seriously. "I've found a part-time secretarial job that I'll start next week. As soon as I get an acting job I'll give that up. I keep going to auditions. I'm sure it's only a matter of time."

"I'm sure," Stuart mused. "Fame and success are probably right around the corner." He sounded stuffy and mocking. To be fair to him, it was difficult having a conversation with Josie about acting. Her enthusiasm and certainty often sounded naïve. She absolutely believed she'd get her big break any day now.

"Definitely." Jack arrived and hovered over them. "She'll be a household name before we know it." He reached out a hand to Stuart and introduced himself. "I've heard a lot about you."

"You too," Stuart said.

There was an awkward silence as they exchanged forced smiles.

Jack sat beside Josie. "We're very proud of her anyway. Not that we were surprised by the two-book deal." He grinned broadly at Emily. "We already knew how brilliant she was."

Emily felt her neck heating up. "We were talking about Josie. The acting."

Surprise registered on Jack's face. He'd obviously not heard the start of the conversation.

"You got a publishing contract?" Stuart said slowly.

"Yeah. It's not really a big deal. It's a small press. The book might be a big flop."

"It won't be a flop," Jack insisted. "And it *is* a big deal."

Stuart smiled uncomfortably. "I can't believe you didn't tell me that. You said the writing was a hobby …"

"It is." She wasn't sure why she hadn't told him about it. It felt like bragging, and she still wasn't sure she really had anything to brag about. "I haven't had anything published yet. It may never sell a copy."

"I'll buy a copy," Jack said.

Josie leaned into him. "Me too."

"Okay." Emily chuckled. "It might never sell more than two copies."

"Your mum will buy one," Josie said cheekily.

"My mum will too," Jack said. "I'm always raving to her about how great it is."

"You've not even read it!"

Jack grinned. "I don't need to. I know it's brilliant." He turned to Stuart. "We've had to start being nice to her since she got the book deal. What's the saying . . .? " He raised an eyebrow at Emily. "Keep your friends close and your famous friends closer."

She extended her leg and kicked him playfully.

"So you're a teacher?" Thankfully, Josie moved the conversation on. "That must be an interesting job. I hope the kids are nice to you. I was awful to my teachers."

"Most of them are pleasant enough," Stuart said, running a hand over the small of Emily's back. "Some of them are really unpleasant."

"So I hear," Jack said. "Emily told us how she had to bring some teenager into line for you when you were visiting the castle."

"It was actually quite lucky that he didn't make a complaint."

Jack frowned. "Seemed more like Emily who should've made a complaint."

"Except the kid was fourteen and only messing around."

"There's always some excuse, isn't there?" Jack sat up straighter. "They're just being boys, or they come from a broken home. Most of the time they're just spoilt little gits."

"I don't know about most of the time," Stuart argued. "Some of the time, maybe."

"It must be lovely to get so much holiday time," Josie said.

"Yes." Stuart smiled. "I can't wait for the end of term – six weeks off."

"Sounds all right to me." Jack turned as Clive called out to him. "Looks like I need to get back to work. I'll see you in a bit." He jumped up. "Anyone want a drink or anything?"

They shook their heads.

"I need to head off soon," Stuart said. "I've got a pile of marking to do."

"Nice to meet you." Jack shook his hand and walked away.

"The marking would annoy me." Josie leaned back on her elbows. "That and all the preparation you must have to do. And the kids. Working with kids would drive me crazy."

Emily chuckled. "Teaching wouldn't be the job for you, would it?"

"No. I'll stick to acting."

"I really should get going." Stuart leaned in and kissed Emily.

"I'll talk to you later," she said.

Josie politely told him it was nice to meet him.

"We should all go out for dinner sometime," he suggested.

"Yes." Josie beamed. "Definitely."

They watched him walk away before Josie let out a long breath and flopped onto her back. "You could've warned us you were bringing him."

"I didn't know," Emily said. "We were out for

lunch and then he asked if he could come and meet you."

Josie stuck her bottom lip out. "I'm sorry."

"Sorry for what?"

"That it was awkward. Maybe if we'd known he was coming, we'd have been better prepared."

"It wasn't awkward." Emily stared out over the water, thinking back on the last ten minutes. "It was fine."

"He hates us."

"No, he doesn't." Emily laughed and had to glance at Josie to see if she was being serious. "You're being weird."

"Maybe it was just me," Josie said. "Anyway I'm in a bad mood. I had two auditions this week and didn't get either part."

"Sorry. What were the parts?"

"The lead in a small independent film. I really thought I'd be perfect for it. And then a voiceover for an advert. I don't know why I didn't get that."

"It will probably be good when you start work next week. It'll give you something else to focus on."

"I'm not really looking forward to it. Being stuck in an office will be annoying."

"You always enjoy any job." It was true. Emily couldn't remember Josie ever complaining about a job. She always just got on with it. She actually seemed to be good at everything. And she always got on well with her colleagues.

"I suppose," Josie agreed. "So long as it doesn't get in the way of my auditions."

"How's it going living with Jack?" Emily asked. She'd helped with the official move a couple of weeks before, and then Josie hadn't really mentioned it since so she'd presumed it was going well.

"It's fine. I was already staying there every night anyway so nothing's really changed. I just don't have to feel guilty about my parents paying rent on a place that was hardly being used."

"Makes sense I suppose," Emily said.

Jack reappeared. "The coffee machine was playing up again. I don't know how Clive would manage without me sometimes."

"You're such a hero," Josie said with a grin.

He looked at Emily and grimaced. "So your boyfriend hates us."

"What?" Emily narrowed her eyes in confusion. "He doesn't hate you. He's also not my boyfriend. We're just dating."

"It was awkward, wasn't it?" Josie asked Jack.

"I've never been so relieved to hear Clive call my name!"

"I don't get it. I thought it went well. Although I was expecting it to be weird so maybe it just went better than I was imagining. I don't think he hates you."

"He definitely doesn't like us," Josie said.

"He was only here for five minutes!"

"Exactly, he left because he doesn't like us."

"He had stuff to do." Emily knew her voice lacked conviction. "He didn't leave because he doesn't like you."

"It was partly your fault anyway," Josie said. "Why hadn't you told him about the book deal?"

"I don't know. I don't want to sound like I'm bragging."

"It's not bragging," Jack said. "It's a fact."

"What did you think of him?" Emily felt deflated now. She'd actually thought it had gone pretty well. "You like him, don't you?" She couldn't think of a reason why they wouldn't like him.

They shrugged in unison.

"He seems okay," Josie said vaguely.

Emily looked to Jack for an opinion. He screwed his face up.

"What?" Emily asked.

"Nothing." Jack waved a hand in front of his face. "He seems like a nice enough guy ..."

Emily glared at him. "Just tell me what you think."

"Well ..." Jack seemed to debating how much he should say. "I kept wanting to tell him you're not a cat."

"What's that supposed to mean?" she demanded.

Jack slowly moved over to Josie and ran a hand over her hair, then down her back. He moved his other hand over her leg. Josie started laughing and shoved him away, but he reached to stroke her cheek, grinning like an idiot.

"He didn't do that." Emily's voice was almost a shout, but she also couldn't help chuckling at Jack acting such a fool.

"He did!" Josie batted Jack away, laughing. "He couldn't stop touching you and stroking you. I had to bite my tongue to stop myself from telling him to get a room."

"No!" Emily screeched.

"Yes!" Jack and Josie said together.

She covered her face with her hands. "It's like we

experienced something completely different. Will you stop it …" She reached over and gave Jack a firm shove as he continued to paw Josie with great amusement. With a dramatic pout, she turned and lay on her front, burying her head in her arms. "I can't believe I introduced you, and now you're being mean."

"Sorry." Jack squeezed her shoulder. "It wasn't so bad. Maybe we misread things. Perhaps he liked us."

"And it wasn't fair to bring him here," Josie put in. "Of course it was awkward. This is *our* spot."

Emily shifted onto her side to look at them. "That's true. I didn't even think about that."

"Next time we can meet somewhere neutral and it will be fine." Josie said reassuringly.

"Oh God." Jack flopped onto his back beside Emily. "We have to meet him again?"

"Yes. You're my friends and he's my … he's the person I'm dating."

She closed her eyes, hoping for an end to the conversation. A moment later she felt Jack stroking her arm. Josie spluttered out a laugh as Emily's eyes pinged open. Jack was lying on his side with a blank expression. His fingers trailed over her hair and then down her cheek and her neck.

"What are you doing?" She swatted his hand away and he finally broke into a grin.

"Checking that your skin actually has sensation because he was doing that the whole time and it was like you weren't even aware of it."

"He wasn't! You're exaggerating. Stop being mean and go and get me an ice cream!"

Jack laughed and stood up.

"I want an ice cream too," Josie said.

"And when you come back we're changing the subject." Emily felt the need to be assertive for once. "No more teasing from either of you."

Jack raised a hand in salute before he walked away.

Emily glared at Josie. "Don't say anything else!"

Chapter 15

Emily was walking out of work the next day when the illegally parked car beeped its horn. It was Stuart.

"Hi!" he said when she peered in the passenger window. "Do you want to have dinner with me?"

"Okay." She opened the passenger door and got in.

"Shall we go out somewhere, or get something at my place?"

"Your place." She sank into the seat. "I just want to relax."

"Long day?" he asked.

"One of the waitresses for the café called in sick so I had to cover for her. Amanda came in to cover the shop. She usually just works at the weekend. It wasn't an awful day. I'm just not used to being on my feet the whole time."

"I'll cook for you and you can chill out on the couch." He gave her knee a squeeze and his hand lingered there until he needed to change gear. When he returned his hand to her leg again, Emily couldn't help but think of Jack talking about how much he touched her. And of course he touched her; it was a new relationship and he was affectionate. It wasn't excessive, though. She'd have noticed before if it was.

She sent her mum a quick message to say she

wouldn't be home for dinner and they drove in silence to Stuart's house. It was a basic two-bedroomed terraced house. He headed straight for the kitchen, and she flopped onto the couch in the living room, where she barely moved a muscle until Stuart brought food through.

"What did you think of Jack and Josie?" She twirled her fork in the spaghetti. "You liked them, didn't you?"

"Yeah." He was unconvincing. "They seemed … fun."

"Fun?" She stopped and stared at him. Jack and Josie were right – he didn't like them.

"Hmm." He put a forkful of pasta in his mouth.

"Didn't you like them?" she asked.

He looked thoughtful for a moment. "There's a weird dynamic between the three of you. I felt a little uncomfortable."

How on earth had she thought the encounter went well and everyone else thought it was a disaster?

"It's probably because I've known them forever," she said.

"I thought Jack and Josie hadn't been together long? Did you know Jack before they got together?"

"No." She paused, thinking. "They haven't been together very long actually. Less than six months." She frowned deeply. "Have we really only known Jack a matter of months?" She realised she was thinking aloud.

"Not quite forever then," Stuart remarked.

She chuckled. "No." It did seem very strange that they'd only known Jack such a short time. It felt like he'd always been around. When she caught Stuart watching her intently, she sensed a change of subject was needed. "The pasta's great," she said. It would help if she was better at conversation.

"Good." He focused on his food and they ate in silence.

A couple of hours later, Emily made a move to go home. Stuart seemed surprised. Apparently he'd assumed she would stay over at his place. She'd stayed over a few times before, but she was surprised by his assumption. Since she didn't have any spare clothes with her and had to work the next morning, she told him she couldn't. It was a handy excuse because she really wanted to sleep in her own bed.

Stuart dropped her home and brought the subject up again as they pulled up outside her house.

"Why don't you leave some stuff at my place? Then you can stay over whenever you feel like it…"

Emily ran a hand through her hair and scratched her head. The way he said it, like it was merely a practical solution to a problem, made it difficult to argue with. It made her anxious. He was moving too fast and she absolutely didn't want to leave her stuff at his house. She should tell him that. It wasn't anything personal – she just felt things were going a bit fast. He'd understand.

"Yeah, maybe," she said instead. After giving him a quick kiss she hopped out of the car and waved him away.

***

The following Sunday she arrived at the Boathouse and grabbed a table inside. The place was quiet. It had been raining and the ground was wet. The sun didn't seem like it was going to put in an appearance.

"I'm really annoyed with you."

"What a nice greeting." Jack planted a kiss on Emily's cheek as she shrugged her jacket off.

"Josie's not here?"

"Not yet. Do you want a coffee before you tell me what I've done to annoy you?"

"Please."

Jack left her and came back a couple of minutes later with coffee for them both. "What did I do then?"

"All the stuff you said about Stuart being overly tactile." She bit her lip as she tried not to laugh. "Now I notice every time he touches me … and it is all the time!"

Jack grinned. "I told you."

"It's so annoying." She picked up her coffee, wrapping both hands around the mug. "I'm not sure how I didn't notice it before."

"I guess there are worse things. It should be flattering. He can't keep his hands off you."

She rolled her eyes.

"Apart from that, everything's good?" Jack asked. "You like him?"

"Yeah." Her voice was flat and unconvincing. Jack raised a quizzical eyebrow. She sighed heavily before she spoke again. It had been playing on her mind all week. "He asked me to leave some stuff at his. So I can stay over more often …" She watched Jack's reaction, but he only gave her a reassuring smile.

"And you don't want to?"

"It feels like things are moving a bit fast." She set

her mug down. "I like him, but we've only been dating a few weeks and it seems like he's ready to move in together, and I'm still a long way from that." She caught the look on Jack's face. "Sorry. I know you and Josie moved in together pretty fast, but I don't feel ready."

Jack glanced around, then leaned forwards, resting his forearms on the table. "I'm not sure I was completely ready for Josie to move in either."

Emily almost laughed until she saw he wasn't joking.

"She said it was temporary," he added. "She couldn't pay her rent so she was going to move in with her parents. Then she asked if she could move in with me for a while instead …" He raised an eyebrow.

"You couldn't say no." Emily looked at him sympathetically. "And of course it's not temporary."

He shook his head. "I can hardly ask when she's planning on moving out."

"Sorry." Emily's smile was part grimace.

"It's fine." He sat up straighter. "I don't mean to complain. It's not like I hate living with her." There was a short silence before he gave her a cheeky grin. "It's actually lovely to go home every evening and have someone waiting to tell me what a mess my place is and that I should do some cleaning. It's a dream come true."

Emily laughed at his sarcastic tone. "Why doesn't *she* clean? She hardly works … what does she do all day?"

"That is a very good question." After a moment, Jack's grin faded. "I shouldn't really talk to you about this stuff."

"It's all right. I know what Josie's like."

"Exactly." He drummed his fingers on the table. "You get it. If I complain to Lee or any of the lads, they look at me like I'm insane for being with her."

Emily nodded. She loved Josie but she knew exactly how pushy and over-bearing she could be. "I definitely understand. Josie's great. But she's also a complete nightmare!"

He nodded. "That pretty much sums her up."

Chapter 16

Emily hurried into the house after work on Friday. The bus had been late and she only had ten minutes to get showered and changed before going out again.

"How was your day?" Her mum appeared in the kitchen doorway, and Emily paused at the bottom of the stairs.

"Fine," she replied. "Same as always. I've got to hurry. I'm meeting Jack for dinner and I need to shower." She continued up the stairs and got ready in record time.

"I waited half an hour for the bus ..." She adjusted her top as she walked into the kitchen ten minutes later. "Stuart will be here to pick me up any minute."

"Stuart?" Her mum eyed her warily. "You said Jack before."

"No, I didn't." Emily dumped her tote bag on the kitchen table, rifling through it to check what she'd haphazardly thrown in. "I'll probably stay at Stuart's and go straight to work in the morning."

"Okay. So long as it's Stuart and not Jack."

"Of course I'm not meeting Jack. You're being weird, Mum. Why would I be meeting Jack?"

"I don't know." Her mum leaned heavily against the sink. "The same reason you talk about him so much?"

"I don't talk about Jack a lot."

Her mum puffed out a quick, humourless laugh.

"Well, why shouldn't I talk about Jack?" Emily stood up straight. "He's my friend."

"He's your best friend's boyfriend."

"So I'm not allowed to be friends with him?"

"If it's really just friendship you feel for him of course it's fine. But I worry that's not all it is."

"Oh my God." She swung the bag onto her shoulder as the sound of a car horn blared. "You're actually serious, aren't you?"

"It's just a bit confusing. Stuart is your boyfriend but you can't go five minutes without mentioning Jack."

Emily opened her mouth but realised the only part of that statement she wanted to object to was the part about Stuart being her boyfriend. It still felt odd referring to him as her boyfriend. This is what happened when you went so long without a boyfriend – even the word felt foreign.

"I've got to go, Mum." She kissed her cheek, wanting to put an end to the conversation. "Stuart's waiting."

"Why doesn't he come in? It's rude to beep the horn and wait in the car. He could come in and say hello. Why doesn't he want to meet your mother?"

Emily sighed dramatically and moved into the hallway. "He does," she called over her shoulder. "I told him not to come in. I want to take things slow. It was me who said we should wait a while before we meet each other's families."

"You're not taking things *that* slow. You're

staying at his place a couple of times a week."

Emily stopped at the door. She turned and raised her eyebrows. Her mum was usually cool. They had a nice, easy relationship, and would chat about most things. Today she was acting like an over-protective, interfering mother hen. Emily didn't like it.

"Sorry." Her mum held her hands up. "Go. Have fun! Whenever you feel like introducing me to Stuart is fine."

"You can meet him soon," Emily promised.

***

Stuart had made a reservation at a French restaurant in the city centre. Gentle piano music played in the background, and candlelight flickered between them in the centre of the table. It was all a bit fancy. And she wasn't really in the mood for anything fancy. Reading the menu felt like hard work. Not used to French cuisine, she ended up playing it safe and ordering risotto. Once she'd ordered, she snapped the pretentious menu shut and handed it back to the waiter.

"Are you okay?" Stuart sipped his water. "You're very quiet."

She shrugged. "I had a bit of an argument with my mum. Nothing major."

"What about?"

"Hmm." She couldn't very well tell him the truth. "She was in a bad mood. Complaining about everything."

"Maybe it's time you moved out."

"It seems like a waste of money. The rent's cheap

with my mum. I'm trying to save. Besides, I said she was in a bad mood. That doesn't mean I need to move out."

"Don't you want to move out? I can't imagine still living with my parents."

"It's just my mum," she mumbled. "She's generally pretty easy to live with."

His mouth twitched into a half-smile. "I could probably comment better if I'd met her." His tone was somewhat jokey. Not jokey enough, though.

When she responded, her voice definitely lacked amusement. "You can meet my mum," she snapped. "Please stop nagging me about it."

His eyebrows jumped defensively. "I'm not nagging."

"Yes you are." She tapped the prongs of her fork. It was annoying because now he'd act all innocent and make her look like the unreasonable one. He definitely nagged, though. Not in an obvious way, but in a constant stream of underhand comments.

"I just don't see why we can't meet each other's friends and family." His calm voice annoyed her. She was definitely going to come out of the conversation sounding neurotic.

"You met my friends," she said. "You didn't like them."

"That's not true. And I only met them for five minutes."

There was a pause. Emily pushed her hands into her lap to put an end to her nervous touching of the cutlery. "We're still getting to know each other. I don't see any rush to bring other people into the equation."

"Because I'd like to show you off." His eyes softened and Emily felt a pang of guilt. "I've been telling my friends and family all about you, and I'd like for them to meet you, and you to meet them."

It made her slightly nauseous when he was sentimental. He'd backed her into a corner – she could hardly say no. How long could she really put it off for anyway?

She reached across the table and took his hand. "Soon, okay? I promise. We can arrange something next week with your friends."

"I think you've been promising next week for a while now," he said lightly.

"Next week. Definitely."

He seemed to be placated and moved the conversation on, telling her about the last couple of days at work. She was starting to know the names of all the kids he taught. Even if she switched off for a minute she could usually accurately guess which kids he was talking about when she zoned back in. It began to be a little game for her. He could talk all night about work, and he didn't seem to notice if she was listening or not.

Emily was in a funny mood. She was tired and irritable. By the time they'd eaten and were leaving the restaurant, she was wishing she'd never agreed to stay at Stuart's place. She wanted to go home and crawl into her own bed.

"Shall we get a quick drink?" Stuart nodded in the direction of a wine bar a few doors down from the restaurant.

"I'm so tired …"

"Come on. It's Friday night. Let's go wild!"

She started to protest but he took her arm and led her down the street. "Just one drink then," she relented.

The wine bar was part of a chain and wasn't as classy inside as it looked from the street. The music was too loud and the floor too sticky. They found a pillar to lean on in the back corner. It had a ledge running around it for drinks.

"Don't forget you're driving." She eyed his bottle of beer.

"I thought I might ditch the car and pick it up tomorrow."

"But we're not staying out long. It's hardly worth getting a taxi for the sake of one more drink. Why didn't you get a soft drink?"

He leaned over and kissed her lips. "Because it's Friday." His lips lingered, brushing against her cheek as he spoke. "I wanted another drink. I'm happy to pay for a taxi. Will you please stop worrying about everything?"

The frown creased her forehead. She really wasn't in the mood for a night out. It wasn't worth arguing, though. If he wanted to pay for a taxi so be it. Her eyes scanned the room. She took a sip of her drink. Stuart was probably right – she should stop worrying. Why couldn't she relax and enjoy an evening out? She slipped her hand into Stuart's and gave a short squeeze. He smiled brightly and kissed her again.

When he pulled away, he held up an arm and waved to someone. "There's Ian," he said. "I work with him." He stared across the room. "There's a whole bunch of people from work. We should have a drink with them. You'll like them."

Emily smiled tightly. She didn't feel she could say no. Interestingly, the group of people walking towards them didn't seem the least surprised to see Stuart.

She had the definite feeling she'd been set up.

Summer at the Old Boathouse

Chapter 17

Emily spent most of Saturday in a daze at work. She was still furious with Stuart and couldn't seem to concentrate. He called her as she was leaving for the day. She didn't answer. As she walked through the front door at home, she ignored another call from him.

Her mum had bright pink rubber gloves on and was scrubbing the inside of the microwave. She stood up straight. "How was work?"

"Okay," Emily replied. "Nothing special."

"Are you seeing Stuart this evening?"

She rubbed an eye. "Maybe. I'm not sure yet."

"Did you guys have an argument or something?" Her mum was obviously wondering why she hadn't stayed at Stuart's place as planned the previous night. Emily had spent an hour with Stuart's friends and managed to pretend everything was fine. Only later, when they were alone, did she let him know what she thought about him arranging for her to meet his friends without telling her. She'd been livid.

Emily took a seat at the kitchen table. "I said I didn't want to meet his friends yet, so he invited them out without telling me."

"Why didn't you want to meet his friends?" Her mum pulled off the gloves and leaned against the counter.

"I think you're missing the point."

"Am I?"

She eyed her mum wearily. "Yes. He tricked me."

When her phone rang, she pulled it from her pocket and set it on the table.

"So now you're ignoring his calls?"

The chair scraped as she stood abruptly. She gave her mum a pointed look as she answered the phone. She went upstairs to talk to Stuart in private and told him she hadn't heard her phone when he called before. He apologised again for the previous evening, and she agreed to go over to his place later that evening.

After ending the call, she pulled out her laptop and got to work on her social media presence. Every post and tweet and comment was an effort. All the cheery words and happy emoticons felt fraudulent. Of course she was excited about the book release, but she wasn't the sort of person to broadcast it to the world. And it was difficult to post every day about a book that wasn't even published yet. Although, she'd actually been advised to keep posts about the book to a minimum and mainly post about herself. It was torture.

It wasn't long before she was interrupted by a knock on her bedroom door. "I'm going food shopping," her mum said as the door slowly opened. "Do you want anything special?"

"No." She sighed. "Just the usual."

"Are you working on the next book?"

"No. I'm trying to take over the internet. Why do I even need a social media presence?"

Her mum chuckled. "The more you do it, the

more natural it will feel. It'll get easier."

"That's what Jack says, but I'm having trouble believing it." She caught the barely there dip of her mum's eyebrows. "Don't start about Jack again. He's my friend. Stop making a big deal of everything."

"Hey!" She backed away with her hands up. "I didn't say anything. I'll see you later. It's probably pasta for dinner, unless you have any better ideas."

She grimaced. "I'm going over to Stuart's."

"Okay," her mum called from the top of the stairs. Emily had the familiar pang of guilt at abandoning her.

"We can have dinner tomorrow evening …"

"Great! Have a fun evening. Love you!"

"Love you too." Her mum was already halfway down the stairs and she had to shout.

After composing a tweet with a meme she'd found about writing, she closed the laptop and unenthusiastically threw a few things in a bag. Hopefully she could manage to have a pleasant time with Stuart. She was worried they'd fall into another argument about the previous evening.

Conversely, when Stuart made a brief apology and then brushed the subject aside, she wasn't as relieved as she might have been. While she didn't feel like talking about it, it did play on her mind. Mainly because she began to wonder why she'd been so against meeting his friends. Stuart had assumed it was because she was shy. He'd said so. Was that the reason? Previously, she hadn't given it much thought, but the more she dwelled on it the more convinced she was that it wasn't the reason at all. She just couldn't quite put her finger on why she'd been so against it.

It didn't really matter, she decided as she cuddled up to Stuart on the couch. He was being very attentive, and she realised she'd probably overreacted. Stuart was a great guy and he had nice friends. It was a simple, easy relationship, and if Emily would relax and stop over-thinking things, she was convinced she'd be very happy with him.

***

"Do you want to do something today?" Stuart asked over breakfast the next morning. It wasn't anything fancy – just coffee and toast. They ate sitting on the couch.

Emily crunched on her toast and ignored the ball of panic that formed in her stomach. "I was planning on meeting Josie and Jack this afternoon."

"Of course." Stuart drummed a finger on the arm of the couch. "Sundays at the Boathouse."

"I don't have to go," she said quickly. The ball of panic intensified. *Please, don't ask me not to go*. She always looked forwards to her days at the Boathouse.

"I've got some stuff to do anyway. I need to do some washing and clean up a bit."

"You could come with me if you want." The suggestion was automatic. She hoped he wouldn't take her up on it.

He frowned. "After last time? I think I'll pass."

"You should meet Josie and Jack again. They're great. I promise. We can arrange something proper – not just hanging around Jack's work."

"That's probably a better idea." He collected up the breakfast things to take to the kitchen, giving her a quick kiss before he went. "Why don't you spend the afternoon with them and we can meet up again this evening?"

"Okay." She leaned back into the couch, then sat up again abruptly. "Actually, I said I'd have dinner with my mum ..." She trailed off. The obvious thing would be to invite him to join them. He hovered in the doorway, his hands full of plates and cups. She should invite him. Her mum would like him. Stuart was the sort of guy you could take home to meet the family. Her hesitation was awkward, and finally he continued to the kitchen.

"Dinner tomorrow, after work?" she said casually when he returned.

"Sure." He flopped down beside her and draped an arm around her. She smiled as he planted a kiss on the side of her head. They spent the next hour chatting and laughing. By the time she left him, she almost wished she'd invited him to have dinner with her mum. She wasn't quite sure why she was putting it off. Maybe she'd call him later and invite him.

Stuart dropped her off in town and she walked the short distance from Folly Bridge to the Boathouse. Emily beamed when she caught sight of Jack walking out of the café. Her stomach felt all fluttery. He didn't see her, and Emily hung back, watching as he walked over to Josie, who was lying peacefully on the blanket in the sun. He crept up and held a cold can of Coke to Josie's exposed midriff. Emily was too far away to hear, but she could tell that Josie squealed as she shot up. Jack was laughing as he lay down on the blanket. They both looked so happy. Josie shoved him playfully and then cuddled up to him.

Emily's smile fell away and she took a step back as though she'd taken a blow to the stomach. A bike skidded behind her and she turned to see an angry cyclist glaring at her.

"Watch where you're going!"

"Sorry," she muttered. It felt like the world around her slowed. Jack and Josie were still engrossed in each other. They hadn't spotted her. It was like the rest of the world didn't exist to them.

Emily sucked in a long breath. Her head spun, her palms were damp. Quickly, she walked back the way she'd come. Everything suddenly made far too much sense. It wasn't a relationship in general that she craved. And she didn't spend all week looking forward to an afternoon in the sun with her best friend. She was such an idiot. Her legs wouldn't take her fast enough. She needed to get away from the Boathouse. Suddenly filled with excessive energy, she didn't wait for the bus but strode through town, dodging shoppers and tourists as she went.

Home. She needed to get home. When she finally burst through the front door, she was bright red and puffing hard.

"I wasn't expecting you until this evening." Her mum was sitting at the kitchen table, eating a sandwich. "Aren't you meeting Josie?"

"No." She sucked on her bottom lip, determined not to cry.

"What happened? Did you fall out with Stuart?"

She dropped her bag by the table. "No."

"Well, don't leave me in suspense …"

There was a glass on the draining board and she filled it with water. She clutched the glass but didn't take a sip. "I'm not meeting Jack and Josie." Her voice was flat, emotionless, but her chest heaved and she knew her turmoil was obvious in her eyes, which couldn't seem to stayed focused on anything.

Her mum looked at her intently. "Why not?"

Emily's eyes darted to her mum. "Because you were right." She walked out of the kitchen and into the living room. Perching on the edge of the couch, she placed the untouched water on the coffee table with a shaky hand. When her mum followed her in, she glared up at her. "You were right," she said desperately. "I'm a horrible person. I was watching them by the river today. I always envied their relationship, but I convinced myself it was their closeness I envied." She dropped her head to her hands. "I like spending time with Jack but I always thought … I thought I just liked his company. I'm such an idiot."

Her mum sat beside her and patted her leg. "Oh, love."

"I can't even figure out if deep down I knew all along. Was I kidding myself that I saw him as a friend? You were right – I talk about him all the time. And I talk about him all the time because I think about him all the time. How on earth didn't I realise it's completely inappropriate? Josie's my best friend."

"But you haven't done anything wrong. Having a crush on your best friend's boyfriend isn't a crime. It's really not the worst thing in the world."

Emily's eyebrows knitted together as she looked helplessly at her mum.

"Not just a crush?" her mum asked softly.

She chewed the inside of her cheek and shook her

head in a series of tiny movements. "What am I going to do?"

"Maybe you should split up with Stuart …"

"Mum! Of course I can't split up with Stuart. I need him around more than ever. If Josie thinks I've got my own boyfriend, she's less likely to notice how I feel about hers."

"It doesn't seem very fair to Stuart."

"It's not." She chewed on a nail. "That's why I didn't want us to meet each other's friends and families. I knew things weren't right between us. It was obvious to you, wasn't it?"

Her mum shrugged. "You talk about Jack so much and hardly ever mention Stuart."

Emily sat up determinedly. "I need to put a stop to these feelings before they go any further. I'm a rational person. Now I'm admitting how I feel, I can get over it and move on."

"Okay." Her mum sounded unconvinced. "So you just need to talk yourself out of it?"

"Exactly! Sort of like aversion therapy or something."

"That could work." Her mum smiled mischievously. "Think about everything you don't like about Jack. Focus all your attention on disliking him, and before you know it, you won't be able to stand the sight of him. It's like when someone annoys you in a dream and you're annoyed with them in real life."

She squinted at her mum. "Do you really do that?"

"All the time! Last week when I was annoyed with you, I'd dreamt that you told me I had to cut down on alcohol and chocolate …"

"You *should* cut down on … never mind, we're getting off topic!"

Her mum shifted until she faced her squarely on the couch. "So tell me everything bad about Jack … Let's be really shallow and start with his looks …"

Emily tilted her head to the side. "Hmm." She couldn't help but smile when she pictured him. It was hard to find anything bad to say. "He's got a lovely face. Kind eyes. He's got great hair … and he's the perfect build: tall but not too tall, well-built but not imposingly so. Just manly, you know. And there's this hint of ruggedness …" She registered the look on her mum's face.

"If that's you describing his bad qualities we might have a problem. So he's good-looking. I suppose that's no surprise; he is Josie's boyfriend. Let's do personality. There must be some flaws there … he is with Josie, after all."

"Mum!" She shoved her playfully. "That's mean."

"Well. I know she's your best friend, but she's kind of flighty and annoying."

Emily couldn't help but smile; she knew her mum liked Josie really. She also couldn't disagree with the description. "Don't be awful," she said lightly.

"Don't look at me like that! You know what she's like, and you'd describe her the same way, if you were honest."

She thought for a moment. "I'd probably say she's wishy-washy and spoilt, but I take your point. She has her good qualities too. She's kind and fun. She's loyal. Why are we talking about Josie? I thought we were picking faults in Jack."

"You're not doing a great job so far. And I was making the point that Josie's far from perfect so unless Jack's a saint, he must have his flaws too. Think hard … does he talk about himself too much? Or interrupt people when they're talking? Does he have a weird tic?"

"No tics," Emily said thoughtfully. "And he doesn't talk about himself too much." Her mind drifted and she remembered all the times she'd spent with him. "He always asks about my writing. But not in a way that makes me uncomfortable, like most people. He seems so interested. And when I feel like it's just a stupid hobby and nothing will ever come of it, he tells me I can do it. That I'll be a successful author."

She paused and looked seriously at her mum. "And when he says it, I believe it. With everyone else I'm self-conscious, but with him I feel so confident. I don't have to worry about what I say. When I'm with Jack, I feel like I'm the best version of myself …" She pushed her hair back off her face. "This isn't going to work, is it?"

Her mum looked at her sadly. "I think we might have to go to plan B."

"We have a plan B?"

"It involves me gently nudging Josie into a busy road … when a bus is coming."

"Oh, my God!" Emily shrieked and stared at her mum, wide-eyed. "I can't believe you said that!" She tried to reprimand her mum with a stern look, but the laughter was infectious and she soon joined in.

"I have an idea," she said finally. "I can sit here,

thinking about Jack, and you do something awful …"
She thought for a moment. "Get a kitchen knife and
stab me!"

"I never realised we were such violent people."

"Somewhere fleshy." Emily kept chuckling as she
spoke. "Nothing life-threatening, but a good amount
of pain. Then soon I'll associate Jack with immense
amounts of pain and I'll be over him in no time."

"And before we know it, I'll be in prison and
you'll be locked up in some institution. I guess being
in love with your best friend's boyfriend won't be
high on your list of worries if you're in a straitjacket."

Emily collapsed back on the couch. She wanted to
argue that she wasn't in love with him.

But she kept quiet.

It didn't seem like a time for lies.

Summer at the Old Boathouse

Chapter 18

Even though her mum refused to go along with her plan of extreme violence, it still wasn't long before Emily associated thoughts of Jack with immense amounts of pain. After finally admitting to herself how she really felt about him, she knew a kitchen knife probably wasn't capable of inflicting as much pain as the knowledge that she could never be with him.

She also needed to find a new best friend. It was unfair being friends with Josie when she spent most of her time having inappropriate thoughts about Jack.

On Wednesday, Josie waltzed into the gift shop. It was quiet, and Emily was reading a crime thriller on her Kindle. She put it aside.

"What happened on Sunday?" Josie asked.

"I told you, I wasn't feeling well."

"It was weird." Josie idly pushed at the postcard carousel. "It's the first time in ages we haven't spent Sunday together. I was worried you'd ditched me for Stuart."

"Nope. I was at home. Mum will confirm it if you don't believe me."

"Has your mum met Stuart yet?"

"Not yet. I met his friends."

"Yeah? What are they like?"

"Nice." Emily moved off the stool. Josie always liked to sit and swivel on it. "We had a good night out with them."

"He managed to get you to go drinking *and* meet his friends? You must be smitten!"

Emily smiled and moved to straighten out a display.

"So things are still going well with Stuart?"

"Yeah. It's all okay."

"That's good." Josie put a hand on the counter when she swivelled too far. "Jack's driving me crazy."

"Is he?" Emily moved souvenir mugs out of place on the display just so she could straighten them out again.

"He's such a slob. The apartment's always a mess. I don't think he even notices."

Emily smiled. She knew for a fact Jack *did* notice, even if it was only because Josie constantly pointed it out to him. "He works a lot," she said. "I guess he doesn't have much time."

"Now you sound like him," Josie said. "I'm sure he thinks I should clean because I work less hours than him. I don't actually have much time either. It's quite stressful looking for acting jobs as well as doing the office work."

"How's the job going?" Emily asked. "Are you still enjoying it?"

"It's all right. The people are easy to work with, and they're pretty flexible if I need to take time off for an audition."

"That's good then. Have you had any more auditions?"

"I've got one next week. Some film extra work. It's for crowd scenes and I'm fairly sure I'll get it. Then I'll have to figure out what to do about the office job. I suppose I'll probably quit."

Emily nodded, unsure what to say. It seemed like such an uncertain career path. She admired Josie's optimism if nothing else. It baffled her the way Josie went into every audition presuming she'd get the part. If she could get through on confidence alone, she'd be a huge success by now.

"I hope it works out," Emily said vaguely. She lingered at the bookshelf, trying to keep herself busy. She swallowed hard and didn't look at Josie. "Jack's okay, is he?"

"Apart from being a slob?" Josie said lightly. "Yeah, he's fine. Do you want to try a double date again? I feel like we should make more effort with Stuart."

"No." The thought of spending time with Jack and Stuart together was about the most unappealing thing she could think of. "Let's not."

"I love how blunt you are," Josie said. "That's quite a skill. Most people feel the need to make up excuses."

"Do you want me to make up an excuse?"

Josie laughed. "Yes, please!"

"Okay." Emily sucked in a long breath. "I'm afraid Stuart has developed an allergy to air and he now lives in an oxygen tent in his house. Otherwise, he'd love to come out and get to know you and Jack better."

"That's very sad." Josie beamed. "Maybe we could visit him instead?"

"I'm afraid that's not possible. A sinkhole appeared outside his front door so no one can get in or out. It's a huge crater, completely unstable. I'm firing food into the house with a slingshot."

"Well, that's a shame! Poor old Stuart isn't having a great week, is he? Maybe when the sinkhole's fixed?"

"Maybe. So long as he doesn't contract a tropical disease inside his tent or something …"

"That's always a worry, isn't it?" Josie hopped off the stool, laughing. "I love your stories. Have you ever thought about writing a book?"

"A whole novel?" Emily said with a grin. "That sounds terribly difficult."

"I'm sure you could manage it. I think you'd make a great author! I'd buy all your books."

The bell above the door tinkled and Emily made her way back to the counter, saying a quick hello to the middle-aged couple.

"I better go," Josie said. "I'll see you at the weekend."

"Okay." Emily was hit by a wave of guilt. Guilt and sadness. "Thanks for coming in."

She went to the window and watched Josie practically skip across the courtyard. How was she always so cheerful? It was annoying. And why couldn't Emily be that happy? She frowned. She'd probably skip everywhere too if she had Jack for a boyfriend. The ridiculous thought made her want to cry.

She only noticed the couple were waiting to pay when the man cleared his throat loudly.

"Sorry," she said, as she went back to the counter.

It was a struggle to focus on work. She kept wondering about the weekend. Should she avoid Jack? Did she even really like him? Was this all something she'd built up in her head? A couple of weeks ago she was spending time with him and it wasn't an issue at all. Now, she'd convinced herself she was in love with him. She probably wasn't at all. It was just her crazy imagination running away with her.

That's what she told herself all week. She was slipping easily back into denial mode. And of course she would go to the Boathouse on Sunday. It would be weird if she didn't go.

She only saw Stuart a couple of times that week. He really was a decent guy. She could do so much worse. It was a shame that was all the enthusiasm she could muster for the relationship. Perhaps her mum was right and she should put the poor guy out of his misery. It was unfair to string him along when there was such a clear imbalance of feelings.

When Sunday finally came around, she was feeling entirely positive. Complete and utter denial is a great thing when you're in love with your friend's boyfriend. She wasn't in love with him, though. Obviously. Denial, denial, denial.

The blanket was already laid out but there was no sign of Josie. Emily dropped her bag down and was about to sit when she heard Jack call her name.

It was only two weeks since she'd seen him, but it felt like way longer. His lovely smile radiated happiness and his eyes sparkled. She didn't love him, though. If she did it was in a purely platonic way. A completely acceptable kind of love. She could even drop it into conversation with Josie: *Hey, I love Jack. He's so great.* It wouldn't be inappropriate at all. Just a declaration of the casual love between friends. That was all.

"What happened last week?" He didn't stop when he reached her, but barrelled in for a hug. He smelled homely. She wanted to bury her head in his neck and inhale deeply. Probably a bit intimate for a platonic friendship. The denial slipped away as his body heat merged with hers. She didn't want to let go. Jack was amazing and she was completely in love with him.

In her defence, she was fairly sure anyone who spent time with him would fall in love with him. How could they not? It was like jumping into a swimming pool and expecting not to get wet.

"I missed you." He pulled out of the embrace but left an arm dangling around her shoulders.

She'd missed him too. She didn't say that, though. What came out of her mouth was a squeak, followed by a grunt. Clearing her throat surely disguised her strange noises. Why on earth did he have his arm around her? And how could she get him off her? The fist bump to his chest wasn't at all planned. Who would plan that? It got him to move away at least.

"Two weeks apart and I completely forgot how wonderfully quirky you are!" He smirked and sat on the blanket.

She joined him, leaving as much distance between them as the blanket would allow. Two weeks apart from him and she'd forgotten how to speak. What was it she was saying to her mum about how confident she was around Jack?

"How's work?" she managed in a squeaky voice.

Almost over-confident really.

"Fine," he said quickly. "I'd ask how the book marketing is coming on, but I've taken to stalking you on social media …"

She laughed and felt the tension leave her shoulders. "Whenever I post anything it seems to be a race between you and my mum to see who likes and shares it first."

"Good old Alison! I feel like I know her already. I'm definitely winning. She's slow on Twitter. You should have a word with her about that. Tell her she needs to up her game."

"I'll let her know."

He looked at her seriously. "I told you it would get easier. The social media stuff."

"It's all so fake." She picked at a daisy and twirled it between her thumb and finger. "And it doesn't make any sense. I'm supposed to let people get to know the person behind the books … for one thing no one has read my book yet so I'm quite sure no one cares. And then there's the fact that I'm an introvert who hates social media. It's kind of ironic that I'm supposed to express my personality on it."

"Maybe you could be really honest and post something like 'All I want to do is write books but I'm being forced to write tweets and Facebook posts and take arty photos of my notebook for Instagram.' You could make it a cry for help …"

"Yes!" She giggled. "I'll be trending in no time … hashtag save the author!"

"Hashtag write books not social media posts." He leaned back and rested on his elbows. His lazy smile made her stomach flutter.

"How's Stuart?" he asked.

"He's fine."

"I heard he lives in a bubble now so we can't double date …"

Her smile took over her face. "I can't believe Josie told you that."

"Was it supposed to be a secret? You're ashamed of your bubble boyfriend? He's really having a rough time of it."

If Emily were close enough, she'd have hit him. Luckily she was at a safe distance. Physical contact was a bad idea.

"She's not supposed to tell you about our insane conversations."

"Josie's the queen of insane conversations. I'm used to it by now." He sat up and stared out at the river. A lady was out watering the plants on her houseboat, and he held up a hand to wave to her. She was a smiley lady who was often pottering around the pretty, brightly coloured boat. Emily waved too.

Jack's tone was serious when he spoke again. "So how *are* things with Stuart?"

"Oh …" She scratched at her neck and ran a hand through her hair. "Okay. I think." The grass beside her was suddenly fascinating. "He's a nice guy. It's all fine."

"Calm down, Em." She could hear the smile as he spoke. "Your enthusiasm's making me feel uncomfortable."

The way he said her name sent a tingle down her spine. When she met his gaze she let out a short laugh. Then she bit her lip. "We had an argument because he insisted I met his friends. He got them to

148

turn up without telling me."

"How was it?" he asked. "What are his friends like?"

"They're lovely and it was pleasant enough. But I hate that he sprang it on me. I like to have a plan. I'm better when I know what's going to happen. And I hate that he thinks he knows better than me. I said I didn't want to meet them, but he thought I should so he arranged it behind my back."

She shrugged and then kept talking. "I keep thinking I'm overreacting. Stuart's a nice guy and there's nothing I particularly dislike about him, but …" She trailed off. Why did she have a habit of over-sharing with Jack? This was why she felt so confident around him. She always felt she could tell him anything and he wouldn't judge her. Unfortunately, it also meant that she told him everything. She definitely needed to tweak the filter between her thoughts and mouth.

"There's no spark?" Jack suggested quietly.

She gave a slight nod. "There's no spark."

"Are you thinking of breaking up with him?"

"Maybe. The trouble is …" She looked away, blowing out a breath as her filter finally kicked in.

"What?" Jack asked.

She couldn't avoid eye contact forever, and when she finally looked at him her filter dissolved again. "The alternative is being on my own." It sounded awful, but there was a part of her that just liked being in a relationship, even if it wasn't the best relationship in the world. Since she couldn't have the relationship she really wanted, maybe it was okay to be in one that had become pretty comfortable. Maybe a comfortable, boring relationship was better than being single. Who needs sparks anyway?

She waved as Josie approached. Perfect timing.

Jack's eyes were still on Emily – so intense it made her nervous. "You can do way better than that, Em." He smiled at her sadly and then turned his attention to Josie.

His words cut right through her. Because somewhere, deep down, she knew he was right. Why did she always take everything he said to heart? When he tells her she'll be a successful writer, her self-doubt vanishes. When he tells her not to settle for less than true love, she immediately thinks of ditching Stuart and downloading every dating app in existence. If only Jack knew the truth: that no matter what happened, she was always going to end up settling for second best.

Watching Josie kiss him in greeting just about finished Emily off. It was all too much. Maybe she should run home and talk her mum into the aversion therapy. It surely couldn't be worse than the metaphorical knife which was currently lodged in her heart.

"I better get back to work." Jack jumped up, turning and shooting Emily a discreet wink.

A wink? Really? A wink?

"I'm a bit hungover." Josie lifted her sunglasses, squinted dramatically and then put them back in place.

Emily dragged her gaze away from a retreating Jack. What was the wink all about? Someone should explain to him that with great power comes great responsibility. He shouldn't be winking at people willy-nilly.

She focused on Josie. "Do you ever consider not drinking so much?"

"That's a great idea." She flopped back onto the blanket. "I'll set a reminder in my phone for next Friday night." She shot Emily a cheeky grin.

"I can't stay long," Emily said.

"How come?" Josie braved a peek out from behind her sunglasses.

"Stuff to do."

"You really should work on your excuses."

Emily lay down and closed her eyes into the sun. What was she supposed to say? *I can't stay long because the sight of your boyfriend sends my insides to mush? I can't stay long because the more I see you and Jack together, the more I like my mum's idea of introducing you to the front of a bus?*

Quite inappropriate, really.

Chapter 19

Emily avoided Stuart all week. It was probably time to break up with him. All she could think about was Jack. At least she'd been developing the skill of making up excuses. She'd told Stuart she had a cold. Not so bad that she couldn't go to work, but bad enough that all she wanted to do after work was go home to bed. Thankfully he didn't offer to nurse her back to health.

By Friday she felt she couldn't keep avoiding him. They spent the evening at his place, in front of the TV. She'd pretty much decided that she was going to split up with him. It would have been best if she'd done it when she first walked in the door, but she chickened out and then spent the evening mentally arguing with herself on his couch.

A little voice screamed at her that it was cruel to drag things out. That she should end it immediately. But there was another voice which feebly pointed out that if she split up with him, it would most likely put an end to the foot massage he was currently giving her. He gave a great foot rub.

Eventually she fell asleep on the couch, and splitting up with him was put off for another day. She wasn't working that Saturday, and they ate a late breakfast at the kitchen table. Stuart had been to the bakery and there was an array of pastries in front of them.

"Do you want to do anything today?" Stuart had a dusting of icing sugar beside his mouth. Emily smiled as she reached to brush it away.

"Yeah." She pursed her lips. "I feel like doing something different."

"We could drive to the coast somewhere?"

"Maybe." Thoughts of splitting up with him had vanished. Being in a relationship with Stuart was definitely better than being alone. She pushed her plate away from her, trying to avoid the temptation to keep eating. "You know what I'd really like to do?" she said suddenly. "Get the train into London. I used to do that with Josie all the time. Just have a walk around. See the sights. Be a tourist."

"Okay." He smiled lazily. "If that's what you want."

**

On the train ride, she stared happily out of the window and wondered why she didn't make this trip any more. It was lovely. Then she recalled why she'd stopped going into London. When Josie had set her up with an internship at the magazine, the novelty of London soon wore off. Getting the train was far less exciting when you were doing it every day. And at rush hour, no less.

It felt like an adventure again now. Like it used to when it was her and Josie going off on one of their little day trips. The train juddered over the tracks, and the wonderfully green scenery rolled past the window.

She happily regaled Stuart with stories of her time at the magazine offices and how she'd loathed everything about it, from the intimidating people to the intimidating atmosphere.

She'd had no clue what she was doing and hated every moment of it. Josie's sister had gone to some trouble to set it up for her, and she hadn't felt she could quit immediately. When Lizzie left the job a couple of months after Emily started there, she didn't feel the need to stick it out and left well before the planned year-long internship was up. It had been an interesting experience, at least.

The weather was glorious when they arrived at Paddington. Emily beamed as she stood on the familiar street in front of the station. The sky was so blue, and the warmth of the sun made her skin tingle.

Stuart slipped his hand into hers, their fingers entwining. "What's the plan then?"

"First we get the most amazing fruit smoothies at that place." She pointed across the road to the tiny smoothie bar. "Then we walk over to Hyde Park and find a nice spot to relax."

"I haven't been to London in years," Stuart said, as they darted through slow traffic. "Are you going to be my tour guide?"

"Yes! This city has the most amazing history of literature. I can show you all the important literary landmarks."

He groaned. "Oh, God!"

She shot a well-aimed elbow to his ribs and he winced dramatically. They joined the end of the queue at the smoothie place. "Don't worry," she said. "I used to spend a lot of time in London with Josie. I'm also well-educated when it comes to trendy pubs and hip dance clubs."

"I will definitely need to see one or two of your trendy pubs. Remind me to thank Josie when I see her."

"I will," she replied happily. It was possibly the first time that she wasn't freaked out by him mentioning meeting up with Josie. Maybe getting them together again wouldn't be so bad. Getting out of Oxford was energising, and she was feeling entirely positive. At least until that moment when thoughts of Josie naturally led her to think of Jack.

For a stupid moment, she let herself imagine spending a day in London with Jack. She squeezed the hand in hers, imagining it was Jack beside her and not Stuart. Her smile evaporated and her positivity morphed into a dark ball of negativity in the pit of her stomach. She took a deep breath. There was no way she would let thoughts of Jack ruin her day out. She absolutely refused to go there.

"I recommend the Mango Magic." Focussing on the menu board behind the counter, she forced herself to smile. "Except don't get that," she said to Stuart. "I'm getting that one. Choose something different and we can share. The Strawberry Sizzle is also good, or the Very Berry Boost ..."

He squeezed her hand. "Why don't you choose for us both."

She smiled up at him. "Okay."

They wandered slowly over to Hyde Park, sipping their drinks as they went and occasionally swapping them between each other. It was busy in the wonderful expanse of green in the middle of the chaotic city. An oasis where the bright sunshine and warm breeze seemed to infect everyone with happiness. They found a spot to sit, and after a few minutes Stuart lay back on the grass. Emily did the same, resting her head on his stomach. Kites wove peacefully above them and children's laughter floated on the breeze.

Stuart ran a hand through her hair. "What's in store for me on your literary tour then?"

"I won't really subject you to that."

"I don't mind."

She closed her eyes to the sun. "You can't do much in a day anyway. It's all quite spread out. We'd spend most the day on the tube, and that would be a waste."

"True. Pick your top spots then …"

"I definitely want to go to Charring Cross Road and browse the book shops. I could spend all day there. You might like some of the museums," she mused. "The Sherlock Holmes museum is good, or the Charles Dickens one."

"Sherlock Holmes," Stuart said.

"Okay. We could go to the George Inn for dinner. You'll like it there. Shakespeare and Dickens were regulars back in the day."

"Well, if it's good enough for them it's good enough for us." Stuart continued gently playing with her hair. "So are these places the hidden gems of the city that no one knows about?"

"No." Emily chuckled. "It's London. Nothing is a secret and everything is a tourist attraction."

"Or maybe you just haven't found the secret places yet."

"I refuse to believe that."

"I've got you worried, haven't I? Maybe you're stuck with the tourist trail while the real literary fans are at the authentic spots chuckling away to themselves."

"Shut up!" She sat up abruptly. "You'll ruin it for me. Come on ..." She stood and tugged on his arm to pull him up. We've got lots to do."

They hardly stopped all afternoon, taking in museums and delightfully dusty old bookshops. They even made it to Poet's Corner in Westminster Abbey and paid their respects to the likes of Chaucer, Dickens and Kipling, all of whom were buried there.

At the end of the day, they sat in the fading sunlight in the courtyard of the George Inn. The old black and white building was stunning, with the hanging baskets providing bursts of colour. The lamps on the front of the building were adorably quaint. Cobblestones made the table slightly wobbly, but Emily didn't mind a bit.

"Do you know this place is the only remaining coach house in London?" She was staring at her phone and didn't look up at Stuart as she spoke to him. "It dates back to the sixteenth century. I could write an essay about how wonderful it is. How am I supposed to describe it in a tweet?"

"You're not struggling so much with social media today are you?"

He was taking a sip of his pint when she looked up. A waiter came and cleared their plates.

"It's easy when I've got so much to talk about. I love London." She positioned herself to take a selfie with the beautiful building in the background, then uploaded it to Facebook with a caption about ending a wonderful day of being steeped in literary history.

"Done?" Stuart asked, looking at her pointedly.

"Sorry." She put her phone on the table, realising she'd spent more time looking at her phone than at him.

"It's fine." He reached across the table and covered her hand with his. "I'm glad you enjoyed the day so much."

"It's been amazing." She beamed and then glanced down when her phone lit up. *Jack Denham commented on your post.* She couldn't resist. Quickly, she picked up the phone to read his comment. Her heart rate increased as she tapped at the buttons to find what he'd written. *A selfie? London is changing you! Come home quick xxx*

Kisses? Why did he add kisses? Why was she focussing on the kisses? And why was she reading the comment over and over again?

Stuart cleared his throat, and she shoved the phone into her handbag. "Sorry," she said again. "This is why I hate social media. It consumes you." As did the knot which had formed in her stomach. She thought she'd done so well, putting thoughts of Jack aside and enjoying her day out. If she was honest, he'd been there all the time, in the back of her mind. She'd pushed him to the edges of her thoughts, but he was definitely still there.

"Shall we make a move?" Stuart said. "By the time we get back to the station and then get back to Oxford, it'll be late."

She nodded her agreement and finished the last of her wine. The journey home was spent mostly in silence. Stuart dozed on the train, and Emily reflected on the day. It had been lovely, and Stuart was such easy company.

If only she could train her mind to stop wandering to Jack, she was sure she'd be perfectly content.

Chapter 20

Back in Oxford, they got a taxi back to Stuart's place. Emily woke up early the next morning and messaged her mum, asking if she wanted to have brunch with her. She was very tempted to invite Stuart to join them, but he'd already mentioned going to visit his parents for the day anyway.

Emily stopped at the bakery on the way home and picked up a selection of fresh bread. Her mum had said she'd put some bacon and eggs on.

"This is amazing," Emily said as they sat at the kitchen table together. She was ravenous and spent a few minutes shovelling food into her mouth before she slowed down enough to chat between mouthfuls. She excitedly told her mum all about her day in London.

"The trouble with Facebook is I already know everything you did," her mum said lightly. "I'm glad you enjoyed it."

"It was brilliant. I forgot how much I love London. Remember when Josie was always talking about us living there and I used to laugh it off? Part of me would love to do it."

"Don't say that." Her mum put her knife and fork down and picked up her cup of tea. "You wouldn't, would you?"

"No. It's a nice thought but I'd be too scared to move on my own. Josie seems to have gone off the idea."

"Can you imagine actually living with Josie?"

Emily chuckled and put a hand to her mouth as she swallowed. "Not really. Although, it might be fun."

"It might be a nightmare!"

"Jack seems to be surviving her anyway." Emily's smile faded and she returned her focus to her food.

"I worry about you," her mum said quietly. "I don't like all this business with Jack. I hate seeing you so upset."

"I'm not upset," Emily insisted. "I had a good day with Stuart yesterday. I'm fine. I don't even know how I really feel about Jack. I think I've built it up in my head. It's probably more of a wanting what you can't have thing."

Her mum sighed and looked at her sympathetically. "Are you going to the Boathouse today?"

She nodded and took a sip of tea. "If I avoid them, Josie will get suspicious."

"No she won't. You just want to see him. You're torturing yourself. You realise that, don't you?"

"It's fine, Mum. Just a stupid crush. I'll get over it." Maybe if she kept telling herself that it would be true. She took her plate to the sink. "Do you mind if I leave you to clear up?"

Her mum shook her head. "Off you go and torture yourself." She moved beside Emily and patted her on the shoulder. "I'm out this afternoon, but I'll be home this evening if you're around?"

"I'll see you this evening." Emily flashed an over-the-top fake smile. "I'll tell you all about my wonderful afternoon with my friends, and how it wasn't at all torturous. Then you'll have to eat your words."

"Fingers crossed! I'd quite like to be wrong on this occasion."

***

It had occurred to Emily to put an end to the Sunday afternoons at the Boathouse. It would probably be the sensible thing to do. At the same time, it was a horrible thought. She loved her afternoons by the river, and when she looked back over the past months, the highlight had definitely been all the lazy afternoons at the Boathouse.

It was only June and the summer stretched out before her. There'd be lots more lovely days at the Boathouse if she could put aside her silly crush.

That's what she kept telling herself as she got ready to go. She ignored the voice in her head which asked why she felt the need to get changed, and why she was trying on everything she owned. Finally settling on a floaty skirt and vest top, she made her way to the bus stop. She got off near the botanical gardens and walked through the peaceful setting, taking in the pretty blossoms and flowerbeds. Then she ambled around the edge of Christ Church Meadow until she finally came to that magical stretch of river that had become so familiar to her.

On the brightly coloured houseboat, the smiley lady sat with a wide-brimmed hat shielding her face from the sun. She waved enthusiastically when she saw Emily and Emily waved back. The path was blocked by a flock of geese. She didn't like to disturb them too forcefully; they were pretty intimidating. Luckily a cyclist whizzed by, sending them scattering and clearing the way for Emily.

"There you are," Josie said when Emily joined her on the blanket. "I was worried you'd decided to stay in London."

"I messaged you and said I was coming." Emily kicked off her shoes and rooted in her bag for her bottle of water. She was parched.

"I know. It looked like you had fun yesterday. I've never known you post on social media so much."

"I might have got a bit carried away," Emily admitted.

"Next time I'll come with you," Josie said. "I miss our trips to London. I bet it wasn't the same with Stuart."

"It really wasn't the same." Emily couldn't hide the amusement in her voice. "Why are you hitting me?" She shrieked with laughter as Josie swiped at her.

"I don't like your tone!" Josie grinned. "It sounds like you prefer going with him."

"No. It's just very different going with Stuart. It was definitely always more fun with you … But with Stuart I got to decide what we did all day. That was great too!"

"Poor Stuart. Did you make him do cultural stuff all day?"

Emily nodded proudly. "I did take him to the pub for dinner."

"I saw on Facebook … The George Inn?" She raised her eyebrows. "That's still cultural."

"But they have beer," Emily countered. "He was happy with it."

"That guy's such a pushover."

It was another hour before there was any sign of Jack, and he looked tired when he joined them. "I just want to lie down." He sat between them and let out a long breath. "But I know if I do I'll fall asleep. It's so busy today. My feet are killing me." He nudged Emily's leg as he smiled at her. It felt like a bolt of electricity shot from his hand through her body, shocking her heart as it went and causing it to beat abnormally. "How was London?" he asked casually.

It was only her who felt the electricity, then. He was clearly oblivious. She swallowed hard and was utterly relieved when Josie's phone began to ring loudly.

"It's Lizzie again." Josie rolled her eyes. "I better answer this time. I'll be back in a minute." She wandered away from them as she answered the call from her sister.

With Josie gone from the blanket, Jack felt inappropriately close. He was so close Emily could feel his body heat and smell the delicious scent of him. How did he still manage to smell so good when he was running around a stuffy café?

"So …" He looked at her questioningly. "London was good?"

"It was great," she mumbled. Why didn't he move over? There was loads of space. Did he really have to sit within touching distance? *Back away, Jack! Back away!* Telepathy obviously wasn't his strong suit.

"And things are better with Stuart I take it?"

His eyes were mesmerising, and she looked down, avoiding eye contact and trying to figure out what on earth he'd said. Her brain had gone to mush. Who was Stuart? She shook her head quickly. Stuart was her boyfriend, that was right. Were things better? That was the question. But what on earth was the answer? And why was he asking about Stuart? It was none of his business.

"It's fine," she whispered.

"Sorry," he said. "None of my business."

So he *could* do telepathy. Her head shot up. There was an eyelash on his cheek, and without thinking she reached out to brush it away. Electricity ripped through her again and she paused. Their eyes locked. He felt it too. She could see it in the intensity of his gaze. The stray eyelash was forgotten, but she couldn't bring herself to move her hand. His skin felt so good. Her fingers trembled slightly as she stroked his cheek. Her heart hammered in her chest. All she wanted to do was kiss him. She'd only have to lean a little closer …

Gently, he took her wrist, pulling her hand away.

"Sorry," she whispered as she came to her senses.

He bit his lower lip but didn't say anything. What on earth had just happened? Did he feel something for her too? He couldn't. He was Josie's boyfriend.

"There was an eyelash on your cheek," she said weakly.

His smile was sad.

"Oh my God!" Josie's high-pitched voice broke the atmosphere and they turned to see her striding fiercely towards them.

Chapter 21

Emily's stomach lurched as Josie stormed towards them with wide eyes. She felt sick. Josie could be a bit gullible but Emily was sure she couldn't come up with an excuse for stroking Jack's face and looking like she was about to jump him right there on the blanket.

"There was an eyelash." She looked back at Jack. If she could find the bloody eyelash, maybe she'd get away with it.

Josie looked puzzled but otherwise ignored Emily. "You won't believe it … Lizzie's getting married!" She dropped heavily onto the blanket. "Max has got a new job. In Hope Cove. He's moving there permanently, and they're getting married." She sighed. "And listen to this … He proposed on the beach in front of their cottage. Lizzie had taken the dog for a walk early in the morning. And when she got back, Max was sitting on the beach with coffee mugs. They often do that, sit and drink coffee and watch the sunrise. But when she took the cup she realised it wasn't coffee …"

Josie paused and put a hand to her chest. Her eyes welled with tears. "It was champagne. So Lizzie asked why he'd got champagne and he said he was hoping they might need it." She paused again as the words caught in her throat. Emily's eyes were damp too. "And then he pulled out a ring! How romantic is that?"

Emily clamped a hand over her mouth, worried she was going to start sobbing. She was a sucker for romantic stories. Especially the real-life ones that happened to people she knew.

"That's so lovely." She beamed and forgot all about eyelashes and notions of kissing her best friend's boyfriend.

"I'm so happy for her." Josie returned her phone to her bag. "I feel bad for ignoring her call this morning."

Emily thought about Lizzie and how happy she must be. It didn't seem any time had passed since Lizzie had been in turmoil, thinking she and Max weren't destined to be together. How quickly things can change.

"They've not really been together long, have they?" Emily regretted the words as soon as she said them. All it was going to do was give Josie ideas. She and Jack hadn't been together long either, but Emily could just imagine it: Josie would get carried away with romantic notions and decide it was a great idea. Before Emily knew it, she'd be looking at Josie in a white dress and Jack in a suit. Emily would be the most ridiculous bridesmaid ever. Hopefully people would assume she was weeping tears of joy rather than tears of grief.

There was no way in the world she could go to Josie and Jack's wedding. She caught the look on Josie's face and waited for Josie to give Jack a nudge and make some comment about how long they'd been together. There was nothing of the sort, though. Actually, Josie seemed to avoid looking at Jack. There was an odd look on her face. Emily could have sworn that Josie was squirming at the thought of marriage.

Or maybe Emily was misreading things. Jack wasn't looking at Josie either. Perhaps they were secretly engaged and avoiding eye contact so they didn't accidentally let it slip.

"That's great news." Thankfully Jack broke the silence.

"They're going to drive up next weekend so we can celebrate." Josie went back to being animated. "Lizzie will no doubt want to start planning the wedding as well. She thinks it will be next spring."

Jack smiled as he stood. "I better get back. Clive will be grumbling."

He didn't look at Emily as he left, and she went back to feeling like a complete fool. Had she really stroked his cheek?

"I'm shocked." Josie got comfy on the blanket, and Emily reminded herself that she was talking about Lizzie.

"It's amazing."

"Do you think I'll have to choose a new bridesmaid dress?" Josie mused. "Or can I wear the one I was supposed to wear for her and Phil's wedding?"

Emily swatted her arm. "You'll get a different dress, I'm sure. There's no way Lizzie will want anything to do with the cancelled wedding."

"I hope so. I wasn't a fan of that dress."

"Do you think they'll have the wedding on the beach? That would be lovely, wouldn't it?"

"I reckon Lizzie would probably have an issue with sand everywhere," Josie said. Lizzie was a bit particular about things. "You should come out with us next weekend and we can quiz her. She always likes to see you. I'm fairly sure she prefers you to me!"

"We'll see," Emily said vaguely. It might be fun. Lizzie was much more sedate than Josie. She was eight years older and way more sensible. "What would your dream wedding be?" she asked suddenly.

"I don't know," Josie said flippantly.

"Don't you ever think about it?" Emily tried very hard to sound casual. The vague questions were actually her way of finding out if a wedding was on the cards for her and Jack. It dawned on her that her mum was right – she was torturing herself.

"Not really."

Great, usually Josie was hard to shut up, but when you actually wanted information from her it was another matter entirely.

"Have you and Jack ever discussed it?"

Josie sat up quickly. "No. Of course not. We've only been together a matter of months."

"I know but you moved in together so quickly."

Josie frowned. "Yeah, and I think that might have been a mistake."

"What?" Emily picked at a stray thread on the blanket and ignored the urge to get up and dance. "It was your idea."

"I know. And Jack said it was too soon. He's always right."

"I don't understand." Emily stared at her. "You're not splitting up, are you?" *Please split up. Please, please, please. A nice amicable split. Realise you're only meant to be friends and go your separate ways.* Except maybe she'd never see Jack again. It was hard to know which was the worst kind of torture.

"No," Josie said flatly. "We're fine. I just wish we didn't live together. It's all a bit full on. What if he starts talking about marriage? I definitely don't want to marry him."

"Never?"

Her nose wrinkled as she screwed her face up. "I don't know." She looked at Emily and her features softened. "Honestly, I can't imagine marrying him. Is that weird? We don't ever talk about the future."

"You love him, though?"

She shrugged. "Yeah." It wasn't the most heartfelt declaration of love.

Emily paused. She had so many questions, but she wasn't sure she wanted to hear the answers.

"Do you tell each other you love each other?" she asked hesitantly.

Josie shook her head and grinned. "I feel like that would be weird. I'm making this sound like a really bad relationship, aren't I? We are happy, I think. I'm just not about to start wedding planning. I'll leave that to Lizzie." Her eyes lit up. "Her wedding will be amazing. We'll have so much fun."

"I don't think I'll be invited." Emily watched a couple of kids picking daisies. "Lizzie and I aren't close or anything."

"Of course you'll be invited. Lizzie thinks you're great. Especially since you helped her out when she split up with Phil. And you helped a lot with her new business."

"I didn't do much." Emily had recommended

Lizzie to some people in her online writer's group when Lizzie was setting up her editing business, that was all.

"She'd invite you anyway because you're my best friend. You're practically family."

"I don't want her to invite me because she feels she has to."

"Why not? It's the only reason Jack will get an invite …"

Emily spat out a laugh. "She still doesn't like Jack?" Josie had said something before about Lizzie being unsure about Jack, but now it sounded like a real issue.

"I don't think any of my family do."

"Why?"

Josie grimaced. "That might be my fault."

"What did you do?" Emily asked amused.

"I didn't do anything. But sometimes I might have slightly misled them. Like the time Jack and I split up. If Lizzie had known it was because I wanted to move in with Jack, she'd definitely have taken Jack's side. So I left that part out."

"I see." Emily glared at her. "So you make yourself look better by making Jack look bad?"

"It's not like they ever say anything to him about it," Josie said defensively. "They're perfectly polite. He doesn't even realise they don't like him so it doesn't really matter."

Emily struggled to get her head around it. "But don't you want your family to know what he's really like? Jack's so lovely, and they have the complete wrong impression of him …"

Josie frowned. "Yes, it would be better. I was

trying to make Lizzie think better of me, but in the end she thinks I'm stupid for staying with such an idiot of a boyfriend."

"I don't know how you're so calm about it." Emily put a hand over her face. "What a mess."

"It's kind of funny," Josie said. "Things do tend to backfire on me."

"Because you're an idiot!" Emily sighed. "No offence."

"None taken," Josie said happily.

"I really don't know how you aren't stressed out about the situation."

"Worrying about things never does any good. Plus, I'm fairly sure you do enough worrying for the both of us."

"That's true," Emily mused. Life would be much easier if she could take Josie's approach to situations.

***

Emily didn't end up staying long at the Boathouse. The next time Jack came over, she made an excuse about meeting her mum. She couldn't stand the way her heart beat so erratically around him and the way her brain went into meltdown mode. Her thoughts were crazy and irrational, and she was so embarrassed by her earlier behaviour. What on earth must he think of her?

The house was quiet when she got home, and she lay back on the couch. Her mind drifted to Jack: looking into his eyes, stroking his face. She was an idiot. There was no way she could be alone with him again. Ever. She was determined not to cry about it.

What good would that do? Unfortunately her tear ducts had other ideas, and her cheeks were damp when her mum arrived home.

Emily looked at her sadly. "You can say 'I told you so' now."

"What happened?" Her mum lifted Emily's feet and positioned them in her lap when she sat down.

"I'm such an idiot," she whispered as she swiped at the tears. "I think I was going to kiss him. And now I'm angry with Josie because she takes him for granted and I don't think she's even in love with him." Her words came fast and were choked with emotion. "And I wish they would split up. But that makes me a horrible friend." She looked desperately at her mum. "I'm a horrible person. And I clearly can't be around him any more and I don't know what to do." She sniffed and wiped her nose with the soggy tissue balled in her hand.

"I think you need to avoid him for a while," her mum said softly. "It's probably best to avoid them both. Find something else to focus on. Stuart or your writing."

"I don't want to be with Stuart," she said through a sob. "I want to be with Jack. It's not fair."

"I know." Her mum rubbed her ankle. "You will get over this, though. One day you'll laugh about it, I promise."

Emily raised her eyebrows. It wasn't what she wanted to hear. Not that anything was going to make her feel any better, but her mum's words sounded so empty. She couldn't imagine how she could ever get over it. And how she could ever laugh at anything.

When her phone buzzed on the coffee table, she

reached for it. It was a Facebook notification – someone had liked one of her posts about London. Automatically, she went into Facebook and stared at the photo of herself grinning into the camera. Was that really only yesterday?

"I was fine yesterday." She held the picture out to her mum. "Then five minutes with Jack and I'm a wreck." She rubbed her eyes. "Maybe I should move to London."

Her mum laughed lightly.

Emily stared at the ceiling. Thoughts churned through her head. Frowning, she reached for her phone again. She really did look happy in that photo. Her heart began to beat faster as the idea implanted itself in her mind.

"I should move to London." Everything seemed to click into place. It was the perfect solution. She sat up and stared at her mum. "I'm going to move to London."

Her mum tilted her head. "You're serious, aren't you?"

She nodded vigorously through a rush of adrenalin. "It's perfect. A new focus, like you said."

"That's not what I meant …"

"But I need to do something. I can't stay in Oxford avoiding my best friend because I can't trust myself around her boyfriend. If I just stop hanging out with them, Josie will ask too many questions. And if I'm in Oxford I'll constantly think about Jack, wondering if I might bump into him. I'll never move on."

"I think you're being rash and impulsive. It doesn't suit you. Think about it for a while."

"Of course I'll think about it." She rolled her eyes. Did her mum think she was going to pack her bags there and then?

She was definitely going to think about it some more.

And then she was going to leave.

Chapter 22

"I don't understand." Emily held the phone away from her ear as Josie spoke far too loudly. "You're moving to London?"

"It will be so much easier when the book comes out." This was the plan she'd come up with: tell them it was all to do with her writing career. "We always said we'd live in London when our careers took off."

"But we were going to move together."

Emily had a sudden panic at the thought of Josie moving with her. It would defeat the purpose of the move somewhat. "You've got your job in Oxford, and Jack. I knew you wouldn't be able to move at the moment. That's why I didn't ask. As soon as you find an acting job we can get a place together." And now it seemed like Emily was going to be sending Josie bad vibes for her career as well as her relationship. Some best friend she was.

"I can't believe you're actually doing it. You really quit your job?"

"On Monday." She probably hadn't taken as much time to think about it as her mum would have liked, but after sleeping on it she'd only been more certain it was the right thing for her.

"What about Stuart?"

"I broke up with him," Emily said sheepishly. She

wasn't overly proud of how she'd dealt with that situation. If she was honest, she should have broken up with him a lot sooner. He'd been upset, and she was still fielding calls and messages from him, but she was sure it was for the best.

"What will you do for money? Where will you live?"

Emily laughed. "I'll get a job and find an apartment. That's why I'm in London this weekend." She took a sip of her takeaway coffee. There was a lot of bustle outside the Great British Library. It had the largest catalogue in the world, and Emily had spent an hour soaking in the atmosphere while she had a break in flat viewings. She'd settled on a bench to call Josie.

"So you've been planning this all week and are only telling me now?" There was a hint of annoyance to Josie's voice.

"It's all been a bit of a whirlwind. I was talking to my editor about the book release. They're talking about a book launch and a few events with other authors. It just made me think it would be great to be in London. And my trip last week already had me thinking about it. I feel inspired to write more here. There's such a buzz about the place."

"Oxford has huge literary significance, you know," Josie sounded indignant now. "Tolkien and C.S. Lewis. They're not good enough for you?"

"I want a change, Josie. I still live with my mum, for goodness sake."

"So you're really leaving me?" Josie said sadly.

"You'll still see me," Emily said. "And you'll be able to stay with me when you have an audition."

"Oh, I didn't think about that." She was suddenly

excited. "We'll have a great time. It'll be like the good old days when we used to hang out in London. Except we'll be able to stay out and party without worrying about catching the last train back to Oxford."

"So you approve now?"

"Not really," she said with a sigh. "But every cloud has a silver lining. Will you come back some weekends so we can hang out at the Boathouse still?"

"Probably not," she said lightly. "I'm going to be busy with the book for a while."

"Don't say that," Josie whimpered. "I've loved this summer. I'll miss the three of us hanging out."

"Me too," Emily said quietly. "I have to go. I've got another flat viewing."

"Where?"

"Shoreditch. It's one of the only ones I've found within my budget that isn't a flat-share. I'm not holding my breath. I saw four places this morning. Everything's so small and so expensive. I was supposed to see five places, but the last one I went to was already taken when I got there." Flat-hunting was already proving demoralising, and it was only day one.

"Shoreditch would be good," Josie said. "Will you be at the Boathouse tomorrow?"

"No. I'm staying in a hotel tonight and looking at more flats tomorrow. I really want to find something this weekend but I'm probably being unrealistic. There are so many people looking for places. Half the time when I ring about somewhere it's already gone. And I'm calling the same day the adverts go up. I can't start job-hunting until I've got somewhere to live." She stood and dropped her coffee cup in the bin beside the bench. "I really have to go."

"Okay. Good luck. Let me know if you find something. We'll meet up in the week and you can fill me in properly."

***

The apartment in Shoreditch was tiny. The small window in the living room didn't let much light in and the paint on the walls was cracked and peeling.

"I need someone to take it furnished," the young bearded guy told her as she stood and surveyed the place. She was trying to find something positive about the place but really it was awful. The kitchenette looked like it was probably growing every kind of mould known to man. She kept expecting to see a rodent run past her. The furniture being included definitely made things worse. It was all musty and worn. There was an ashtray on the windowsill, which explained some of the bad smells.

"And I need to be out quick," he said. "Like in the next week or two."

She didn't like to ask why. He seemed like a slightly dodgy character, though she realised it was wrong to judge him by his many missing teeth.

"I ... Erm ..." She walked to the bedroom again. It was only big enough for a single bed and a small wardrobe. She thought she could probably fit a narrow bookcase in the corner. Maybe. "I've still got a few places to see today." She turned and smiled at him. Maybe weeks from now when she still looking for a place, she'd curse herself for not taking it.

"Just give me a call later," he said.

"Okay." Outside the thick door, she waited in the hallway. The lift was out of order and it was on the eight floor. Maybe she should have taken it. She could still look at the others today, then call and say she'd changed her mind if she found anywhere better.

Her phone pinged with an email. It was from the people at the flat she was viewing next, saying it had already been taken.

Turning back, she knocked on the door. Toothy guy answered with his phone to his ear and held up a finger to indicate she should wait a minute.

"I decided I'll take it," she said when he hung up a moment later.

"Too late," he said holding his phone up. "That was the guy who looked round before you. He's taking it. Sorry."

"No problem." She backed out of the doorway. "Thanks."

Back to square one. She dragged herself to the tube station and spent the remainder of the day travelling all over London. It seemed she couldn't afford to be picky so she expressed interest in every flat she looked at. They were flat-shares for the rest of the day. So she was supposed to win over a bunch of strangers and convince them she'd be a great flatmate. They all politely told her they'd be in touch but she didn't hold out much hope. She was well aware of the fact that she didn't make a great first impression.

On the train home on Sunday evening, she called her mum and complained about her exhausting weekend. She wondered how many more similar weekends she had ahead of her.

Her phone rang a few minutes after she'd finished talking to her mum. An unknown number. She answered hesitantly.

"You looked at my apartment yesterday," the gruff voice said in introduction. "In Shoreditch. It's available again if you're interested?"

"Yes," she said quickly. "I'm definitely interested."

Chapter 23

After worrying that the move to London would be a long drawn-out process, everything fell into place very quickly. The apartment was available from the following weekend, which coincided with Emily finishing work. She'd given two weeks' notice assuming she wouldn't have an apartment but would be able to dedicate all her time to finding one if she wasn't working. For once, luck had been on her side.

On Friday evening, Emily walked into the Eagle and Child pub for farewell drinks with Josie and Jack.

"I know you don't like busy pubs." Josie was sitting alone at the bar and swivelled on her stool so she was facing Emily. "Jack chose it. You can blame him."

"The Inklings used to meet here," Emily said, looking around the charming, historic pub. It was small and busy, but the atmosphere was relaxed and pleasant.

"The what?" Josie said. Was she slurring her words?

"It was a writers' group. Tolkien and C.S. Lewis were part of it. How can you live in Oxford and not know that?"

"It rings a bell. I didn't know it was this place. That's why Jack chose it then."

Emily scanned the pub. "Where is he?"

"Here's not here yet. I don't even know if he's coming. He's in the worst mood."

Emily was torn between being relieved and grief-stricken by the thought he might not come out. It was probably easier not to see him, but it was supposed to be her leaving drinks. The last time she'd see him for a while.

"Did you have an argument?" She raised her voice a little and leaned into Josie.

"Yes. But what's new? He called and said he had to stay late at work. Then he wanted me to make him dinner for when he got home. Like I'm some 1950s housewife."

"I take it you said no?"

"I'm not going to cook his dinner. We were supposed to go out for dinner."

"How long have you been here?" Emily noticed the almost-empty pint glass with an empty shot glass beside it.

"About an hour I think. I was so annoyed after I spoke to him, I had to get out of the apartment."

"So you skipped dinner and went straight to drinking alone?"

She waved at the barman. "Dale! This is my friend Emily. She's an author."

"Hi," Emily said weakly. So Josie came out on her own and made friends with the bar staff. And she was obviously well on the way to being drunk. Emily had the distinct feeling the evening was going to be a disaster. She ordered a glass of wine and declined when Josie told her to get a shot so she could catch up.

"I guess we'll have to stay at the bar." Emily scanned the room but there were no empty seats. Jack was coming towards them through the crowd. She reminded herself she only had to get through the evening, then she'd be living in London and could start afresh without the torture of seeing him.

He grinned and said hello to her before moving to Josie and kissing her cheek. "How was your day?"

"Fine," Josie replied flatly.

Jack reached over the bar and shook the barman's hand. Apparently they already knew each other. "Did you reserve us a table?" Jack asked.

Dale nodded across the pub towards the entrance. "Over near the window."

"Thanks." He ordered drinks. "I told you I'd got us a table," he said to Josie.

"I was quite happy at the bar," she replied tersely.

He ignored her tone and turned his attention to Emily. "I can't believe you're leaving. I saw you a couple of weeks ago and you didn't mention anything."

"I'd been thinking about it for a while." That was a lie. "And then it fell into place really quickly. It's been a bit of a whirlwind."

"It sounds like it." Jack paid for the drinks when they arrived on the bar. "Shall we go and sit down."

They followed him to the little table by the window, where he politely gestured at the reserved sign to the young guys sitting there. They didn't seem to mind being ousted from their seats.

"It's much more fun at the bar," Josie complained. "Everyone chats to you when you're by the bar."

"You could talk to me," Emily suggested with a grin. "I'm leaving tomorrow, after all."

"You're moving to London. It's like an hour on the train. I'll still see you all the time. Let's not get all sentimental."

"Okay." Emily placed her wine down in front of her.

"I need the toilet," Josie said loudly. "I'll be back in a bit." She picked up her drink and wandered through the crowd, stopping to chat with a couple of middle-aged guys at the bar.

"How many drinks has she had?" Jack asked.

"No idea. I only arrived a few minutes before you. Seems like she's been here a while, though."

Jack took a long swig of his beer. "This could be a fun night," he said flatly.

"She said you had an argument ..."

"I got stuck at work and asked if she could put some pasta on since we wouldn't have time to go out for dinner." He frowned. "Apparently that makes me a chauvinist."

Emily's gaze roamed to Josie. She was laughing, and her beer sloshed out of the glass as she gesticulated along with whatever story she was telling.

"She's driving me mad." Jack leaned forwards. "The other day—"

"I don't want to know." Emily didn't look at Jack. "Sorry. I know I asked about your argument, but I really don't want to spend the evening stuck in the middle of your stupid quarrels."

"Sorry," he said, seeming taken aback by her outburst. He chewed on his bottom lip and looked as though he wanted to say something else.

"I'm going to drink this and go," she said.

"What? Why? We only just got here."

Emily sat up straighter. "Josie's so drunk she won't notice whether I'm here or not. You don't really want to be here. I don't want to be here …"

"Who said I don't want to be here?" he said indignantly. There was a short silence and his expression softened. "I chose the place. It's known for its great authors. Perfect for you."

Emily managed a tight-lipped smile. For a moment she hated him. Why did he have to be so nice to her? If he weren't so nice to her, she'd never have fallen in love with him and wouldn't be uprooting her whole life to avoid seeing him. It was all his fault.

"If you don't want to be here," he said, "then don't, but I wanted to hang out with you before you leave."

She really did want to leave. Josie was clearly going to spend the evening talking to anyone but them which meant she'd be alone with Jack. She couldn't cope with sitting and chatting to him all evening. It would be far too lovely.

"Sorry." She felt bad. It wasn't Jack's fault. "I'm just stressed about the move and everything."

"I understand," he said. "And Josie told me you split up with Stuart?"

Now she wanted to scream. Instead she shook her head and let out a low growl which she seemed to have no control over. "Will you please stop?"

"Stop what?" he asked slowly.

"Being nice," she snapped. "You're annoyingly nice." Ranting incoherently to Jack probably wasn't a great idea, but she couldn't seem to help herself. "Stop asking me stuff. I'm not going to sit here and dissect my relationship with Stuart. You talk to me about inappropriate things. I don't want to hear about your relationship with Josie and I'm not going to talk to you about my relationships. It's weird." She clamped her mouth shut and looked out of the window.

"I thought we were friends. Why are you suddenly making rules about what we can and can't talk about?"

"We're not friends." Her voice was raised and choked with emotion. "I'm your girlfriend's best friend. That's all. It makes us acquaintances. Nothing more."

"I have no idea what's going on today." He looked at her sadly. "I think I'm making normal conversation and somehow I keep offending people."

She was being irrational and should probably apologise, but all she could focus on was getting out of there. "I'm going to go. Josie insisted I come out and now she can't even be bothered to talk to me. I'm going to say goodbye to her." Picking up her handbag, she stalked across the pub. She pulled on Josie's arm to get her attention. "I'm going home."

"You can't leave yet. I got chatting but I was just coming back to talk to you."

"I've got a headache," Emily said. "You stay and have fun. I'm going to hop in a taxi."

"If you're sure?" Josie pouted. That look drove Emily mad. It always had done.

"See you!" She turned and headed for the door. "Good luck with her," she called to Jack as she passed. "She's completely drunk."

He called out to Emily but she didn't stop. All she wanted was to get away from him before she started crying, which felt inevitable.

Unfortunately, he followed her outside.

"Em!" His hand was on her arm and she had no choice but to turn to him. "What's going on? What was that all about?"

"I just want to go home." She turned, looking up and down the road for a taxi.

"You really don't see me as a friend?"

Her toes were at the curb and she put a hand to her face, squeezing the bridge of her nose.

"I'm sorry." She let out a breath as she turned to him. "I'm really sorry. I shouldn't have had a go at you. I'm the worst company in the world tonight."

He wrinkled his nose and glanced back at the pub. "I think you're second in the running actually."

She couldn't help but smile. "I'm sorry," she said again.

"You don't need to apologise. I don't care. But if I did something to upset you I'd rather know."

"You didn't," she said. "You never did anything to upset me. You're ..." She stopped, wondering where she was going with the sentence. Amazing? Perfect? Her favourite person in the world? From the corner of her eye, she saw Josie stumble out of the pub.

Jack looked at Emily intensely, but she was saved from finishing the sentence as Josie draped an arm around his shoulders. It seemed she'd forgiven him.

"Where are we going now?" Josie's words were barely recognisable, she was slurring so much.

"I'm going home," Emily said.

"Oh no!" Josie did the annoying pout again. "Why?"

"Headache, remember?"

"Oh yeah." More stupid pouting. "Where are we going, Jack?"

"Let's go home too."

"No," she whined. "It's still early …" She lifted her wrist and then giggled. "I don't have a watch." Pulling on Jack's hand, she squinted at his watch. "What time is it?"

"Really late," he said. "They already called last orders."

"No!" Her eyes were wide. "Really?"

Emily nodded. "Everything's closing. Time for bed."

"Let's do something tomorrow," Josie said, wrapping her arms around Emily.

"I'm moving tomorrow," Emily said tersely.

"Do you need any help with the move?" Jack asked. "We can load up my car if you want?"

"Thanks but I'm fine. Mum's helping me and I'm not taking much this trip. Just the basics."

A taxi arrived behind her and she smiled at Jack. "I'll see you next time I'm back."

He engulfed her in a big hug, and she fought off tears as she squeezed him too tightly. She loved the scent of him and the feel of his arms around her. Taking a step back, she pasted on a smile. This was why she was moving. Because a hug at the end of the evening would never be enough.

"Call if you need anything," he said.

In the taxi, she pushed her head back into the seat.

Time to get over him and get on with her life.

Summer at the Old Boathouse

Chapter 24

Emily's mum failed to muster much enthusiasm for the flat when they arrived the next day. "It's not so bad," she said. "With a good clean and some nice furnishings it will be fine."

Emily sat on the couch with her head in her hands, contemplating what on earth she'd done. "It's expensive too," she said. "Not only am I living in a hovel, I'm paying a fortune for the privilege."

"It's London. What did you expect? At least it's a place to yourself."

"I don't know if that's a good thing or a bad thing at the moment. I could rot away in here and no one would even notice."

"I'll notice," her mum said softly.

Emily's phone vibrated in her pocket. It was Josie. Emily's greeting was frosty.

"I'm so sorry," Josie said. "I'm a terrible friend. I ruined your night out."

Emily was annoyed with her and couldn't be bothered to pretend otherwise. "What's going on with you?"

"I was in a bad mood, and I didn't eat and then I drank too much. I'm so sorry. I'll make it up to you. Don't be angry with me. Jack's furious. I can't cope with you being angry with me too."

"Of course I'm angry," she snapped. "You're the one who insisted we go for a night out and then you couldn't even be bothered to speak to me."

"I had an argument with Jack and then—"

"You had a stupid argument with Jack because you take him for granted and get annoyed with him about nothing. It's not his fault you were in a foul mood. I don't even know how he puts up with you." She caught her mum glaring at her and put an end to her outburst. Now she felt like apologising. She wouldn't, though. It was all true.

There was silence for a moment down the phone. When Josie finally spoke, she didn't argue with Emily. In fact, she didn't react to her words at all.

"Should we come and help you move? Jack can take the day off and we can drive you to the new place and help you unpack."

She laughed. "I already moved this morning while you slept off your hangover. Mum drove me."

"So you don't need us to help?"

"Nope."

"I'm sorry. I really wanted to help and see your new place."

"You should have got up earlier then," Emily snapped. "I've got to go. I'll talk to you later." She pressed end and threw the phone on the couch beside her. "Don't look at me like that," she growled at her mum. "She's so annoying."

"She's the same as she's always been. You usually have more patience with her."

"Well, I've run out of patience. I'm going to find a new best friend who isn't so selfish."

"No you're not. But you can sort things out with

Josie later. We need to focus on making this place liveable. I suggest getting rid of these black curtains …" When she tugged on them a puff of dust shot out, making them both laugh.

"Okay. I can do this," Emily said optimistically. "Let's write a list and go shopping." She pulled her trusty notepad from her handbag and ripped out a page. "We'll need a lot of cleaning supplies. And new curtains, a nice rug, a throw blanket to cover the couch …"

"Cushions," her mum suggested. "Maybe a plant."

Emily felt much more positive as she scribbled her list.

***

On Friday afternoon, Emily answered the door to Josie.

"I'm so sorry." Josie dropped her bags and hugged Emily tightly. "I hate it when you're angry with me."

Emily relaxed into the embrace. She'd been feeling bad for being so terse with Josie. It wasn't all her fault. Her mum had been right about Josie being the same as she always was. It was Emily reacting differently that changed things.

"Come in," she said. "How was the audition?"

"I think it went well. Hopefully Michaela will call me soon with some news. Fingers crossed." She stopped and looked around the apartment. "This is nice."

Emily laughed at her attempt at diplomacy. "You

should have seen it a week ago. It looks so much better now." She was actually quite happy with it now that she'd made it her own. The black curtains had been replaced with cheerful yellow ones and there was a lovely bohemian style rug in front of the couch. "I need your help too. I ordered a bookcase and it arrived this morning. It's flat pack so you can help me assemble it. You're better at that stuff than me."

"I like a bit of DIY," Josie said happily. Moving across the living room she took in the tiny kitchen, then went and checked out the bedroom. "It's cosy."

"I'm happy I don't have to share with a bunch of strangers. And the location's good."

"It's great."

"Not the best view," Emily admitted as Josie peered out of the window.

The atmosphere between them was slightly strained, and Emily hoped she wouldn't regret telling Josie she could stay for the weekend. She'd had an audition in London and asked if she could visit.

The silence was shattered by the sound of Josie's phone ringing loudly.

"Oh my God!" She went to her backpack and fumbled with the zip. "I put it on really loud so I'd hear it if Michaela called." Panic swept over her features as she pulled out the phone. "Cross your fingers," she said quickly, then answered the phone.

"Hi, Michaela." The false cheer in her voice did little to disguise her nerves. Emily clasped her hands together and squeezed. She felt nervous too. Did Josie go through this after every audition? Emily would be a nervous wreck.

Josie was nodding and chewing on her lower lip.

She turned away abruptly and Emily heard the slight tremor in her voice. "Okay, then. Yes, of course. I'll talk to you next week. Thanks a lot."

There was a pause and Emily held her breath, waiting for Josie to turn back to her. When she did, the smile was so forced it made Emily want to cry. Her best friend could be a pain in the bum, but she really did want the best for her.

Josie shook her head. "Not this time. They said they want to go in a different direction …"

"Sorry." Emily stroked her arm and wished she could offer more comfort.

"Something better will probably come up next week." Josie walked over to the couch. "Shall we have a cup of tea?"

Emily went to the kitchen. It was difficult seeing Josie trying so hard to stay upbeat when she was obviously so disappointed. When she placed mugs of tea on the table, there were tears in Josie's eyes.

"Sorry," she said wiping them away. "I'm being pathetic."

"No you're not. It must be so hard. I can't imagine."

Josie sniffed and leaned back on the couch. It was a moment before she spoke again. "I know I was awful last weekend, and I'm honestly not trying to make excuses … but I wasn't just in a bad mood because I'd argued with Jack …"

"What then?" Emily asked, puzzled.

Josie glanced sadly at Emily. "You have everything in order. Your life is perfect. And I'm so jealous. It makes me sound like a horrible friend. I am happy for you. I think it's great that things are going so well for you, but it really highlights how crappy my life is at the moment."

"My life isn't perfect." Emily was actually struggling to comprehend that Josie was being serious. "It's so far from perfect."

"But we always said we were going to move to London and follow our dreams. And you're doing it. You've got a book deal, for goodness sake. In a few months your first book will be published. I can't even get a crappy part in a crappy soap opera."

"But I live in a tiny, horrible apartment. And I'm on my own ..."

"Yes! Because you chose to be. You're so brave. You knew things weren't right with Stuart so you ended it." Josie reached for her tea and blew gently on it. "Sometimes I think things aren't right between Jack and me, but I'd be too scared to split up with him. Plus, I stupidly gave up my apartment so if I split up with him I'd have nowhere to live."

Emily hated herself. All she felt when Josie talked about problems between her and Jack was hope. She was a terrible best friend. She was also completely deluded. It wasn't as though the situation would change if Josie and Jack split up. It would just mean she'd probably never see him again.

Picking at a piece of fluff on a couch cushion, Emily struggled for something to say. It was strange to think Josie was envious of her. "I always want your life," she said honestly. To her, Josie had it all. "You're so confident and positive about everything ..." And she had Jack.

"We're a right pair, aren't we?" Josie chuckled, then looked at Emily seriously. "It's good to have a proper chat with you. We don't really do that any more." She looked thoughtful and a frown wrinkled her brow. "It's my fault, isn't it? I'm one of those awful girls who ditch their friends when they get a boyfriend."

"You didn't ditch me," Emily insisted. "You always try and involve me in everything."

"Yeah but we don't hang out just the two of us. Jack's always around."

"I didn't mind that." At least until she realised she was probably more in love with him than Josie, but she could hardly blame Josie for that.

"I always like how well you two get on. I think it's really sweet how he asks about you."

"Does he?" Again, Emily had an awful pang of hope, which was quickly replaced by guilt.

"I think he's more upset about you leaving than me!"

"That's daft." Emily turned away. Was she blushing? She was an idiot, that much was for sure. "I only really saw him on Sunday afternoons."

"Yeah but he says he can have a sensible conversation with you, which makes a change from me wittering on about nothing!"

"It's going to be weird not seeing you and Jack every Sunday."

"He did offer to come and pick me up on Sunday," Josie said. "We could all have dinner together …"

Emily opened her mouth, wondering how she could politely avoid that.

"I'll tell him it's strictly a girls' weekend," Josie said firmly. "We don't want him crashing the party."

"A girls' weekend sounds good," Emily agreed.

And it *was* good. They spent the weekend exploring London – visiting their old haunts and finding new places. Josie even agreed to go to the National Gallery with no complaint at all. She seemed to enjoy it too. There was no mention of any wild nights out. It was all lovely and sedate: exactly what they needed, Emily realised. Time for the two of them with no one else around. A rejuvenation weekend for their friendship. They laughed and chatted and enjoyed each other's company.

It reminded Emily why Josie was her best friend. Despite her flaws, Josie was a great friend.

And Emily would never do anything to jeopardise that.

Chapter 25

For the first few months in London, Emily's mood seemed to match the weather: bright and hopeful at first, then getting gradually darker and colder as summer came to an end and autumn took over. Her social life, which had been fairly quiet when she was in Oxford, had faded to non-existent.

If it weren't for the waitressing job she'd found a couple of weeks after she arrived, she was sure she'd hardly ever speak to anyone. The Italian restaurant was a pleasant enough place to work. It was a small, family-owned operation, without a lot of drama. The perfect setup for Emily. It also meant she had her mornings free to write, which suited her well.

The book launch happened in October. If she was honest, Emily found it fairly underwhelming. She wasn't sure what she'd been expecting, but other than a few congratulatory phone calls and messages, it was just a flurry of activity on social media. It meant she had to be social with strangers on the internet. Definitely not her favourite thing.

It should have been a momentous day, one she'd been dreaming about for years, but it fell flat somehow. The high point of the day was when Jack called to congratulate her. Unfortunately it was quickly followed by the low point of her day.

She was so touched that he called, and after not seeing him for over two months it was a thrill to hear his voice. They spent a few minutes chatting – he was his usual cheerful self and she was her usual mumbling nervous self.

Ending the call was the low point of her day. Tears automatically filled her eyes as she realised how much she missed him. She'd been trying so hard to put him out of her mind, but that brief phone call set her back. The following weeks were difficult. She thought about him constantly. On the phone he'd asked when she'd be back to Oxford for a visit. She'd told him soon, and she was tempted. It wouldn't do her any good, though. The couple of times she went home to see her mum, she kept the visits quiet.

Josie turned up in London fairly regularly, either because she had an audition in the city or just for a night or weekend away. Their friendship was as strong as ever.

Those first few months in London dragged so slowly, but eventually Christmas came around and Emily packed up some things for a few days with her mum back in Oxford.

***

She met up with Josie on Christmas Eve. Josie had already mentioned that Jack had to work in the morning, so that was when Emily suggested they meet. She had the feeling that spending time with Josie and Jack together could ruin the whole Christmas period for her and was keen to avoid it.

They met in the city centre. Josie had been doing

her last-minute shopping and arrived at the café with an armful of bags. Emily had arrived a few moments before her and was taking her coat off. She blew on her hands. It was icy cold outside and her cheeks were bright red from the whip of the freezing wind.

"Perfect timing," she said when she caught sight of Josie.

"I've done it!" She proudly held up her shopping bags. "I finished my Christmas shopping."

"I should hope so." Emily rolled her eyes. "The shops close soon."

The bags were shoved under the table. "It's so good to see you," Josie said.

"You too," Emily said. They embraced tightly.

"I'm so cold." Josie's eyes darted around as they took a seat. "I need something warm to drink." She caught the eye of a passing waitress and ordered a pot of tea for two.

"I can't believe you do all your Christmas shopping on Christmas Eve," Emily said.

Josie laughed. "I bet you had all yours done by about September."

"Not quite," Emily said, amused. It also wasn't too far off the mark. "Don't you get stressed doing it all at the last minute? What if you can't find everything?"

"I always find things. I have to. Shopping is much quicker when you're against the clock. Anyway, I got it all. Hang on a minute." She rooted around in the bags. "There's one for you here somewhere."

Finally, she pulled out a leather-bound notebook and a neatly boxed pen. She'd never been one to bother about wrapping presents. Emily was used to it by now.

"Thank you," she said looking it over.

"Do you like it? I thought it would be useful for your writing."

"I love it," Emily said.

"Good." Josie drummed on the table. "Come on then, where's mine?"

Emily smiled. She reached into her bag and pulled out a neatly wrapped gift for Josie.

Josie untied the ribbon and then tore off the wrapping. Pulling out the turquoise scarf, she immediately put it on.

"I love it, thank you."

The waitress arrived and balanced the tray on the edge of the table as she offloaded the cups and the pot of tea. As she left, Josie took a teaspoon and stirred the tea in the pot before pouring it. Impatient as ever.

"Jack was sorry he wouldn't see you," she said.

"Me too," Emily said. "Everyone's so busy over Christmas. I thought we'd have time to catch up on Boxing Day. I completely forgot you're going down to Hope Cove." Actually, she hadn't forgotten at all.

Josie looked thoughtful. "You could come with us. Lizzie would like to see you, I'm sure. You'd probably have to sleep on the couch, but it would be fun."

"I can't," Emily said. "Mum is already complaining that she doesn't see me enough. I'm only here a few days and then I have to get back to London for work."

"That's a shame. It would've been fun to show you Hope Cove. Anyway, what about tonight? Why don't you come to the pub with us?"

"I promised Mum I'd stay in with her."

"Jack's going to think you're avoiding him."

"I'm not," she said, too quickly. Josie had only been joking, and she'd responded as though she was being accused.

There was a pause and Josie eyed her over her cup. "We'll have to get together in the new year. I could finally bring Jack into London and we can have dinner together …"

"That would be nice." Emily made an effort to sound normal. "It'd be good to catch up with him." It wouldn't. It would be awful. Like the phone call from him, but worse. She thought about him every day, and seeing him would only make it so much harder.

"Is everything okay with you?" Josie asked.

"Yes." The smile was forced and unnatural. "Why?"

"I worry about you. I know you're busy with writing and working at the restaurant, but do you have any sort of a social life in London?"

Emily laughed. "Of course I do. I have my writing groups. I've made quite a few friends there."

"Oh. Okay. You never mention anybody. Whenever I think of you, I imagine you all alone in your apartment."

"No, I go out with my friends from the writing group. And I sometimes hang out with Tina from work. I probably don't mention it because I don't want you to think you're being replaced."

"As if I could ever be replaced," Josie said. "I'm glad you have a social life. I always worry you'll get a couple of cats and become a recluse."

"Oh you don't need to worry about that," Emily

said lightly. "I'm not allowed pets in the apartment."
They both laughed.

Chapter 26

Emily's catch-up with Josie left her feeling melancholy. Josie had been spot on about her life in London. There was no social life. When she wasn't at work, she was generally alone in her flat. The writing groups she'd talked about didn't exist. Actually, they *did* exist, but Emily wasn't a part of them. She hadn't made any friends, and while it was true that she worked with a girl called Tina, she'd never seen her outside of work.

It was a lonely life she'd created for herself, and she realised what a fool she'd been. The plan was to move to London and forget about Jack. She was supposed to be moving on. But how could she do that when she spent so much time alone in her flat? She should be out dating and meeting new people. That was the only way she'd really get over Jack.

She said as much to her mum while they sat watching a terrible romantic comedy on Boxing Day afternoon. Christmas Day had been pleasantly uneventful – the two of them in the morning, and then over to her uncle's house in the afternoon to meet with the extended family.

"Of course you should get out more." Her mum lowered the volume on the TV. "I keep telling you this."

"I did have plans to join a writing group when I moved. I just never got round to it. The thought of it terrifies me."

"Why? What's the worst that can happen? You make a fool of yourself and never go back? Who cares? You worry about stuff too much."

"Over-thinking does seem to be a problem of mine. This is going to be my New Year's resolution – I'll get out more and be sociable."

"It sounds like a good plan to me." Her mum looked at the TV for a few minutes before turning back to Emily. "Shall we go out for dinner or get a takeaway?"

"Takeaway," Emily said automatically.

Her mum's laugh was high-pitched. "You just said you're determined to get out more!"

"It's not the new year yet. I can continue being a lazy recluse for another week."

"Let's go out."

"You realise that will involve getting dressed?"

"You could go crazy and shower too …"

"Fine." Emily chuckled.

***

Once they settled on a bar meal, Emily chose the Fox and Greyhound. She might be going out of the house but she'd choose somewhere familiar. It was odd being there, though. She was flooded with memories of the couple of times she'd been with Josie and Jack. If only she could go back to those days – before she had feelings for Jack and when everything was easy. She missed those days.

They enjoyed a pleasant meal in the back room of the pub. It was fairly quiet when they arrived, but soon filled up as the evening wore on. Emily would rather have had a takeaway in front of the TV. She didn't mention that to her mum, but was glad when they decided to head home.

A group of guys were coming in as they were walking out. Emily kept her head down and didn't properly register them. She quietly thanked the guy who held the door for her.

"Hey!" he said forcefully.

Her head shot up. And there was Jack.

He kept a hold of the door with one hand, while the other grabbed her waist and pulled her to him. She didn't protest. Her arms automatically snaked around his neck and she squeezed him hard. He smelled good. She'd missed him so much.

The grin took over his face as they broke apart and edged away from the crowded doorway.

"It's great to see you," he said. "It's been too long. How are you?"

"Fine," she mumbled, struggling to recover from the shock of seeing him. "I thought you were in Hope Cove?"

"I was supposed to be. Long story." He frowned and tipped his head in the direction of the pub. "Let's get a drink and I'll fill you in."

"I was just leaving …" She looked to her mum, who was hovering nearby.

"You can stay for a drink," her mum said. Her attention switched to Jack. "Her boring mother was dragging her home early …"

Jack's eyes lit up. "It's nice to finally meet you.

I'm Jack."

"I've heard a lot about you."

"That's worrying!" They moved aside as a group of girls filed out of the pub. Jack grinned. "You must be very proud having a brilliant author for a daughter …"

"I'm so proud," her mum agreed.

"It looks like the book's doing well?" Jack said to Emily.

"Yeah." Emily felt the heat in her cheeks. "It's doing okay."

"Stay for a drink and tell me all about it," Jack suggested.

She really shouldn't stay for a drink with Jack. The sensible thing to do would be to go home. It'd been amazing to see him, but now she should walk away.

"I'll see you at home," her mum said as she hesitated. "Nice to meet you, Jack."

"You too." He smiled, then took Emily's elbow and gently nudged her back into the pub.

"It's quieter in the back room," she said. The main room was busy now, and there was a crowd three-deep at the bar.

He took her hand as they squeezed through the throng. Her heart hammered wildly. She hated herself for how much she enjoyed the feel of his hand in hers.

"Wine?" he asked when they reached the smaller bar in the back room.

"Please." He'd released her hand but she still felt the warmth of it. While Jack waited at the bar, she spotted a couple leaving and took their table. She definitely needed a seat. Her legs felt wobbly. A few deep breaths did little to calm her down before he came and sat opposite her.

"Cheers!" He clinked his glass against hers. Hopefully the wine would calm her down. "I'm so glad I bumped into you," he said. "I can't believe I haven't seen you since you left. How's London?"

"It's good. I was talking to Josie about you guys coming over for a visit in the new year sometime." She was going to have to bite the bullet and actually have them both over sometime, and she did feel guilty for cutting Jack out of her life so abruptly. It would be fine for them to visit, though. Her plan to develop a social life would make everything easier.

"I'd love to. But I think Josie enjoys visiting you alone. She always says it's a girls' weekend or whatever, but I think she just likes to get away from me now and again." He was smiling, but it didn't quite reach his eyes.

"Things are fine between you two?" Why was she asking that? She knew from Josie that their relationship was fine. Aside from their stupid petty squabbles.

"Yeah." He chuckled. "But you're asking on a bad day."

"Oh. You're supposed to be in Hope Cove … what happened?"

"I'm surprised you haven't heard about it from Josie," he said.

Emily was pretty surprised too. She was usually inundated with messages from Josie if she'd had an argument with Jack. She shook her head.

"She'll no doubt fill you in later. Tell me about the book … It's the first time I've seen you for ages, I don't want to bore you with the latest drama with me and Josie."

She smiled, also not really wanting to hear it, even though part of her was intrigued. "The eBook's been selling well," she told him. "And it will be available in paperback from March. It'll be online retailers at first, but the publisher will try and get it into regular shops too."

"That's amazing." He seemed genuinely impressed and threw questions at her, asking about the whole writing and publishing process. Normally, she only really spoke to her mum about it, and it was great to be able to chat it all through with someone else. Once she got going, it was hard to stop talking. Not a problem she usually had.

She only registered their empty drinks when Jack's friend Lee arrived at the table. "I wondered where you'd got to," he said to Jack. "We're moving on. Are you coming?"

"I'll catch you up later. I'm going to have another drink with Em."

It was as though Lee only just registered her. He smiled politely.

Part of her wanted to tell Jack that she needed to go home. Unfortunately that part was overruled. It was so lovely chatting to him that she didn't want to leave yet. And there really wasn't any harm in chatting to him.

"All right," Lee said. "I think we're heading to Wetherspoons but give me a call …"

"Will do." Jack waited until Lee had gone. "You've saved me. I didn't even want to come out but I got talked into it. I'll be able to slip away now."

Her heart dropped in her ribcage. "I should probably be heading home too," she said quietly.

"Not yet." There was mischief in his eyes. "I didn't mean right now. Another drink at least? It's still early."

"Okay," she said, brightening again. "One more."

Another hour passed without her registering the time. Her drink was long gone, and she refused the offer of another. She was tipsy as it was. Jack made her laugh with stories about work, and she smiled when the conversation moved to his mum and he talked so affectionately about her.

When Emily's phone beeped in her pocket, she opened the message from Josie, automatically telling Jack who it was.

"She'll be telling you what a terrible boyfriend I am, and how I ruined her Christmas because I won't make any effort with her family ..."

Emily's eyebrows knitted together as she read the message. "That pretty much sums it up." When she met his gaze, he looked intense. "What happened?"

"She just told you." He flashed a half-smile and indicated the phone.

"I'm not sure this is the truth." She waved the phone and then placed it on the table. "Do you really not like her family?"

"They're okay," he said hesitantly. "I spent all day yesterday at her parents' place. They're not really my kind of people but it's okay. I just never fully relax."

"It doesn't sound like the best Christmas." Emily thought of the day at her uncle's house with all the younger cousins running around the place. It was full of noise and fun, and she'd felt completely relaxed.

"It's not terrible," he said.

It didn't seem like he was going to offer any more information and Emily played detective in her head, trying to figure out what they would have argued about. Then she was intrigued enough to ask.

"So you had Christmas Day with Josie's parents and then you'd planned to go to Hope Cove today?"

He nodded.

"So when do you see your family?"

When he smiled sadly, she knew she'd found the issue.

"We were supposed to have brunch with my mum this morning, but we overslept and Josie said we didn't have time …"

"Oh," Emily said slowly as it all slotted into place.

"It's very boring," he said. "This is why I didn't want to talk about it. There's always some drama."

"That's not fair … if she expects you to spend Christmas with her family and not see yours."

"I wasn't going to cancel on my mum at the last minute. I already felt terrible for not seeing her on Christmas Day. And I really wanted to see her. We could've gone down to Hope Cove later. Sometimes I think Josie enjoys the drama. I can't be bothered with it."

"If only she could find an acting job," Emily mused. "Then she could direct all the drama into something productive."

She was actually being serious, but when Jack started laughing, she joined in too. At least it lightened the atmosphere.

"I don't suppose I can tempt you to another drink?" Jack asked as the laughter faded.

He could definitely tempt her. He wouldn't, though. "No. It's been lovely but I really should head home."

The crowd in the main part of the pub had thinned and Emily was slightly disappointed that there was no need for Jack to take her hand again.

They walked down the road to the taxi rank, where he wrapped her in a big hug. She embraced him tightly, hating the fact that she probably wouldn't see him again for a while.

"Maybe I'll visit you in London one of these days," he said with a lopsided smile. "Take care, Em!"

She smiled as she stepped into the waiting taxi.

It was amazing how quickly the smile disappeared as the taxi took her further and further away from him.

Chapter 27

Emily was on the train back to London the following day when Josie called. She contemplated ignoring the phone. They'd been exchanging messages that mostly consisted of Josie complaining about Jack, and Emily wasn't sure she could cope with an actual conversation.

Finally, she answered and stared out of the window, as though the other people on the train couldn't hear her if she looked away from them.

"Are you still in Oxford?" Josie asked.

"No. I'm on the train. I've got a shift in the restaurant tonight."

Josie sighed. "I just got back. I thought we could hang out. I'm trying to avoid Jack."

"Where are you?"

"At my parents' house."

"You'll sort things out with Jack, won't you?"

"I don't know. I'm so angry with him. It was embarrassing to turn up at Lizzie's place without him and have to explain why he wasn't there. Did he say anything when you saw him?"

Emily had already mentioned in her messages that she'd bumped into him. "Not really," she said. "Only that he wanted to spend time with his family and you wanted to spend time with yours."

"I don't understand why we couldn't see his mum today. He was just being awkward. I swear he did it on purpose to get out of going to Lizzie's. He probably forgot to set the alarm on purpose ..."

Emily struggled to keep up with the conversation. Poor Jack was doomed when it came to arguing with Josie.

"Couldn't you set your own alarm?"

"Yes!" she said loudly. "I should have done. But I forgot and I thought he'd do it."

"Well ..." Emily caught her reflection in the train window and was amused by the look of absolute puzzlement. Most of the time it wasn't worth getting into these discussions with Josie. "What are you going to do then?"

"I'm not sure. Sometimes I think we should split up. We spend so much time bickering."

"Maybe," Emily mused.

"Do you think so?"

"Erm ..." Emily sat up straighter. "What?"

"You think I should split up with Jack?"

"Maybe," she said again. "If you think it's not working out any more ..." Oh my God. Was she seriously advising Josie to split up with Jack? Her eyes darted around the train carriage, sure that people would be looking at her with contempt. She was an awful person after all. No one paid her any notice. They were all busy staring at their phones or laptops.

"I don't know what to do," Josie whined. "I spend a lot of the time annoyed with him."

"That's probably a sign that things aren't working any more then. There's no point staying together if you make each other miserable." Wow. She really was a bad person. A bad person and an awful friend. She took a breath and tried to think rationally. It wasn't actually terrible advice. And if she didn't have feelings for Jack, she'd probably have said this to Josie a long time ago. It was a very dysfunctional relationship.

"I don't think we make each other miserable," Josie said firmly. "We have loads of fun. Sometimes it's great. But then sometimes it's not."

"You should probably have a proper talk with Jack. Get everything out in the open …"

"You're so sensible," Josie said cheerfully. "This is why I ask you for advice."

"Anytime," Emily said.

When she finally got off the phone, she felt emotionally drained. She was annoyed with herself for suggesting Josie break up with Jack. Even if it *was* good advice, her motives were all wrong. It wasn't even that she was deluded enough to think anything could ever happen between her and Jack, but she thought he deserved better. That seemed like a terrible thing to think about her best friend.

***

Thankfully, Emily had a shift at the restaurant that evening to take her mind off all things Jack and Josie. It was late morning when she woke the next day, and she was determined to get started on her plan to develop a social life.

She'd only just opened her laptop when the incessant banging on the door started. After squinting through the peephole, she let a manic-looking Josie in.

There wasn't even time to ask how she'd got into the building. People often left the front door open, and it drove Emily crazy.

"We've split up," Josie said tearfully. She barged inside and planted herself on the couch. "He wouldn't apologise so we ended up arguing even more. I threw some things in a bag and left. And I'm not going back."

"I'm so sorry." Emily took a seat beside her and placed a sympathetic hand on her shoulder.

"He's such a selfish prick," Josie spat.

"I thought you were going to talk to him and sort everything out ..."

"I tried. But he's so stubborn. He wouldn't apologise for not coming to Lizzie's. He didn't even seem to think he'd done anything wrong."

"Did he explain why he didn't go?"

"No. I didn't want to listen to more excuses. It's all I ever get from him: a load of pathetic excuses. I've had enough of it."

"I really thought you'd make up," Emily said.

"No. You were right. You said I should break up with him. I decided to take your advice. If I let you take over all my decision-making, my life might be as easy as yours."

"Erm ..." Emily opened and closed her mouth in quick succession.

"I'm joking." Josie rolled her eyes. "Don't look so scared."

"But I didn't tell you to split up with Jack. I only meant, if you felt it was the right thing to do."

"I think it was the right thing." She sounded confident as she wiped tears from her cheeks. "It'll just take a bit of getting used to, I guess. Is it okay if I stay here for a couple of days?"

"Of course. I've got to work in the evenings but you can make yourself at home."

"Thanks." She frowned. "I'm going to have to move in with my parents for a while. Temporarily anyway. I know this year is going to be my year. My career is going to take off. I just know it."

"I think you're right," Emily said. "I have a feeling about it too." At that point, she'd say anything to make Josie feel better. It felt like the least she could do since she was so instrumental in Josie's breakup with Jack. She should have kept her mouth shut and not got involved.

The worst of it was that the thought of Jack being single made her tingle with happiness.

Summer at the Old Boathouse

Chapter 28

Josie stayed for two days. She was surprisingly upbeat for someone getting over a breakup. Mainly, she stayed on the couch, flicking through the TV channels, reading magazines and drinking cups of tea. When she left it was to go back to her parents' house. She really did seem okay about it all. Emily had expected her to make it a huge drama and wallow in self-pity, but she'd underestimated her. Josie was being entirely positive about the situation and looking to the future. It was something Emily definitely needed to get better at.

It was New Year's Eve when Emily heard from Josie again. She called in the afternoon as Emily was getting ready for work. "I wanted to wish you a Happy New Year! I know you'll be at work later so I thought I'd get in early."

"Happy New Year," Emily said unenthusiastically.

"You won't believe what happened." Josie sounded excited. "I went to pick up my stuff from Jack's place and we got chatting. We got back together."

"Oh. Wow. That's good." Her words were flat.

"I know you think we should split up—"

"I didn't say that," Emily protested but Josie

spoke over her.

"I took your advice in the end. We actually sat down and chatted everything through. I think Jack really did just want to spend time with his family. And I was probably being a bit selfish. I've said that next Christmas we'll organise it better so we see everyone."

"That's good." Emily sat heavily on the couch. "I'm glad you're happy."

"I am," Josie said. "I think we probably needed a bit of time apart. It might have done us good."

Emily felt a wave of anger course through her. "I've got to get work," she said quickly. "Have a good evening."

"Talk to you next year." Josie's voice was full of amusement. Of course she was amused – she got everything she wanted. Always. Even when she didn't deserve it.

***

Emily was at work for the start of the new year. It was surprisingly fun. After feeling so deflated by the phone call from Josie, she was sure she'd struggle to be cheerful at work, but it was hard not to laugh around such a wonderful group of people. The private party who'd taken over the restaurant were so much fun. Between courses, they kept insisting she sit and have a drink with them. She couldn't as she was rushed off her feet, but after desserts had been served she managed to relax a bit. When she protested that she had to refill people's drinks, one of the older gentlemen took the wine bottle and did it for her.

It was a lovely atmosphere, made even better by the fact she was being paid for double time. With the generous tips, she made almost as much as she usually made in a week. And the money was well-needed.

With the new year came her resolution, and she was determined to stick to it. There was a library in Shoreditch which hosted a writing group once a week. She usually had Tuesdays off so it was perfect. There was no excuse not to go. It was the second Tuesday in January when she first went along. She made it as far as the information desk and registered for a library card.

The following week, she made it a little further. Casually browsing the shelves, she located the group in a quiet corner in the back. They were partially hidden by strategically placed bookshelves, but she was convinced that was them. On her third visit she browsed the bookshelves nearest the writing group. Peering through the stacks, she got a good look at them. There were seven of them, sitting around a large oval table. Some of them had paper or notebooks in front of them. A middle-aged man was reading from a sheet of A4 paper.

Oh, would she have to read something she'd written? That hadn't occurred to her. She hadn't thought beyond introducing herself, and that scared her quite enough. She'd imagined them asking questions as they tried to gauge whether she was a proper writer, worthy of being in their group. And now she realised that if she survived, she might have to read aloud something she'd written. Being a miserable recluse really didn't seem so bad.

On her fourth visit to the library, she bit the bullet

and wandered through the shelves to the scary area where the writers met.

"Hi," she said nervously when all eyes landed on her. "Is this the writing group?"

"It is." A grey-haired man with a beard stood and offered his hand. "Welcome. Please take a seat."

"Thank you." She smiled around the group. There were only five of them today. "I'm Emily, by the way."

"Lovely to meet you, Emily," the grey-haired man said. "We were about to listen to Janet read an excerpt of the short story she's been working on. Would you mind if we carry on with that and do proper introductions after? It'll help you get a feel for how we operate too."

"Of course," Emily stammered.

She barely registered a word of Janet's reading; she was too worried about the so-called proper introductions. Why was she doing this to herself? She hated meeting new people. Why put herself through the torture?

Once Janet finished her reading, the others weighed in, giving their opinions and having some gentle discussion. It was all very positive. Maybe reading something out wouldn't be so bad.

"What did you think, Emily?"

She was in the spotlight and she cursed herself for not listening properly. "It was great," she said vaguely. "I really enjoyed it."

"It's hard to give your opinion to a bunch of strangers," the grey-haired man said. "I'm sure you'll feel more comfortable after a few weeks." He shook his head. "We haven't even introduced ourselves. I'm

Phillip ..." He went round the others and she nodded a greeting to Janet, Mary, Jonathan and Becky. They were all older than her but seemed to be a friendly bunch.

After some discussion, she found she was one of the only published authors in the group. Apparently most of them were hobbyists. Jonathan cleared his throat loudly at that point and proceeded to spend ten minutes telling Emily about his published article in a men's magazine describing how to change a carburettor on a certain type of lawnmower. The rest of the group openly rolled their eyes.

"I'm going to look out for your book," Mary said when Jonathan finally stopped talking. "Are you working on something at the moment?"

"Yeah." Emily felt herself turning red.

"What's it about?" It was Janet who asked the inevitable question. Stupid Janet.

"Well. It's a little complicated ..."

"What genre?" Phillip prompted. "More romance?"

"Yes. Women's fiction with a bit of humour."

"One-line description," Janet said beaming. "Go ..."

Emily gritted her teeth and shook her head. Bloody Janet. "It's about..." Argh, she really couldn't sum it up in one sentence. She'd have to improvise and make something up. "It's about a young woman who's in love with her best friend's boyfriend."

There was a lot of sucking in of breath and puffing breath from cheeks. That certainly knocked the positivity out of them.

"It doesn't sound like your typical romance,"

Phillip said.

"It's not really," she agreed.

"And it doesn't sound particularly humorous …"

"I throw in a few jokes," she said.

"Romance readers like things to end happily," Becky said quietly. "I'm not sure how you'll get a happy ever after from that scenario."

"I've not figured that out yet either," she said drily.

"It's difficult," Mary mused. "Because for the protagonist to get her happy ever after, she's going to have to lose her friend."

Janet jumped in next. "And if she treats her friend badly, she's going to be a very unlikeable protagonist."

"That's a problem I'm struggling with," Emily said. If she managed not to laugh manically she'd be doing well. Why couldn't she just have told them about her book?

"Usually we don't like to be discouraging," Phillip said. "But as you're writing for mainstream publishing I think it's worth considering the points made."

"I'll probably scrap the idea. Now that I think about it, it's really a terrible idea for a book."

Mary reached over and patted her arm. Her eyebrows were raised sympathetically. "I'm sorry. It's your first time here and we've trampled all over your plot."

No, not my plot, Mary, just my life. "I haven't even started writing it. It was only an idea. But you're right: there's no way to get a happy ending from it. Not that I can see anyway."

"I know what you could do," Jonathan said enthusiastically. "Kill off the best friend. Make the hero sad for a chapter or two, then your protagonist swoops in to comfort him and they live happily ever after ..."

Janet clicked her tongue. "Still not really a happy ending, Jonathan."

"Best I could come up with," he said with a shrug.

"I'm definitely going to put the idea aside," Emily said, hoping to put an end to the surreal conversation.

"It might be for the best," Becky said kindly. "You don't want to ruin your writing career when you're just starting out."

Emily smiled politely and was thankful when they switched their attention to Phillip, who wanted to get their opinion on a poem he'd written.

She nodded along for the next hour and was glad when the meeting finally came to an end. It was pleasant enough but utterly boring.

They were right: there would never be a happy ending for her with Jack. She needed to put the thoughts of him behind her and find a way to be happy without him.

Chapter 29

Emily spent the next few months forcing herself to be optimistic. She told herself that anything could happen. Unfortunately, not much did. She went to work and she got on with her writing, increasingly nervous about meeting the deadline for book two. With some effort, she forced herself to go to the library writing group until it became habit – and a pleasant one at that. There were some livelier characters who hadn't been there at the first meeting. She even met one or two of them outside of the group.

In March she proudly took in a copy of her book in paperback to show her friends at the writing group. It was amazing having the book in print. It seemed more real then. She spent a long time after she'd received the books just staring at the pretty pink cover.

As winter tailed off, Josie visited more often, and every couple of weeks they'd spend a day or a weekend together. There was no mention of Jack joining, which saved her from having to think of excuses or to endure what would surely be a painful meet-up. Apparently he was busy with work so never had time to visit when Josie did.

About once a month Emily would get back to Oxford, but spent the time with her mum and kept a low profile, going to places she was sure she wouldn't run the risk of bumping into Jack.

From what she could tell, things were good again between Josie and Jack. There was still the usual complaining from Josie, but generally she seemed content and happy with the relationship.

At least up until one Friday in May when Josie called in floods of tears. It was the weekend of Lizzie and Max's wedding so Emily was surprised to hear from her. Emily had made up an excuse for not going to the wedding. She'd said her deadline was coming up and she was snowed under trying to get the book finished. It was partly true: she did need to have the book finished soon, but it was almost done and she definitely could have taken the weekend away from it.

She just couldn't face the wedding. It would be too hard watching Jack and Josie all dressed up and looking like the perfect couple while she sat in a corner not knowing anyone. That's what she imagined anyway. A day of watching Jack and Josie slow-dance to romantic music. No thanks.

At her desk, she brought the phone to her ear. She expected to hear Josie's squeals of excitement about the wedding. Josie seemed to have been looking forward to the day almost as much as Lizzie.

"Jack broke up with me," she said sadly.

"What? Where are you?"

"I'm in Hope Cove. At Lizzie's house. I'm standing on the beautiful beach but Jack's not coming." She cried gently. "It's definitely over between us."

"I don't understand. I thought things were better."

"It's always the same. We're fine for a while and

then we're not. He said we're not right for each other. He sounded so definite." Her voice cracked and a sob echoed down the phone.

Emily's eyes filled with tears at the sound. "I'm so sorry."

"I hate him," Josie spluttered. "Any time we're supposed to do something with my family he ruins it. Now I have to go to the wedding on my own. Tomorrow I need to spend the whole day smiling and being happy for Lizzie. I don't know how I'm going to manage it."

"You'll be fine." Emily tried to sound positive. "You're an actress, remember! It'll be easy for you."

That got a laugh from her. "I'm actually unemployed, but thanks for reminding me."

"Sorry," Emily said. She'd forgotten that Josie's secretarial job had come to an end. It was only a temporary contract to cover maternity leave so it was expected, but still, Josie must feel like everything was going wrong. "Don't worry. This is your big year, remember? You're going to get an acting job. You'll have more time to focus on that without the office job holding you back …"

Josie laughed again. "You really do have a great imagination. What am I going to do about Jack?"

"What do you want to do? Do you think you'll get back together? It's not the first time you've broken up … you usually manage to sort things out."

"I can't believe he won't be at the wedding," she said. "I'm so angry with him. But I also can't imagine not being with him any more. What if it really is over this time?"

"Maybe it's for the best," Emily said gently. She

knew as soon as the words were out that it was the wrong thing to say.

Josie's annoyance seemed to radiate through the phone. "You never thought we were right for each other, did you?" She didn't wait for an answer. "You don't get it. You think we should split up because we argue sometimes, but relationships are complicated. Things aren't always perfect, that doesn't mean you give up on them."

"I didn't mean it like that." Emily went on the defensive. "Of course if you want to be with him you should try and work things out."

"Sorry," Josie said. "I'm taking it out on you." She took an audible breath. "I worry about your love life too, you know. You never date any more. I never understood why you broke up with Stuart so abruptly. I thought you liked him."

"He was okay, but I didn't see it going anywhere. Why are we talking about my love life?"

"Because you don't have one and it's sad. You should start dating again."

"I'm not exactly inundated with requests."

"Who's going to ask when you barely leave your flat? And even if someone asked you on a date you'd say no."

She chuckled. "Are we focussing on my love life to make you feel better about the state of yours?"

She could hear the smile when Josie spoke. "We're both as bad as each other, aren't we?"

"Maybe."

"I wish Jack would make more effort. I want him to just turn up for the wedding. That would be romantic."

"Maybe he will."

"No," she said matter-of-factly. "It's Jack we're talking about. He doesn't do romantic. That's part of the problem."

"Don't let it ruin your weekend," Emily said. "Enjoy the wedding."

"I'll pretend to enjoy the wedding," she said. "Like you said, I am an actress."

They were both smiling when they ended the call.

Emily felt bad for Josie. She hated hearing her so upset. And she was annoyed with herself about her comment about it being for the best. Why did she always say the wrong thing? A thought occurred to her then. She could call Jack – suggest that he go down to Hope Cove to surprise Josie like she wanted. Before she knew what she was doing she had the phone to her ear, listening to it ring.

Panic hit. She should definitely have stopped to think it through. Maybe she shouldn't interfere. It was a relief when he didn't answer. What on earth had she been thinking?

She opened her laptop, determined to get some writing done and not spend the weekend thinking about Jack and Josie.

It was the next morning when he called her back, and she panicked at the sight of his name on the display. It was tempting not to answer.

"Hey," he said cheerily. "I missed a call from you yesterday."

"Yeah. I just wanted to say hi …"

"Hi!" he said, chuckling. "You heard me and Josie split up, I presume?"

"I'm sure it's only a temporary glitch." It was so

good to hear his voice. She hadn't spoken to him for so long but he sounded casual, as though they spoke all the time.

"Not this time," he said. "She's furious with me."

"Yeah but I'm sure if you apologise …"

"Apologise for what? For her being a drama queen who creates issues for no reason? All I said was I couldn't call in sick to work just because she wanted to change the plans at the last minute and drive down a day early. I don't think I was being unreasonable."

"Oh," Emily said. It was always interesting to hear the other side of things.

"Sorry. I didn't mean to take it out on you. She drives me crazy sometimes."

"I'm sure it will be fine."

"No." He sounded as though he was moving around and she wondered where he was. "It's over. And it's probably for the best." Silence for a moment. "Besides she'll never forgive me for not going to the wedding. I should probably have driven down there, but I'm so sick of all the drama."

Emily stayed quiet for a moment, nodding to herself. "Make her laugh," she said without thinking.

"What?"

"Call her tomorrow. Ask her how the wedding was and when she's coming home. Make light of the whole situation."

He chuckled. "That won't work."

"It will," Emily insisted. She knew Josie so well. What she loved most about Jack was when he was joking around and doing his whole cheeky chappy routine. "Make her laugh and she'll forget anything ever happened."

He didn't respond, and the silence was uncomfortable. She didn't even know why she'd said that.

"Everything okay with you?" he asked.

"Yeah, fine. Busy."

"That's good. I should probably get on. I've got some stuff to do. It was good to talk to you."

"You too," she said, ending the call with a quick goodbye.

***

On Monday, Emily began getting cryptic messages from Josie about the wedding. Apparently Josie had loads to tell Emily but needed to speak to her in person. It seemed that she and Jack were back together. Fairly predictable.

It was Friday when Josie called from the train saying she needed to meet with Emily. She was rambling manically about having a new job and moving to a farm in Devon. Emily agreed to meet her for a quick lunch.

"You're moving to Devon?" she asked when they were settled on a bench in Regent's Park.

"Yes. Max's aunt owns a dog kennels and she offered me a job."

"Wow."

"I know. It's in the middle of the countryside, but I think the change will be good for me."

"Won't you miss the city?" Emily was struggling with the idea of Josie living a quiet life in the middle of nowhere. "I can't imagine you living in the countryside."

"I'll give it a go," she said. "It might be fun."

"I suppose it might." Emily wasn't at all convinced. It was typical Josie – she'd get a crazy idea in her head and jump in with both feet.

"You're not making me feel better," Josie said. Emily obviously hadn't managed to hide her hesitation about the idea. "Tell me about the book ..."

Oh yes, Emily was supposed to be stressed about deadlines and meetings with editors. "I'm officially a starving artist." She really would be starving too if it weren't for her savings. "And this next book is killing me. I can't seem to get it right."

"You said that about the last one and it came out brilliantly. I can have a look if you want. I reckon I'll have lots of time for reading in the back of beyond."

"I just sent it to Lizzie. She's going to have a look over it while she's away." They'd exchanged a few emails about the wedding, and Lizzie had offered to look over the next book. She said it would be nice holiday reading while she was on honeymoon. Emily had taken her up on the offer.

"I see. Ask the pro!"

"How was the wedding?" Emily asked. The messages she'd got from Josie hadn't made a lot of sense, but it seemed as though Jack's absence hadn't ruined the weekend. "I can't believe I couldn't make it." It occurred to her that if she'd known Jack wasn't going to be there, she might have gone. Not that it mattered now.

"It was amazing." Josie's smile was wide and her eyes sparkled happily. It confused Emily.

"I thought Jack had split up with you and you were upset about going alone?"

"It turned out to be fun going on my own."

"What happened?"

"Nothing. The best man was pretty cute, that's all."

"You're terrible." Emily forced herself to laugh with Josie. But she didn't find it at all funny. Surely Josie hadn't cheated on Jack? "You don't waste any time," she said, in an attempt to coax more information.

"It wasn't like that." Josie turned serious as the laughter subsided. "He's actually a really sweet guy." She paused, a small smile playing on her lips. "He's Max's best friend. And it was only a bit of flirting. He lives next door to the kennels so I guess I'll be seeing him again."

There was something about Josie that Emily couldn't quite put her finger on. It seemed like there was more about this guy than she was letting on. She had a bad feeling. "This sounds like it's about to get complicated. Didn't you say you worked things out with Jack again?"

"Yeah. It's not complicated. Jack and I made up. The thing with Sam was just a momentary weakness. You know how it is at weddings ... So much champagne and romance. It was nothing."

"I might have to come and visit then ... if there's a hot guy going spare."

"You should!" Josie said. "Definitely. There's a pub in the village. We can go wild!"

"You know me so well," Emily said with a faint eye-roll. "What happened with Jack then? You just decided to give it another go?"

"Yeah. I thought things might be over for good

this time. But he's so sweet and funny. And if I'm honest, the argument before the wedding was as much my fault as his."

"What's going to happen if you're living in Devon?"

"I'll be in Devon during the week and then go back to Oxford on the weekends. I think it'll work out okay."

"I hope so," Emily said quietly. One of them should really have their life in order.

She spent a couple of hours with Josie before leaving to get ready for her shift at the restaurant. She was working all weekend and it went by fast. By Monday she was exhausted. Josie messaged her in the evening saying she'd arrived at Oakbrook Farm and everything was going well so far.

They were messaging back and forth when a Facebook message popped up on her phone. Emily had to read it a couple of times before it sank in. It was a guy that she went to school with. Glenn Edwards. She checked his Facebook page and vaguely remembered him. Apparently he'd seen that she'd published a book and wanted to congratulate her. Weird. He also asked if she still lived in Oxford and if she'd fancy meeting for a drink sometime if she did. Very weird.

It was tempting to immediately tell Josie about the message but she resisted. Josie would tell her to go out with him. Their previous conversation played on her mind: Josie had been adamant that Emily would say no even if someone did ask her on a date. Maybe she should prove her wrong. A date might be good for her, and who knew what would come of it.

She wasn't working the following Friday or Saturday and could definitely pop back to Oxford for the weekend.

Not wanting to seem too keen, she waited until the following evening to reply to Glenn. He messaged her straight back and after a few more messages she'd arranged to have dinner with him on Friday evening.

The remainder of the week was spent in a state of mild panic.

Chapter 30

It was Glenn's suggestion that they meet at a little Italian restaurant in the Castle Quarter. Emily hadn't liked to say she was sick of the sight of Italian food. It was strange to be back in that part of town too. Walking past the castle made her feel nostalgic. It had been a great place to work, and she missed it.

Glenn was standing outside the restaurant when she arrived, and she brushed the memories of her old life aside and pasted on a smile as she greeted him.

The restaurant belonged to a chain, and Emily was slightly underwhelmed, given the lovely authentic Italian restaurant where she spent so much of her time. It didn't matter; she took a seat and focused on getting to know Glenn.

They spent a little while reminiscing about school and swapping snippets of information about what had happened to the rest of their classmates. Emily had lost track of everyone apart from Josie and a couple of people she still kept in touch with through Facebook.

Over the meal they talked about work and their lives. Emily knew early on in the date that she wouldn't see him again. It was pleasant enough, but there was definitely no spark between them. She wasn't deterred by the fact. It had been an interesting little experiment, and it actually might encourage her to date more. Just not Glenn.

She'd had two glasses of wine by the time they finished the food. When Glenn suggested they move on to a bar, she only hesitated for a moment. Another drink would be okay.

It was her who suggested the Wetherspoon's on George Street. In the back of her mind she knew that on a Friday night, there was a good chance Jack might be there.

They found a table and she soon felt stupid for the time she spent scanning the room for Jack. She was supposed to be moving on from this stupid obsession. Forcing herself to focus on Glenn, she listened as he told her some story about his car breaking down the previous week.

After two more drinks, she was well on the way to being drunk.

"Do you want another?" he asked, looking at her empty glass.

"No." She shook her head and reached for her handbag. "I think I've had enough. I should get home. It's been fun …"

That's when she spotted Jack walking in with his crowd of friends.

"Maybe just one more," she said to Glenn without much thought. Her heart felt like it was going to explode out of her chest. She wanted everyone else to disappear and it just be her and Jack.

When Glenn returned from the bar, the conversation continued to plod along. Emily was only half concentrating. She kept glancing at Jack. He was laughing and joking with his friends and hadn't noticed her at the other side of the room. Glenn seemed oblivious to the fact that she wasn't really listening to him. She barely registered drinking her drink. It was only when Glenn laughed and made a comment about her thirst that she realised she was empty. She'd really downed that one.

The sensible thing would be to go home, but the alcohol in her system made her anything but sensible. Glenn got her another drink.

She wasn't sure how much time passed, but Glenn was in the bathroom and she was openly staring at Jack from afar. Her head was spinning – from the alcohol or the sight of Jack she wasn't sure. He was mid-laugh when he finally caught sight of her. Their eyes locked. His laughter faded, but a smile remained and he immediately headed towards her.

"Hi," he said happily, his adorably boyish grin giving Emily butterflies.

"Hi." The giggle was alcohol-induced.

Jack's grin widened. His eyebrows twitched together. "Are you drunk?"

She giggled again. "I'm on a date," she blurted.

"Really?" She could have sworn he frowned, but her eyes weren't focussing properly. "Where's the lucky guy?"

She glanced around. "He's around here somewhere."

"I should probably leave you to it then …"

She hiccupped. "You can sit and have a drink with us if you want."

"It doesn't sound like the best idea you've ever had." Jack took a swig of his drink. He looked suddenly serious. "Don't get too drunk."

She watched him walk away and went from

feeling giggly drunk to melancholy drunk in less than a second. How dare he tell her what to do? If she wanted to get drunk it had nothing to do with him.

Glenn returned and she forced a smile. He wobbled slightly as he reached the table. "Are you having a good time?" he asked.

"Yeah," she said flatly. "But I should probably go home soon."

Glenn looked at her hopefully. "One for the road?"

"Go on then," she said. "I suppose one more won't hurt." Famous last words.

It turned out one more would hurt, and not only her head the next day. About half way through that one last drink, her vision started to blur. Her eyelids drooped. She could barely keep them open. The room began to spin. She needed to get to the bathroom, and quick. When she moved from her chair, the floor seemed to sway. Nothing was steady.

Glenn's voice echoed in her ears. "Are you okay?" he asked, unconcerned.

She definitely didn't feel okay. She should've gone home three drinks ago. Forcing her eyes to focus, she caught sight of Jack watching her with an odd look on his face. So if it wasn't enough to embarrass herself on her first date in goodness knows how long, she also had Jack to witness it.

Her hand clutched the back of a chair as she paused on the way to the bathroom. Nausea swept through her and she put a hand over her mouth. She needed to get to the bathroom. Fast. But her legs were about to give away. She could feel them turning to jelly beneath her.

"I've got you." Jack slipped an arm around her waist, taking some of her weight. She closed her eyes and leaned into him. When they reached the bathroom, Jack lowered her to the floor in a cubicle. He pulled her hand from the mouth and her body convulsed. Everything that she'd put into it was reappearing. She fought for breath. Her body felt so heavy.

"Stay awake." Jack's voice was gentle in her ear as he held her up and pulled her hair back.

The vomiting finally stopped. She shuddered as she gulped a much-needed lungful of air. Then she flopped to one side, landing full force on Jack. He toppled backwards, hitting the cubicle wall with a thud. Her head was on his chest. She was vaguely aware of his heartbeat and could just make out the scent of his aftershave through the stench of vomit.

"I'm sorry," she whispered.

"Don't worry." He pushed the hair from her face. "Just try not to pass out on me."

"What happened to my date?"

Jack took a deep breath. "I think he left."

Emily clutched Jack's shirt as tears streamed down her face. She couldn't lift her head from his chest. "I'm such an idiot."

"You're just drunk." He idly ran a hand over her hair. "Let's get you home."

"I don't know if I can walk." Her words were a slurred jumble. Since her head was suddenly too heavy for her neck, it seemed unlikely that her legs would cooperate and take the weight of her body.

"I'll help you." Jack pulled her up with him and then awkwardly manoeuvred them through the cubicle door.

It was loud back in the pub, and Emily breathed deeply through another wave of nausea. Surely there couldn't be anything left inside her. Her legs buckled and she slouched onto Jack.

He shouted something over her head. A man's name. "Help me get her in a taxi, will you?"

More arms made her feel lighter and she was moving quicker. Cool air hit.

"Do you know her?" A male voice. Jack's friend.

"Yeah. She's my girlfriend's best friend."

The leather seats of the taxi were cool on her cheek.

"One of you better be getting in here with her." The angry voice rattled round her. "And if she pukes you pay for cleaning."

"Of course I'm going with her." Jack's voice was low and gruff. He was angry too.

"Get her home and come back out," the other voice said.

"I doubt it." Jack slid into the seat next to her, talking loudly to the guy outside. "I've got puke down my shirt."

"Go home and change. It's still early."

She didn't hear Jack reply. The car door banged shut and the driver asked where they were going.

"What's your mum's address, Em?"

She tried to speak, but the noise that came out didn't sound right. She tried again. "I want to go home."

"I know." His hand was on her chin, pushing her head up off her chest. "I'll take you home. But you need to tell me where that is."

"Home."

There was a snorted laugh, but when her eyes flicked to his, he didn't look amused.

"Sorry," she mumbled.

"I'll call Josie," he said. "I'll get the address from her."

Her arm didn't feel like it belonged to her as it batted at his phone. "No."

He let go of her to retrieve his phone from the floor. "I need to ask her where to take you."

"Don't," she insisted, but couldn't find enough words to form any sort of an argument. Her eyes closed.

When she opened them again she didn't know where she was. She was lying on a couch and Jack was at her side.

"I'm going to be sick."

She stood and Jack led her to a bathroom. This time she managed to hold her own hair back as she threw up. Jack left and came back with a glass of water while she was still retching. He set it beside her and then lowered himself onto the bathroom floor opposite her, leaning his head back against the wall.

"Where are we?" She wiped her mouth and took a sip of water.

Jack looked exhausted. "My place."

She'd only been there once before, when Josie first moved in. That seemed like forever ago. "Did you call Josie?"

He shook his head. "I decided it would be easier to bring you back with me than turn up on your mum's doorstep and have to explain to her."

Emily flushed the toilet, then slumped against the

wall. She put her head in her hands and cried.

"Come on." Jack was in front of her, taking her hands and pulling her up. "You need to sleep it off now."

He led her back through the living room and into his bedroom.

"I can sleep on the couch," she mumbled.

"Take the bed," he said wearily.

She sat on the edge of it. "You can go back out and meet your friends. I'm fine."

"I've got to be up early for work anyway."

"I'm sorry," she said as he started to move away.

"Don't worry about it."

"I ruined your night and I'm taking your bed." Her hand went to her mouth as a sob formed. "And you're really angry with me."

He sighed and came back to sit beside her. "I'm not angry. You worried me, that's all. What would have happened to you if I hadn't been there? Your date didn't seem too keen on sticking around to look after you."

"I wouldn't have been in that state if you hadn't been there." She hiccupped through her tears.

"What?"

"I was about to leave and then I saw you." The tears came in a steady flow. She knew she should stop talking, but the filter between her thoughts and mouth must have drowned in alcohol. "I never see you any more and I wanted to see you. I wanted to talk to you. But I was on a stupid date, and I can't talk to you because you're Josie's boyfriend—"

Jack stood abruptly. His eyes were full of kindness. "You really need to sleep." He patted the pillow and she lay down. There were a couple of tugs as he pulled off her shoes.

"Jack …"

"No more drunken rambling. Go to sleep."

She sniffed and buried her head in the pillow.

There was click of the light switch and she could just make out Jack's silhouette in the doorway.

The pillowcase was damp with tears in no time.

Summer at the Old Boathouse

Chapter 31

Daylight hit her eyes, and Emily's head throbbed. There was a noise nearby, like glasses clinking together. It took a few seconds to remember where she was and then memories came flooding back. She wished she was still asleep. Slowly, she sat up and swung her legs off the bed. She waited a moment. After a deep breath she stood up.

Jack didn't notice her at first. He raked a hand through his hair then continued tidying up the living room. With an armful of takeaway boxes, he disappeared to the kitchen. When he returned he stopped short, finally catching sight of her in the bedroom doorway.

"Morning," he said. One side of his mouth twitched to weary smile. "How are you feeling?"

"Embarrassed. Humiliated. Disgusting."

"And how's your head?"

"Pounding."

He scooped discarded clothes from the couch, along with a blanket and pillow. "Sit down," he said, and moved to the bedroom with his bundle.

Emily did as she was told, and Jack came back a moment later with a glass of water and a couple of paracetamol.

"You'll feel better," he said, handing her the

tablets as he sat beside her.

She gulped them down. "Thank you." For the briefest moment she closed her eyes, then turned to Jack. "I'm so sorry," she said.

"These things happen."

"Not usually to me." Embarrassment was all encompassing. "I don't know what I'd have done if you weren't there." Though she knew for a fact it wouldn't have happened if she hadn't seen him in the pub. Then she remembered telling him that and felt herself flush. It was like she'd been trying to see how many ways she could embarrass herself in front of him in one evening.

"I'm just glad you're okay," he said.

"Do you think you could do me a favour," she blurted, "and not tell Josie about this?"

He leaned back on the couch and let out a frustrated growl.

"Sorry," she said quickly. "I shouldn't have asked you. Of course you'd need to tell Josie. You shouldn't keep secrets from her because of me."

"It's not that." His lips twitched to cheeky smile. "I was hoping we could make me sound heroic and get me out of her bad books. I'm not her favourite person at the moment."

Emily's brow furrowed in confusion. "Why? I thought you'd sorted everything out after the wedding?"

"Oh, we did. But I was in the pub when she got home last night so she wasn't very happy. And the place is a mess."

"Why were you in the pub if you knew she was coming back?"

"I lost track of time." He sat up straighter as his gentle tone turned gruff. "I'm working every hour of overtime I can get, and I just went for a quick drink with the lads and the next thing she's calling me, furious because I'm not at home and the place is a mess."

"It is kind of a mess." Apparently Emily's filter had yet to resume normal service.

"I know." He stood and continued cleaning. His voice was loud and made her head hurt. "But I'm working as many hours as I can, which means I generally come home knackered. I'm too tired to cook so I get a takeaway and pass out on the couch. And before I know it my alarm goes off and I'm jumping in the shower and running out the door again."

Jack was pacing the living room, randomly tidying as he went. She wished he'd talk quieter. "And do you know why I'm doing all the extra hours?" He stopped and glared at her as though it was all her fault. "Because Josie's so airy fairy with money that I've basically been supporting us both for as long as we've been together. She doesn't pay for anything. She's never paid a penny towards the rent. Even when she *was* working it was only part-time, and she kept taking time off to go to acting auditions. And it didn't matter that she was barely earning anything because she has her own personal Bank of Jack." He took a deep breath and stretched his neck. "Sorry. I shouldn't be telling you all this."

"I didn't realise," Emily replied vaguely. She'd assumed Josie didn't pay much rent, but she hadn't realised she didn't pay anything. Although it made sense. She hardly seemed to work any hours.

"No one does," Jack said. "Josie's too busy telling people what a lazy slob I am."

That was true. Josie had complained to Emily about him countless times.

"I don't mind the money." He was calmer as he picked up a dirty mug and plate from the coffee table. "But she's so unappreciative. I don't think she has any idea of the strain it puts on me."

"Why don't you tell her?"

He smiled and his features softened. "Because she lives in some sort of happy bubble, and I don't want to burst it. She's completely oblivious, and while it can be really annoying, it's also not a bad trait. She's so carefree. I love that about her."

Emily's gaze dropped from Jack to the floor. It felt like someone had punched her and knocked the wind out of her.

"Do you want a coffee?" Jack called as he went to the kitchen. "Or toast or anything?"

"No." She groaned at the thought.

"You'll feel better soon," he said when he returned.

She dropped her head to her hands. "I'm so embarrassed."

"Don't be."

She managed a humourless laugh. How could she not be embarrassed? She kept having flashbacks to Jack propping her up in the ladies' toilets while she vomited what felt like her entire body weight.

"What happened to Josie last night?" she asked.

"She went to stay with her parents. She said she'd be here this afternoon." He checked his watch. "I've got to get to work but it's only eight o'clock. Why don't you go back to bed for a bit? You'll feel better after more sleep."

He was right – sleep would probably be good, but a part of her also thought she didn't really deserve to feel better. This was her punishment for drinking too much and causing Jack so much stress.

"Or you could call Josie," Jack suggested. "Catch up with her this morning."

"I didn't tell her I was back in Oxford." She hadn't mentioned it because she didn't want Josie adding to her anxiety about her date. The plan had been to tell her about it afterwards. Obviously that wasn't going to happen. It was a story she'd rather keep to herself.

She couldn't face Josie anyway. She was annoyed by what Jack had told her about Josie freeloading off him. If Josie started complaining about Jack again, Emily might struggle to hold her tongue.

"It was only supposed to be a quick trip," she said. "I'm getting the train back to London today." She didn't want to hang around in Oxford any more.

"Okay. I won't mention I saw you then." Jack nipped into his room and came back a few minutes later dressed for work in a pair of jeans and a white shirt with the company logo. He picked up his wallet and shoved it in his back pocket. "I've really got to go." He surveyed the room. "This place will have to do. No doubt I'll still be in trouble with Josie, but it's all I've got time for. You can let yourself out. Help yourself to anything. Have a look through the wardrobe for some of Josie's clothes if you want …" He trailed off, looking slightly sheepish.

Emily looked down. She was still in the previous

night's clothes and there were some dubious-looking stains down her front. "Thanks." She folded her arms across her chest. "And thanks again for taking care of me."

"No problem." He paused at the door. "It was good to see you."

She smiled. He was far too kind. How could it possibly have been good to see her?

Alone in the apartment, she contemplated going back to bed. She knew she wouldn't be able to sleep. It was weird being there: in the apartment that Jack and Josie shared. She was also worried that Josie would arrive, and she didn't feel like hanging out with her or explaining how she'd come to stay at their place.

After a quick shower, she had a rummage around and helped herself to some of Josie's clothes. She couldn't quite fit in Josie's jeans, but there were a pair of jogging bottoms that would do. At the bottom of a drawer she found an old T-shirt – things she thought Josie was less likely to notice were missing.

She was about to leave when she glanced around the living room. The coffee table was adorned with ringed coffee stains and crumbs, and the carpet looked like it hadn't been vacuumed in weeks. Throwing her bag on the couch, she went in search of cleaning supplies.

Not quite what she wanted to do with a hangover, but she supposed it was the least she could do.

Chapter 32

A little over a week later, she had a phone call from Josie.

"I've split up with Jack," she said without emotion.

Emily couldn't help herself. She laughed. Moving the phone away from her ear, she glared at it for a moment.

"Are you still there?" Josie asked.

"Yeah. I'm not sure I can have this conversation with you again."

"It's different this time."

"Hmm." Emily peered out of the small window of her apartment. The road below was busy with cars and people going about their lives. "I highly doubt that." She should probably try to muster at least a little bit of sympathy. Or some patience at least. She seemed to have run out. "I think I can tell you how this story ends."

"I've met someone else."

Emily walked to the couch and perched on the arm. She wasn't expecting that. "What?" She shook her head. "Who?"

"The guy I met at Lizzie's wedding. Sam."

"You cheated on Jack?"

"No," Josie said impatiently. "Nothing's

happened with Sam. Well, I kissed him at the wedding," she added flippantly. "But Jack and I had broken up so it wasn't cheating. Anyway, I've split up with Jack because I really like Sam, and I think he likes me too."

Emily sighed heavily.

"I know, I know. It sounds like me being fickle and impulsive, but it's not like that. It's different with Sam. Everything I feel for Sam made me see what was missing in my relationship with Jack."

"How did Jack take it?"

"Okay, I suppose. I didn't tell him about Sam ..."

"So Jack probably thinks this is a regular three-day break up?" That was a little harsh, but she really had lost all patience for Josie's drama.

"No," she replied slowly. "Jack understands. He's okay with it. All he's worried about is that we stay friends. We shouldn't have got back together after the wedding. We both knew that, really. I don't know why Jack decided to brush everything under the carpet and carry on as normal."

That might have been Emily's influence, but she didn't like to mention that detail.

"So it's definitely over?" Emily was still finding it hard to comprehend.

"Yes. And I really need a favour from you ..."

"What?" she asked dubiously.

"Could you collect my stuff from Jack's place?"

"No." She spluttered out a laugh. "No way."

"Please." Josie's voice had taken the tone of a little girl pleading for ice cream. Emily could imagine her making big eyes.

"Why can't you get it yourself?"

"I can, but it'll be awkward."

"You just said he still wants to be friends …"

"Of course we're still friends. It's Jack. I can't imagine not having him in my life. But I don't want to have to deal with all the awkward end of relationship stuff."

"I think you have to, Josie. It's called being an adult."

"You know how terrible I am at grown up stuff. You do it for me… please!"

"I'll think about it."

"Thanks. It'd be nice for you to catch up with Jack anyway. You don't have to stop being friends with him because I'm not with him any more."

"Hmm." She couldn't form a response to that.

"Just give him a call and arrange to pick it up next time you're in Oxford. He said he'll box it up. There's no rush. There's nothing I need urgently."

"Okay." She was sure it would be weird to collect Josie's stuff. If it wasn't urgent she'd definitely put it off for a while.

Summer at the Old Boathouse

Chapter 33

Life was quiet for Emily. Her second book was with the editor – there would no doubt be changes she'd need to make, but the bulk of the work was done. It was strange not to be writing, but she didn't have any ideas for the next project. She wrote some flash fiction and short stories for her writing group, but it was nothing that inspired her. Hopefully, she'd come up with something new soon.

Josie called her regularly, keeping her up-to-date on her new life in the country, and Sam, who she was completely smitten with. It was hard for Emily to digest that things were definitely over for Josie and Jack. They'd broken up so many times that she kept assuming they'd get back together, but it really didn't seem like it this time.

It was one evening in June when Josie called and told her she'd been offered her old acting job. Apparently the military soap opera was finally going ahead. They'd offered Josie the same part as before, and she was debating whether or not to take it.

"When did you find out?" Emily asked.

"Yesterday. Jack came down to give me the news."

"Really?" Emily asked surprised. "He drove all the way down to you?"

"Yeah." Emily could hear the eye-rolling even down the phone. "He just turned up. Sam was here and Lizzie and Max. It was so awkward."

"I can't believe he drove all the way down there. Why didn't he call you?"

"He tried." Josie's voice muffled as she shouted something to a dog in the background. "I hadn't been answering his calls so in the end he drove down with my mail."

"Wow."

"That will teach me not to ignore my phone," Josie said.

"It's quite a long round trip," Emily mused. She remembered Jack telling her how unappreciative Josie was, and it rang true now as well.

"He didn't want me to miss out on the job," Josie said. "I guess he thought I'd be really keen but I'm so torn."

"Take some time to think about it," Emily said. "You'll figure it out."

"I guess so. I wish they'd offered it to me six months ago. The timing feels all wrong."

"It would be nice to have you closer again," Emily said. "Why don't you come for a visit? Or we could meet in Oxford next weekend …"

"I don't have time at the moment, but I promise I'll come soon." There was more background noise and Emily waited for Josie to concentrate again. "By the way," she finally said. "Jack said my stuff is still at his place. I thought you were going to pick it up."

"I haven't been back to Oxford," Emily said. It was a lie. She had been back but she couldn't face seeing Jack. She'd still not got over the embarrassment of her drunken night.

"Don't worry about it. I can get it myself sometime."

She panicked now that her opportunity to see Jack was being taken away. "I can get it," she said quickly. "I told you I would and I will. Next weekend."

"Thanks." She gave a little squeal. "Oh, my God. I almost forget to tell you … Lizzie's pregnant!"

"Aww. That's lovely."

"Yeah." Josie's laughter drifted down the phone. "It's twins!"

Emily had a huge grin on her face when she finally got off the phone. It was amazing news, and she was so happy for Lizzie.

***

Emily went back to Oxford the next weekend intent on picking up Josie's things. When she messaged Jack, he told her he'd be at home on Saturday afternoon.

She borrowed her mum's car and was a bundle of nerves when she rang Jack's doorbell and waited for him to buzz her up. Instead, he told her through the intercom that he'd bring everything down to her. She ignored the wave of disappointment that washed over her. He didn't want her to come up?

A moment later the lift arrived. Emily's heart went into overdrive when Jack stepped out and opened the front door for her. The boyish smile was so wonderfully familiar. He gave her a hug, told her it was good to see her. He was his usual charming self. She mumbled random words. Her usual awkward self.

"I thought I could throw this stuff in the car and then you could come up for a coffee. If you've got time? And lunch maybe?"

Finally, her smile took over her face. "I've got time."

Loading the car was a quick job. There were only a few boxes. They were drinking coffee on Jack's couch in no time. She knew it was probably the last time she'd see him for a while, and she wanted to savour the time.

"Josie was telling me about the acting job," she said. Why had she immediately brought Josie into the conversation? The one topic she'd like to avoid with Jack.

"Yeah. I thought she'd be more excited. She seems pretty settled. Got a new boyfriend too."

Emily nodded.

"You know that already, of course."

"Yeah. I thought she'd have told you. Was it awkward, going all that way and finding her boyfriend was with her?"

"A little bit. I think it was more awkward for her." He grinned cheekily. "I did try calling her about ten times."

She pulled her legs under her on the couch. "It was good of you to drive down."

"I was interested to see the place." He looked slightly embarrassed and she felt sorry for him.

It seemed like he'd probably driven all that way hoping to get back together with Josie only to find her with her new boyfriend. Emily wondered how Josie managed to have everyone falling over themselves for her.

"Max and Lizzie were there too," Jack said. "So that was awkward."

Emily chuckled. "You really don't like them, do you?"

"I don't dislike them." His eyebrows knitted together. "But they don't like me, and they're not great at hiding the fact. And I swear, every time I meet up with any of Josie's family, within ten minutes someone will ask if I still work in the phone shop. As though it's not a proper job and I should be looking for something else."

"Well, to be fair ..." The words were out of her mouth before she knew it.

Jack's face fell and she immediately felt awful.

"Sorry." She swallowed hard. "I just meant you can probably do better, that's all."

He raised his eyebrows and she realised she'd dug her hole a little deeper.

"Thanks. Come round my place and belittle my job. That's nice."

"I wasn't belittling your job. It came out wrong."

"But you think working in sales is beneath me? Why? I do my job and I get paid. I'm not overly ambitious but so what? I pay my own way."

"That's not what I meant," she said desperately. All this time she'd thought about seeing Jack again and somehow she'd started an argument. He'd taken it the wrong way. Her eyes filled involuntarily with tears.

"Why are you upset?" he asked, confused. "You're the one who insulted my job."

"But I didn't mean to." She wiped tears from her cheeks and wished she had more control over her emotions. "I always say the wrong thing. It feels like every time I speak I either say the wrong thing or something stupid. And then I think maybe I should join a convent. Find a silent order and that way I'll never risk offending people or making a fool of myself ever again."

Jack's mouth twitched at the corners. "It seems slightly drastic." There was a short silence before he spoke again. "I never had great career prospects. I'm okay with my job. It's frustrating when other people make an issue of it."

She sniffed. "I meant it as a compliment. You're so kind and caring. I feel like you should do a job where you help people."

"I help people choose the right phone!"

"You know what I mean."

"Well, I'll think about becoming a doctor if it'll please you." His tone was annoyingly sarcastic. "I can't promise anything."

"I didn't mean you should be a doctor. I just think you've got a lot of potential. I was honestly trying to give you a compliment. It came out all wrong."

"I think they call it a back-handed compliment." He smiled. "I appreciate the sentiment."

"I'm going to go before I open my mouth and say something even more idiotic."

He shook his head when she stood, and his hand on her arm stopped her in her tracks. "I'm sorry. Don't rush off. I'm being overly sensitive. Don't worry about it."

"No. You're right, I was rude."

"Let's forget it." Jack's hand was still on her forearm and when his eyes pleaded with her, she sat back down. "You can't leave before lunch anyway."

"I was only really expecting to collect Josie's things. You didn't need to rearrange your day for me."

"But we never see each other any more. I cooked and everything."

"Really?"

He laughed. "Did you just sniff? As though the smell of my home-cooked meal might just hit you now?"

She couldn't help but grin. "But you said you cooked and it doesn't really smell like it."

"I've been at work this morning." He shook his head in amusement. "I cooked last night. I just need to heat it up."

"You were cooking on a Friday night?"

"Yes! I don't get many visitors. No one respectable anyway. The lads from football don't count. You're a VIP. I hope you're hungry?"

"I am actually." She'd been so nervous about seeing Jack that she hadn't eaten anything that morning. Now that she'd managed to relax around him, her stomach was starting to complain of neglect.

"The oven's on." He stood and moved to the kitchen. "It shouldn't take too long to heat it through."

Emily joined him in the kitchen as he pulled a dish from the fridge. "What are we having?"

"Chicken and mushroom pie."

Emily's lips twitched to a smile. "That's my favourite."

He frowned. "I know."

"How do you know?"

"Because we're friends. Don't you know what *my*

favourite food is?"

She thought for a moment. "Shepherd's Pie."

"See. You didn't even realise how well you know me."

She watched him put the pie in the oven and set the timer. "You really stayed in on a Friday night to make chicken pie?"

"Well, don't tease me about it!" He looked adorably vulnerable. "I didn't feel like going out last night. And it's nice having someone to cook for."

Emily bit her lip and took steps back to the living room. He'd really cooked for her. She needed to move so he wouldn't catch the look of elation on her face.

"Anyway, I felt like I owed you for cleaning my apartment." He sat on the couch again and she joined him. "I still can't believe you did that. And with a hangover."

"But I only did that to repay you for looking after me that night ..." She glanced away, not quite over her embarrassment.

"It seems like we're stuck in a vicious circle then. I've cooked for you so now you owe me, I'm afraid."

"Maybe it's time to break the cycle."

He wrinkled his nose. "Nope."

She laughed. "I presume you didn't tell your friends you were staying in to cook on a Friday night?"

"I can't believe you're teasing me for that." He looked at her intensely. "What were *you* doing last night?"

She should never have teased him. "I was working," she said quickly.

"At the restaurant or writing?"

"I was actually reading," she admitted.

He laughed. "What's happening with your next book? Have you written another bestseller?"

"It's with the editor," she said. "And my first book isn't a bestseller."

"Yet," he said pointedly. "It's doing well, isn't it?"

She shrugged. "The publisher seems happy with it. I think it's selling pretty well but I don't have much to measure it by. The publisher is currently in talks with WHSmith's about distributing through them." Previously the book had only been available for purchase from online retailers so she was excited by the prospect of seeing it in shops. She was also trying not to get her hopes up too much, to avoid disappointment.

"That's amazing." Jack was suddenly animated. "I'll drag you into every WHSmith's around to sign all their copies, and I'll brag that I'm friends with the author."

"Knowing my luck I'd get kicked out for writing in books."

"No way." He looked her right in the eyes. "That will be so exciting, to walk around a shop and see your own book on the shelf."

"I still can't quite believe they published it in the first place," Emily mused.

"Why? It's great."

Emily grinned. "Josie's biased, by the way. When she tells you how great it is."

He rubbed at the stubble along his jaw. "I wasn't saying it's great because Josie told me so. *I* think it's great."

"You read it?" Surely not. No way Jack read her book. Her heart raced.

"Of course I read it."

"I don't believe you," she said automatically.

"Why? You wrote a book. Why is it so shocking that I would read it?"

"I don't know." She shuffled in her seat. "Do you read?"

His eyes went wide. "Do I read? It's like you're on a mission to offend me today."

She couldn't help but laugh at the mock horror on his face. "That's not offensive," she insisted. "If I'd asked if you *can* read it would have been offensive. I only asked *if* you read. There's a huge difference."

"It's offensive how you looked at me like it's unimaginable that I ever read books."

"I didn't." She reached over and gave him a friendly shove. She couldn't stop laughing. "You're such a football and pub kind of guy. I never imagined you reading much."

"I have a bookcase and everything." Standing, he gave a quick flick of the head to indicate she should follow him.

In the corner of his bedroom was a tall broad bookcase. She scanned the contents. Lots of Terry Pratchett and Lee Child. Some Harlan Coben and James Patterson. And then neatly tucked between a battered copy of *The Hobbit* and the *Game of Thrones* boxset was her book. She pulled it out, fighting off her emotions. Jack owned a copy of her book.

"And you actually read it?"

He leaned casually against the bookcase. "Cover to cover. It's funny."

Automatically, she flicked through the pages, then gave a sharp intake of breath. "What did you do to it?"

His eyes narrowed and she held out the book, indicating the crease in the page. "You fold the corners down?"

He grimaced. "You're one of those people who uses bookmarks?"

"And you're the devil. You mutilated my book, Jack Denham! How could you?"

He laughed loudly. "If the corners weren't creased how would anyone know how well-loved it was?" Pulling *The Hobbit* from the shelf, he leafed through the pages. "See ... this one's so well-loved that there's hardly any pages that haven't been turned down. It's been read a lot."

"Oh, so now my book doesn't seem very well-loved. There aren't really many destroyed pages after all."

"They're not destroyed." His smirk made his eyes sparkle. "And I didn't need to fold many pages because I read it so fast. See ..." He took the book from her. "Look how much I read without a break. It was hard to put down."

She looked away and hoped her face wasn't as red as it felt. "Flattery will get you everywhere," she muttered, giving the bookcase her full attention. Her gaze finally landed at the top shelf.

"Ah, you've noticed my collection of jigsaw puzzles!" Jack's voice rang with amusement. "That's embarrassing."

"They're not yours," she stated confidently.

"Okay. You got me." He pulled them from the

shelf. "They're Josie's. Maybe you should help me look around for anything else of hers I've missed."

She ignored the suggestion, it not being something she was the least inclined to do. She really didn't need to be reminded that Josie used to live here too.

"They're *my* puzzles," she said. "*My* embarrassing collection!"

"I didn't mean—" His eyes met hers and he bit his lip sheepishly. "I think lunch might be ready …"

Chapter 34

In the living room, Jack left the stack of puzzles on the coffee table and continued to the kitchen. There was still ten minutes on the timer, and he poured Emily a glass of water and they chatted as they waited. When he finally pulled the pie from the oven it smelled delicious. They sat at the kitchen table to eat.

"I'm impressed," Emily said after the first mouthful. "It's delicious."

"No need to sound so surprised," Jack said.

"I'm pleasantly surprised." Their gaze locked for a moment and then she shifted her focus to the food. They ate in silence after that, but Emily felt completely at ease, which was surprising considering how she'd worked herself into a state about seeing Jack. She'd been excited too, of course, knowing how precious it was to spend a few moments with him. Even if it was just collecting Josie's belongings.

She never imagined that she'd have long hours with him chatting, and browsing his bookcase and sharing a meal that he'd made especially for her. Her favourite food.

Then she remembered her plans to meet Josie later and was struck by a familiar pang of guilt. She knew she shouldn't really be there. She shouldn't really be enjoying Jack's company so much. But she also knew she'd have to leave soon and she didn't know when she'd see him again. That bothered her far more than any guilt.

She thanked Jack profusely as he cleared the plates away, and when they moved automatically to the living room, a feeling of dread pulsed through her. The silence which had been so comfortable felt suddenly charged.

Jack shifted his weight as he stood behind her. "I don't understand the appeal of puzzles." They adorned the coffee table like a centrepiece. An obvious conversation starter.

"It's fun," Emily said, turning in time to catch his smirk

"Fun?"

"That might not be quite the right word," Emily said. "Sometimes when Josie and I had no money to go out we'd buy cheap wine and stay in doing a puzzle. They're kind of absorbing and addictive. It's a bit like a good book: you forget about everything else."

He crouched beside the coffee table and browsed the stack of puzzles then pulled the bottom one out. "I like this scene." It was a picture of Slovenia. Lake Bled and the castle.

"That one's my favourite."

He moved the rest aside then opened the lid. "Show me how this is fun."

"It's a thousand pieces, Jack." She stood over him and chuckled. "It takes days, not an hour or two."

He shuffled the pieces on the bottom of the box and picked one up, turning it over. "For average people maybe, but I reckon we can get it done pretty quick." He grinned at her. "I might be some sort of puzzle genius and we'll get it done in no time."

"I'm meeting Josie this afternoon." She glanced at her watch but crouched opposite him nonetheless. Automatically, she reached for a straight-edged piece and placed it on the table before repeating the action with another piece. "You have to find all the edge pieces first," she said. He joined in searching them out.

It turned out that fun was exactly the right word. They chatted and laughed as they worked on the puzzle. She hadn't laughed so much in a long time. Her stomach muscles would surely ache the next day.

"They don't actually fit together," she said as Jack put pieces of blue sky together along the top edge.

He looked confused. "Don't they?"

She looked more closely, then reached over. "They look like they do, but they wobble a bit. It's annoying when you have pieces like that."

He chuckled and scanned the box for another piece. "It's like me and Josie. We almost work. But not quite." A look flashed across his face that she struggled to read.

"Do you miss her?" She was on dangerous ground, she knew. She couldn't bear to listen to Jack gush about Josie. If he missed Josie, she really didn't want to hear about it.

"No." There was no hesitation, and Emily looked at him searchingly. It wasn't what she was expecting to hear. "That sounds harsh," he said. "But I don't."

Emily was confused. Was he lying? "But she broke up with you. You wanted to work things out, didn't you?"

His focus was on the box of puzzle pieces, and for a moment Emily thought he wasn't going to reply.

"I was reluctant to give up." His voice was even. He didn't look at Emily. "It felt like we'd been trying to make things work for so long. It was hard to admit that it wasn't going to work."

"I never really understood you two," Emily mused. "You always seemed so happy. But then you'd bicker and split up, and that never seemed like a big deal."

"That's an accurate evaluation. We were mostly happy when we were together. Aside from the stupid arguments, it was fun. But it also wasn't a big deal for us to be apart. I never missed her." He plucked a piece from the box and finally met Emily's gaze. "I realised it's not enough to love being with someone. You should also hate not being with them." He smiled and clicked the blue piece into place. "Is that better?"

"Perfect," she whispered.

Three hours passed. The quickest three hours of her life. And then she glanced at her watch and panicked. "I really have to go," she said. "I'm meeting Josie for dinner in half an hour."

The edge pieces of the puzzle lined the coffee table, and Jack was making good progress on constructing the castle in the middle.

"I guess I'm not a puzzle genius after all," he said. "You were right – it would take days." His smile didn't reach his eyes. "I might have to leave the room while you put it back in the box. I'm not sure I can stand to watch all our efforts undone."

"I could always leave it for you to finish," Emily

offered.

He dipped his eyebrows. "I thought it was your favourite?"

"I wasn't planning on doing it again. Plus it's been sitting on your shelf for goodness knows how long and I haven't missed it."

"Okay then. If you really don't mind?"

She laughed. "I know you'll swipe it back into the box as soon as I leave. But it's sweet of you to pretend you enjoyed it."

She was about to pack it away when Jack took the box from her. His features were serious. "Leave it. Please."

Her heart quickened. She said nothing but stood and collected up the rest of her puzzles.

"Thanks for lunch." She'd been so relaxed, but now she felt herself go to mush again. Her heart thundered against her rib cage and her brain wouldn't communicate with her mouth.

"Have a nice evening with Josie," he said at the door.

She nodded and stood looking at him. Words escaped her. She leaned into him when he kissed her cheek, annoyed by the stack of puzzles between them. Then her hand was on the door. She was out in the hallway. She turned, smiled, whispered goodbye.

On the way to the car, all she could think about was running back to him. The feel of his lips lingered on her cheek.

She wanted so much more.

Chapter 35

Emily drove straight from Jack's place into the city centre to meet Josie for dinner. On the drive, all she could think about was Jack. After spending a whole afternoon alone with him, he was well and truly on her mind. If she'd known that morning that she'd get to spend so much time with him she'd have been over the moon, but now one afternoon was nowhere near enough.

She wanted to see him every day. Every day for the rest of her life. Then she'd be satisfied. Only then. She loved being with him. She hated not being with him. If only he felt the same about her. Maybe he did. He'd cooked her favourite meal. He'd read her book. It was *him* who'd got out the puzzle and prolonged their time together. But surely not. Jack liked girls like Josie. He would only ever see Emily as a friend. He'd been kind to her and she'd read too much into it. But he'd always been kind to her, that was nothing new.

And it didn't matter anyway. Even if he felt something more than friendship for her, they couldn't do anything about it. Josie would freak out.

The fantasy took over her thoughts regardless. She imagined being with Jack. A whole life with him. Waking up to him every morning. Cuddling up to him every evening. Reaching out in the night to find him beside her. Kissing each other goodbye as they left for work, and embracing on their return. Lazy weekends. Holidays together. A nice little house. A wedding. A baby. Maybe two. Everything she'd always wanted.

If she could have that, couldn't she live without her best friend?

Tears filled her eyes as she drove into the multi-storey car park in town. How could she think of hurting Josie?

Outside The Head of the River, Josie flung her arms around Emily in greeting, and Emily felt like the worst person in the world. Of course she could never hurt Josie. And the thought of not having her in her life was ridiculous. Josie might be hard work sometimes, but her friendship meant the world to Emily. She knew Josie would do anything for her, and she often took that for granted.

They sat on the terrace outside the pub, and Emily listened as Josie filled her in on her news. She was so excited about the acting job.

"It's perfect," Emily said, not stopping to think it through. "You could come and live with me." After spending a year coveting Josie's boyfriend and on occasion fantasising about her quick demise under a bus, the least she could do was offer Josie her couch while she was looking for a place of her own.

Josie eyes widened in surprise. "What?"

She couldn't back down now. "Yes!" Reaching over, she squeezed Josie's hand. "My rent is killing me, and it'll be so much fun living together. I've missed you."

"I missed you too," Josie said slowly. "Isn't your

place a bit small for two?"

"You'd have to sleep on the couch," Emily said. "But it would be so much fun. Didn't we always talk about getting a place together in London? You were going to be a famous actress and me a famous author." And it *would* be fun. So much fun that she wouldn't have the chance to think about Jack and conjure up wild fantasies about living happily ever after with him.

Josie chuckled. "I think we've got a way to go still."

"I know but it'll feel like we're at least trying to do what we planned. It'd be such an adventure. And after all those times you came crying to me because you'd got rejected from some acting job, how can you even think of turning it down?"

"I was just feeling settled at last. I'm worried I'll just turn my life upside down for what might end up being another dead-end job."

"But I thought Michaela said it could end up being a speaking part." She was actually amazed that Josie was having to consider whether she should take the acting job. It was what she'd wanted for so long.

"It *might*," Josie said. "It also might not." She paused. "Things are going so well with Sam. I don't want to mess everything up."

"But you keep telling me what a great guy he is. Surely if he's that great he'll be supportive? You don't have to break up with him." No guys ever split up with Josie. Generally, they'd cross oceans for her. A few hours in the car wouldn't put anyone off seeing her.

"I think you might be simplifying things," Josie

said.

"That's because it all looks pretty simple from where I'm sitting."

"Maybe we should swap seats," Josie said drily.

The more Emily thought about it, the more she thought it was a great idea. Josie would get her dream job, and Emily could ease her guilt by being the best friend anyone could ever wish for.

Chapter 36

Josie moved in two weeks later, and Emily realised it was a massive mistake about three minutes after she arrived. The one thing Emily loved about living alone was the quiet. Josie was anything but quiet.

And she had so much stuff. There was only one suitcase, but it didn't take long before the contents of the suitcase were scattered all over her previously tidy apartment. It was like a bomb had exploded inside the suitcase and thrown everything out all over the place. It occurred to Emily that she might be a neat freak and had gone her whole life without noticing it. The stuff everywhere annoyed her so much.

Josie swanned around the apartment, trying to find space for her things. But there was no space. And what was really worrying was that no matter how much Emily commented on the lack of space, Josie never once made reference to it being a temporary arrangement. She seemed to think she was there for good, and the cramped confines didn't seem to be an issue for her at all. Nor did the fact that she didn't have a bed to sleep on, just the couch.

Emily hadn't thought things through properly. She'd never be able to get any writing done with Josie around the apartment. The editor had sent the manuscript back to her and asked for way more changes than Emily had expected. She had a lot more work to do on it and needed peace and quiet so she could concentrate.

She zoned back in to Josie's endless monologue. She was telling her about Sam, the boyfriend who she'd left at Oakbrook Farm. Apparently he wasn't interested in a long-distance relationship and had broken things off. Josie was sure he'd change his mind. She seemed to be expecting a call from him any minute. It was typical Josie – always so full of optimism.

They sat together that evening, chatting over a glass of wine. It was nice to spend time with Josie, but it occurred to Emily that they'd never spent more than a weekend together. She was increasingly nervous about the new living arrangement.

***

It was a few days before she saw Josie again. But that didn't mean the living situation wasn't driving her crazy. Her stuff was everywhere, and the bedding on the couch was a constant annoyance. And how on earth had Josie ever had the cheek to complain about Jack being a slob?

Josie couldn't even manage to put tea bags in the bin, but dumped them in the sink as though they'd magically fly to the bin from there. A pile of dirty clothes was building in the corner of the living room, even though Emily had given her a laundry bag and hung it on the back of the bathroom door for her. She wondered how long it would be before she would give in and pick up the clothes for her.

Emily had been working in the restaurant in the evening for the first few days after Josie's arrival. Josie left for work at the TV studio early in the mornings so they missed each other completely. Josie would be snoring on the couch when Emily came back from work, and gone again when she got up in the morning.

She was surprised to find Josie on the couch when she got up on Wednesday morning. It was early, but she really needed to get some writing done. She wasn't working at the restaurant and was happy to have a full day set aside for writing. Hopefully Josie wasn't going to ruin her plans.

Emily contemplated taking her laptop and sitting on her bed to work, but it was so uncomfortable, and she had everything set up on her little desk in the corner of the living room. If she was quiet she probably wouldn't disturb Josie anyway.

She was rewriting her opening paragraph when Josie stirred ten minutes later. She mumbled something about the birds which used to wake her on the farm. A dig about Emily disturbing her with her typing. It annoyed her. This was *her* apartment and she had work to do. Did she have to apologise for that now? Probably.

She swivelled in her chair and tried to keep calm. "Sorry. I end up with a stiff neck if I write in bed for too long."

"It's fine," Josie said.

"Are you working today?" *Please be working.*

"No, I've got a few days off." A few days? She couldn't hang around the apartment for a few days. It would drive Emily crazy. "But I'll get out of your way," she added, to Emily's relief.

"Thanks," Emily said. "I've got loads to do."

"Are you sure it's okay me staying here?" Josie looked at her with concern. "I don't want things to get weird. If it's a problem just say."

"It's fine." It wasn't fine, though. The apartment was too small, and Emily needed her space. But she couldn't say that. "I could really use the help with the rent," she said instead.

That much was true at least. After what Jack had told her about Josie not paying rent, she thought the suggestion might make Josie realise how good she had things at Oakbrook where she had free accommodation with the job. But Josie seemed determined to give the acting another go, so she was unlikely to leave London.

Josie sat up and stretched. "And that's a subtle hint for me to give you some money."

"There's no hurry," Emily said with what she hoped was a sweet smile.

"I'll go to the bank today."

That at least meant she'd definitely have to leave the apartment. And if Josie gave her some money, it might soften the blow of having her apartment taken over.

"Thanks," Emily said. She felt bad for being short with Josie. It was her who'd invited Josie to stay after all. "Sorry I'm no fun at the moment. I'm snowed under. Maybe we can have a night out at the weekend?"

"Sounds good," Josie said.

"How's it going with the filming?"

"It's okay. Jack was there yesterday so that

livened things up."

Emily's heart rate took a dramatic increase. "How's he doing?" There was the slightest wobble to her voice. Thankfully Josie didn't seem to notice.

"He's the same old Jack. He was off out on a date last night."

Emily swivelled back around to her desk and told herself to keep breathing. She randomly removed a Post-it note from the edge of her laptop screen, then replaced it in almost exactly the same spot. Jack was on a date. Of course he was on a date. Why was it a shock that he was dating? What did she expect, that he was sitting at home thinking about her?

"That must be weird," she said, trying her best to sound casual. "It's a shame things didn't work out with you two. I always thought you made a good couple." That was a lie obviously, but it made her next question more plausible. "You're not tempted to try and get back with him since things didn't work out with Sam?"

"No!" Josie wrinkled her nose. "Of course not."

Thank goodness. Emily couldn't take it if Josie and Jack ended up back together again. "Have you heard anything from Sam?"

"Yeah." Josie sighed. "I spoke to him, but it seems like it's really over."

"He sounds like an idiot." Emily was trying to be helpful, but the look on Josie face told her she'd said the wrong thing. He did sound like an idiot, though.

"He's not," Josie replied.

"Don't get all defensive." Emily was sure Josie just needed to realise how badly this guy was treating her. "I'm just telling it like it is. If he can't make the effort to try and make things work, he's probably not worth it." It sounded like a similar situation to when she was with Jack. He liked being with her, but being apart was obviously also okay for him.

Josie stood abruptly. "I'm going to have a shower and I'll get out of your way."

"Sorry." Emily had clearly hit a nerve, but maybe it was one that needed to be hit. "I just hate you moping around because of some guy. You can do much better."

Emily got back to the writing and only vaguely registered Josie saying goodbye a little while later. At least she hadn't banged around the kitchen making breakfast. She'd quietly slipped away and left Emily to it, as she'd promised. Emily was hit with the feeling that she was being entirely unreasonable. It was supposed to be fun, having Josie live with her. She'd nip out later and grab a bottle of wine. She'd make time for Josie that evening and hopefully things would be better. They just needed to get through the settling-in period and adjust to living together.

She was probably worrying about nothing.

Chapter 37

Things did get better. They fell into some sort of routine. Josie found a second job in a café nearby and between that and the acting she was working seven days a week. Long hours too. She was barely in the flat. Emily was actually a bit worried about her; all she seemed to do was work and sleep. The guy she'd left behind at Oakbrook Farm had clearly hurt her. Emily tried to talk to her about him a few times, but she always seemed to say the wrong thing. At least she still had that skill.

About a month after Josie moved in, Emily was tapping away on her laptop when she heard voices outside the door. She'd been taking advantage of the peace, knowing that Josie didn't work late at the café on Sundays and would be back any minute.

Emily paused at the voices. She heard Josie loud and clear but the male voice confused her.

Even when Josie burst into the apartment with Jack right behind her, Emily was still bemused. Why was Jack there? And why was she suddenly so light-headed?

"Look who I found," Josie said, delighted.

"Hi." Emily forced herself to get up. She didn't know how to greet him. She never did. He kissed her cheek as he always did.

"So …" Josie's expression was set in a comedy grimace. "We're both filming tomorrow and I told Jack he could stay here tonight instead of driving from Oxford at crazy o'clock tomorrow. But I think I forgot to ask if that was okay with you." She looked sheepish. "You don't mind, do you?"

Emily looked around the tiny living room. "I'm not quite sure where he'll sleep." She caught Jack's eye and realised it was rude to talk about him as though he weren't there. "Where *you'll* sleep," she corrected herself.

He smiled. "I'm fine on the floor."

She could hardly say no.

Josie beamed. "I'm so excited about us hanging out together again. It's just like it used to be. What shall we do, go out for dinner or stay in? We could do a pub crawl later. It'll be such a laugh!"

"I can't," Emily blurted. Her head swam as she fought to conjure an excuse. "I've got a writing workshop this afternoon." She glanced at her watch for good measure. "I have to leave soon."

Josie groaned. "But we're never together any more. Can't you cancel?"

"No, sorry." She moved back to her desk and closed her laptop. She'd have to go and find a coffee shop to write in. There was no way in the world she could spend the afternoon with Jack and Josie. It would feel like torture.

"Meet us for drinks after the workshop then?" Josie said.

"I'll try. It might go late. And there's the social bit afterwards. I need to start networking more."

She ignored Josie's pout and headed to her

bedroom. "Next time," she murmured vaguely.

She was throwing some things in her backpack when she registered Jack in the doorway.

"I thought Josie had asked you about me staying over," he said quietly.

"No." She grabbed her notepad and a couple of pens from her bedside table.

"But it's okay?"

Of course it wasn't okay. But she could hardly say so. All she could do was wander the streets and come back after they were asleep. They'd be gone before she got up in the morning. She was sure she'd never be able to get any sleep with Jack in her apartment, but that was hardly the end of the world.

"It's fine." She was doing her best to avoid eye contact. It worked well until he stepped into her path.

"You do owe me after all." His mouth twitched to a smirk. "Not that I'm necessarily keeping track but if I remember rightly: I cleaned up your puke, you cleaned my apartment, I cooked lunch for you. And that's as far as we got. So you owe me …"

When her eyes finally met his, she couldn't help but smile. "That's true," she said. "I owe you. I suppose you can stay then." Suddenly, Emily found it hard to believe she'd been about to give up the chance to spend an afternoon with him. He was her friend, and if that's all they ever were, so be it. It was enough just to be around him.

"Owe him for what?" Josie's voice broke the atmosphere between. As she walked up behind Jack, she snaked an arm around his waist and rested her head on his shoulder.

Emily's smile slipped and she turned away. "Jack

made me some lunch the day I picked your stuff from his place. I told him I owed him a favour."

"What delights did he rustle up for you? I hope he went all out and made you cheese on toast. That's about his limit when it comes to cooking."

Emily thought back to the lovely chicken pie. He'd even made the pastry from scratch.

"You love my cheese on toast," Jack said, extricating himself from Josie and dodging the question at the same time.

Emily pulled her backpack onto her shoulder. "I'm sorry I'm rushing off. I'll see you later." But she had no intention of coming back until late. She remembered how awful it was being with the two of them. Josie was all over Jack even though they weren't together any more. Maybe she wanted to get back with him. That was quite likely. She seemed happier with Jack around than she had in a long time.

"See you later," they called after her.

***

Emily jumped on the tube to put some distance between her and home. It would be slightly awkward if Josie and Jack went out for dinner and bumped into her along the way. Her plans for a productive afternoon of writing were out the window. Even when she found a quiet coffee shop and tucked herself away in the back, she still couldn't get anything done. Her mind wouldn't focus on anything but Jack. She'd missed him so much, and now he was in her apartment and she was avoiding him. Part of her wanted to go back and spend time with him. Even if it meant watching Josie fawn all over him. Even if she knew she could never have him.

After a couple of hours and too much coffee, she walked along the banks of the Thames, stopping on a bench and watching the world go by.

When the sun set, she took herself to the cinema and sat for two hours staring blankly at Matt Damon as he tried to save the world or uncover state secrets or whatever it was he was doing … she wasn't actually sure. She'd lost the plot in every sense of the phrase.

It was after midnight when she slipped quietly into her dark apartment. She went to the bathroom and then picked her way through the living room to get to the bedroom. She almost tripped over a pair of Josie's shoes. With a hand on the back of the couch, she regained her balance. Her eyes adjusted to the dim moonlight which filtered in through the window. Josie's gentle snores echoed round the room. Her blanket lay discarded at the end of the couch, leaving her exposed but for her tiny shorts and skimpy vest top. The small room was warm and stuffy.

Jack was sprawled on a blanket on the floor. Jogging bottoms covered his lower half. His toned chest was bare. One arm was hooked behind his head.

Somehow, she realised he was awake a fraction of a second before his eyes opened. Not enough time to avert her gaze.

"Hi."

"Sorry." She continued towards the bedroom. "I didn't mean to wake you."

"You didn't. I couldn't sleep." He sat up, wrapping his arms around his bent knees. "How was your evening?"

"Fine, thanks." She gave a little nod in Josie's direction and then a quick wave indicating that she was going to bed.

As she turned to close her bedroom door, she found Jack behind her and gave a start. He leaned on the doorframe. His voice was low.

"I just wanted to say I'm sorry."

She swallowed hard. "What for?"

"For whatever I did to annoy you."

"I'm not annoyed with you," she said.

"But you can barely look at me, and when I arrived you shot out of the building like it was on fire."

"No I didn't," she insisted.

"Well, you stopped to grab your laptop and your notebook. But knowing you, you'd do that even if the building was on fire."

He knew her so well. She couldn't help but smile.

"I thought you knew I was coming," he said. "Josie made it sound like we'd all spend the day together. I got the impression you knew the plan. If I'd have known you weren't around I wouldn't have come so early." He lowered his voice a little further. "Josie's a bit intense at the moment."

Emily gave a half-smile but didn't comment.

"I was looking forward to seeing you," Jack said. "It would've been good to have a drink together and catch up."

"Next time."

"So you promise you're not annoyed with me?"

"I'm not."

"And you didn't just go out today to avoid

spending time with me?"

Her mouth was dry. She swallowed again. Shook her head.

"Wait there." He turned and walked across the living room.

"What are you doing?" Emily asked in a loud whisper.

He glanced back. Flashed his cheeky grin. "There's wine in the fridge."

She wanted to protest. Opened her mouth to do just that. Nothing came out.

He was back a moment later with two glasses and the bottle of cheap white. Thankfully, he'd put a T-shirt on. They sat side-by-side on her bed, and she held the glasses while he poured the wine. The first gulp calmed her nerves. Had Jack been waiting up for her to get home?

He stood and crossed the room, stopping in front of the bookcase.

Emily shuffled back on the bed, leaning on the headboard with her legs stretched out in front of her. "You're making me nervous. Looking at all my things."

He raised an eyebrow. "I showed you my bookcase."

She took another sip of wine as he casually went to the door and pushed it until it was almost closed. Then he placed his wineglass on the bedside table and lay across the end of the bed, propping himself up on an elbow.

"So how've you been?" he asked.

"I've been okay," she said, nodding. "Busy with the restaurant and writing."

"How's the book coming?"

She frowned. "Not as well as I'd like. I'm still making changes and my deadline is looming. I'm worried it won't be finished in time."

He looked at her seriously. "I'm sure you'll manage it."

"I hope so." She twirled the wineglass. Her book deadline was becoming more and more worrisome. It wasn't something she wanted to think about at that moment.

"How's everything with you?" she asked.

"Well, I don't know if you've heard, but I've been doing a bit of acting." His boyish smile was adorable. "You'll be asking for my autograph before you know it."

She grinned. "The way Josie described it, it didn't quite sound like you're the star of the show."

"Josie's just jealous," he said lightly.

"Why are you doing the acting?" she asked seriously. "I thought you weren't interested in it really?"

"I'm not sure," he said with a sigh. "They offered it and it wasn't a problem to get the time off work. I thought it'd be fun."

"And? Are you enjoying it?"

"It's all right," he said. "I've only done the odd few days here and there."

"Josie said you're dating someone you met there. Some hot actress, no doubt." She forced a smile and hoped he didn't notice how uncomfortable she was. Why had she said that? She told herself so many times that she didn't care if he was dating someone. But she did. Of course she did.

His gaze bored right into her. "I'm not dating anyone."

"You *were?*" She should have dropped the subject. He could do what he wanted, after all. But she couldn't stand him lying to her.

He sat up and took a sip of his wine before lying down again. "I had a drink with one of the women there. Once."

There was a hint of annoyance to his voice. She should never have brought it up. But a part of her needed to know if he was seeing someone. Especially when he was creeping into her room for midnight chats. What was he playing at?

He didn't say any more about his date. His eyes scanned the room, and Emily was thankful it was reasonably clean and tidy. "When Josie told me your place was small, I didn't realise quite how small."

"Yeah." She smiled. "It's not ideal."

"Why did you invite Josie to live with you?" His expression was puzzled, as though he'd been trying to figure out the conundrum for some time.

She shrugged. "She needed a place to stay. That's what friends do, isn't it?"

"Yeah. But this place is really small. She'd never have expected you to offer. Besides, I know what you're like about people and your own space and stuff."

"I'm not sure how to take that," she said, grinning.

"Liking your own space and your own company isn't necessarily a bad thing." He paused. "Anyway, you're a good friend, letting her stay with you."

She laughed then and put her wine glass down as

she spluttered on the sip she'd taken. "I'm not a good friend." She wiped at the drip of wine that had spilled down her top. "I'm an awful friend. That's why I said she could stay."

"Well, that makes absolutely no sense," he said, confused.

"I felt so bad for being such a crap friend that I offered her a place to stay in an attempt to redeem myself. Except it's not really working."

His expression was questioning and intense. When would she learn to keep her mouth shut?

"When have you ever been a bad friend to Josie?" he asked.

Why was she having this conversation with Jack? She either needed to kick him out of her bedroom or do something to lighten the atmosphere.

"Do you remember the time we went out for dinner, and I put black pepper round the rim of Josie's glass when she was in the toilets?" She smiled at the memory. She'd not wanted to go out with them because she thought she was in the way, but it had ended up being such a fun evening. "I was a pretty bad friend that day."

He smirked and turned onto his back, staring up at the ceiling. "I'm fairly sure I dared you to."

"That seems likely," she agreed. "But still."

"Doesn't quite seem like the sort of thing that would require drastic measures to redeem yourself."

"It's not," she said. "But I don't really want to talk about it."

He turned his head to her. "Okay."

"Tell me about work," she said in a bid to change the subject.

"You want to know about my job? I work in a mobile phone shop and apparently it's beneath me ..."

She kicked at him gently and then scooched a little further down the bed to get comfy. "I meant tell me a story. You always used to have funny stories about work. What interesting characters have you had in the shop recently?"

"Now you mention it ..." He scooted up the bed and she shuffled over so he could lie beside her. Then he launched into anecdotes about the customers in the shop. Emily kept remembering funny incidents from the restaurant, and they laughed together as they exchanged stories.

They stayed like that, lying on Emily's bed and chatting, into the early hours.

"What time do you have to get up for work?" she asked when Jack yawned for the third time in as many minutes.

"I think we have to leave at 5.30 a.m."

She checked the time. "Oh dear."

"I don't think I even want to know what time it is. Is it even worth sleeping now?"

"You could get a couple of hours," she said.

"Maybe I should." But he made no move to go anywhere. Emily didn't want him to leave. She wanted him to stay beside her and wrap his arms around her. Instead, his hand crept around hers and their fingers gently entwined. For a moment Emily forgot to breathe. Then she snatched her hand away and sat up on the bed, staring at the floor.

Jack stood and picked up the empty wine glasses.

Their eyes locked as he paused in the doorway. Emily waited for him to say something, but he just smiled sadly before he left.

She couldn't fall asleep and lay in the darkness listening for sounds and wondering what on earth was going on. It wasn't long before she heard Josie getting up. Then a little while later Josie shouting at Jack to get up. A tear rolled down her cheek as she listened to their muffled voices and heard them moving around to get ready.

Her eyes stayed fixed on the door, as though he might come back in. She imagined him grinning and saying he was too tired to work and crawling into bed with her.

It didn't happen, of course. A few minutes later, the front door banged and they were gone.

Chapter 38

Emily slept all morning. Her alarm woke her just in time to grab a shower before work. The restaurant was busy as always, but in every spare moment her mind drifted to Jack, lingering on the feel of his fingertips trailing over her hand. It was hard to let herself imagine that he felt something for her too. The potential for disappointment was immense, but the glimmer of hope taunted her nonetheless.

He was on the living room floor again when she returned home that night. This time he was fast asleep, and Emily stood for a moment watching the gentle rise and fall of his chest. Sleep didn't come easily that night. Knowing he was so near made her anxious, and she imagined him coming into her room and lying beside her, gently stroking her hand and pushing it to his lips. Her fantasies mingled with her dreams and she tossed and turned all night.

In the morning she was surprised to see Jack sitting on the couch, staring into a cup of coffee.

"Morning," she said. Hopefully she sounded more confident than she felt.

He stood. "Do you want a coffee?" It only took him three steps and he was at the kitchen.

"Yes please." That would at least give her time to get out of the terrible pyjamas. She backtracked to her bedroom while he made coffee.

"Aren't you working today?" she asked as they sat on the couch together five minutes later.

"I'm supposed to be, but I called in sick. We didn't finish filming until late last night. I had breakfast with Josie down in the café. She's filming again today. I thought I'd hang around here for a bit."

The silence was loaded, and Emily was intensely aware of her rapid heartbeat. Why was he hanging around instead of going back to Oxford?

"Is that okay?" he asked.

"Yeah." She paused, completely confused. "Sure."

Calmly, Jack set his coffee mug down on the table then turned with a look so intense it made her insides flutter.

"I wanted to see you again."

She shifted her weight to the edge of the couch, feeling utterly self-conscious.

"I thought maybe we could do something today," he said. "We could have brunch somewhere or go for a walk and have lunch later?"

"I've got loads of work to do." Her voice was quiet and uncertain.

Jack moved along the couch and took her hand. Her heart pounded fiercely.

"Take a day off," he said. "You can show me your favourite places. We can go to a museum." He smiled. "Or anywhere. I'll bet there's some huge library round here that you love?"

She pulled her hand from his and stood. The apartment was far too small. It was impossible to put enough distance between them. She hovered at the kitchen doorway and tried her best to keep her voice light.

"If I spend the day with you, Josie will say it sounds like a date and tease me forever."

He smiled softly. "It would be like a date."

Pain shot through her lip when she bit down on it. Staring at her bare feet, she shook her head.

"Go on a date with me, Em." He was in front of her, his hand reaching for hers again.

When she stepped back, she collided with the wall. Sidestepping, she dodged around him and stood beside the couch. "I can't go on a date with you."

He stayed where he was. "Why not?"

"Because you're my friend and it would be weird," she said anxiously. Not to mention that he was Josie's ex. And the fact that she couldn't actually believe he was asking her. "And I don't understand …" She looked at him in earnest. "I don't understand why you're asking me on a date."

He tilted his head to one side. "Because I think you're amazing."

She shook her head and turned away.

"I mean it, Em." His voice was pleading. "You're funny and intelligent. You're beautiful. I love being around you and I miss you when I'm not. I can't stop thinking about you." She could hear his footsteps as he moved closer to her. There were tears in her eyes when she turned.

"That's not true," she said quickly. "You were going on dates a couple of weeks ago. How can you say you're thinking about me?"

"One date," he said sadly. "And only because I convinced myself you'd never be interested in me. I was trying to forget about you. But I can't. I walked out of the date after half an hour because I kept wishing I was with you." He paused and moved close to her. This time she made no move away from him. "I just need to know how you feel. If you don't feel the same, tell me and I'll go."

She was so torn; part of her wanted to kiss him and cling to him and another part wanted to march him out of the apartment as quickly as possible. The silence stretched out. "Of course I feel the same," she whispered finally. Surely it had been obvious.

His arm gently circled her waist, and she allowed herself a moment to breathe him in and savour his embrace. "I need you to leave, Jack."

"But—"

"Josie would be so hurt."

"Josie will be okay," he said. "If we talk to her, she'll be all right with it, I'm sure."

"No, she won't," Emily said firmly. "I'm living with her and things are strained enough as it is."

"She might be a bit uncomfortable with it at first," he said. "But she'd get used to the idea."

"She'd hate me," Emily insisted. "It's not worth it."

"Thanks," he whispered.

"I didn't mean it like that." She put a hand on his arm. It was hard to believe this was a real conversation. "I don't know what to think, Jack. You've sprung this on me and I'm so confused."

"Spend today with me?"

"I can't." She took a step away from him.

He took her hand tenderly in his. For a moment she thought he was going to kiss her. She looked away, not wanting him to kiss her. Not there. Not like that.

"I don't want to leave not knowing when I'll see you again. Can I at least call you later?"

She nodded and he untangled his fingers from hers.

"Jack?" she called when he reached the doorway. She couldn't quite believe what had just happened. "You really want to date me?"

"More than anything," he replied with a slow smile.

Chapter 39

Jack messaged her every day. It gave Emily such a thrill to know that he was thinking of her. She was dying to see him. First, she needed to talk to Josie. She decided she should get everything out in the open and hope that Josie could be happy for them.

Unfortunately, Josie was in a terrible mood that week. She came home late on Monday after a long day of filming. Emily knew that the acting work wasn't turning out as Josie hoped, but it was the first time she'd talked about quitting. It seemed like she really hated it and it was getting her down. Emily was sympathetic. Josie had given up the job at the kennels *and* the guy she liked for the acting job. For it to not work out must feel so deflating.

It didn't seem like the best time to bring up the situation with Jack. Emily was at work in the restaurant on Friday when she got a message from Josie saying she'd decided to go back to Oakbrook for a visit for the weekend.

Emily casually relayed the information to Jack. He didn't mention coming over, but she assumed he'd turn up at some point and she didn't tell him not to.

The doorbell rang mid-morning on Saturday.

"You should have messaged me to check Josie wasn't here," Emily hissed as she opened the door.

"I thought you might tell me not to come. I called Josie instead."

"What did you say?" she asked in a panic.

"Nothing. I asked her what she was up to. She was driving to Devon."

"You shouldn't call her when she's driving. She always answers and she never puts the phone on speaker. One of these days she'll kill herself. Or someone else ..." She realised she was babbling and that Jack was still standing in the doorway, looking at her in amusement.

"Hi," he said softly.

It felt like her heart stopped beating for a moment. Then she opened the door wider for him. He walked to the middle of the tiny living room and Emily's heart kicked in again, apparently now trying to compensate for any missed beats.

"This feels weird," she blurted out. "Having you here. It feels wrong. I hate having secrets from Josie." Obviously she'd been keeping her feelings for Jack a secret for a long time, but actions were a lot different to feelings.

"I just wanted to see you," he said. "I won't stay long if you don't want me to."

"I've got to work later," she said. "I've got a shift at the restaurant."

"Okay," he said calmly.

Every muscle in her body felt tense. She didn't know how to act around him or what to do. It felt so intense and unnatural.

"Shall we go out?" she suggested quickly. The apartment seemed like it was closing in on her. Fresh air would be good.

He nodded and she slipped her feet into a pair of shoes and grabbed her purse. Outside, she immediately relaxed a little. They wandered aimlessly, keeping conversation neutral, mostly chatting about London and whatever sights they passed.

They stopped for lunch in a café and then walked down to the river. The sun was partially covered by hazy clouds when they sat on a bench and looked out across the Thames and the Millennium Bridge. When he'd first slipped his hand into hers shortly after they left the apartment, Emily had felt uncomfortable. Now she thought they may need a crowbar to pry them apart. She never wanted to let go.

"I'll need to go and get ready for work soon," she said reluctantly. It was the last thing she wanted to do. "Why aren't you working today?"

"I called in sick." He pulled his hand from hers and ran his arm along the bench behind her.

"I've never called in sick in my life," she said.

"Not even when you were actually sick?"

She shook her head. "I've never been ill enough to take a day off work."

Jack's eyes shone with amusement, and she couldn't help but laugh. It wasn't even very funny.

"I don't even know how to ring in sick. What would I say if I decided I didn't want to go to work today?"

He looked at her quizzically. "Migraine usually works well. Then you only need one day off."

Before she could change her mind, she pulled out her phone. Jack grinned as she moved away from him to make the call. She peered over the wall and into the murky water of the Thames as she lied to her boss. When she ended the call, she turned around and laughed.

Jack regarded her from the bench, then walked slowly over to her.

"What?" she said as he smirked. Her grin was making her cheeks ache.

He put a hand on her hip and it sent shivers up and down her spine. As he leaned closer, his breath tickled her ear when he spoke. "If I don't kiss you soon, I think I'm gonna die."

She laughed loudly and pulled back. "You are so cheesy! I can't believe you said that."

He grinned and hooked his thumb over the top of her jeans. "It's true. I'm about to drop dead. I don't know why you're laughing."

She couldn't stop the laughter. "You're an idiot."

A look of vulnerability flashed in his eyes, and he drew ever so slightly away from her. Any minute now he'd crack a joke and laugh it off. He wouldn't kiss her. How many times had she wished she could kiss him?

She stopped laughing. "You'd better kiss me quick, if you're going to die."

At the rate her heart was beating, she thought it was she who might die. Her body was nestled against his, and she waited, panicking that he wouldn't kiss her at all. He did. But there was nothing quick about it. His hand moved up to caress her cheek as he looked at her with absolute intensity. She wondered how she'd been laughing just a moment before. Nothing seemed funny now. He was so serious.

When his forehead came down and gently rested

against hers, she inhaled sharply. His breath danced on her lips and she closed her eyes. Her stomach fluttered, and she moved her shaky hands from his chest up to his neck and into his hair. He teased her, gently brushing his lips against hers. When she couldn't take it any more, she gripped the back of his neck and pushed her lips into his. Their lips moved in perfect unison, and when he finally pulled back, she gasped.

Her whole body felt shaky, and she prayed he wouldn't step away. Her legs felt so wobbly she worried she'd drop to the ground without him to prop her up.

She turned in his arms and gazed out over the water.

"Thanks," he whispered as he kissed her cheek.

"Did I save you from certain death?" She smiled as she rested her head against his.

"You did," he replied lightly. "How about you?" He put a hand across her forehead. "How's the migraine?"

Her eyes opened wide as she finally came back to her senses. "Did I just call in sick to work?"

"I think so," he said, chuckling.

"Oh my God! You're such a bad influence."

He stepped away and held up his hands. "It was nothing to do with me."

"It was everything to do with you." Pulling him back to her, she kissed him again, and it felt like the most amazing thing in the world. It was only when she pulled away that thoughts of Josie popped into her head.

"What's wrong?" Jack asked.

"Nothing."

"You look nervous."

Probably because she was nervous. She felt out of control. She was wandering around London with Jack, acting as though they were a couple. They shouldn't be doing that. She'd also called in sick to work. On top of that, she wondered if he was expecting to stay at her place that night. Because he absolutely couldn't. They were being crazy.

"We need to talk," she said finally. "About Josie."

***

Back at the apartment, Emily made coffee and then sat at the opposite end of the couch to Jack.

"I kept trying to talk to Josie but she's so down about work and this guy Sam, I didn't dare say anything."

"You know there's a chance she'd be excited for us."

Emily shook her head. "You're deluded."

"We're her two best friends. It's perfect."

"It's anything but perfect."

A mischievous smile played on his lips. "I had this idea that you could complain to her about your love life and I'll complain about mine. She might decide to play matchmaker and set us up … It's the sort of thing she'd do."

Part of her wanted to laugh, but part of her was annoyed with him for making light of the situation. "Don't tease," she said. "It's not fair to Josie."

"I was only joking," he said. "I love Josie."

The words were uttered so casually, but there was

panic in his eyes as soon as he said it. "I didn't mean—"

"It's okay," she said, cutting him off. "I know you love Josie."

"I meant as a friend."

She swallowed hard as all her fears and insecurities bubbled to the surface. "It's more than that, isn't it?"

"No." His eyes were as serious as his tone. "It's not."

She still couldn't quite allow herself to believe he really wanted to be with her. "Is it that you can't have Josie so you'll make do with me instead?"

"No." His features softened. "Not at all."

"But there's so much that doesn't make any sense to me. You didn't even want to break up with her."

"I did," he said with a pained expression. "But when you told me I should get back with her, I thought you had no interest in me whatsoever. It was pretty comfortable being with Josie. Most of the time."

"But even after you broke up you drove all the way to Devon for her. And I know you said it was so she didn't miss out on the job, but I think, if you're honest, it's because you're still in love with her."

"I didn't drive down there just to tell her about the job," he admitted. He ran his hands roughly through his hair. "I was thinking about you. I couldn't stop thinking about you. And I had this crazy idea of telling Josie that. I thought maybe she'd laugh and tell me to ask you out. Except she never answered her phone so one day I got in the car to drive down there. But when I saw her, everything that had sounded so rational in my head seemed ridiculous."

"So you understand why I'm having problems raising the subject with her?"

"Yeah." He smiled. "It was very awkward, by the way – that day at the farm."

"What's it like there?"

"It's amazing. The place is stunning. And the old woman Josie was living with, Annette, she's so lovely. I think she spent about ten minutes trying to suss me out, then she warmed to me and I spent three hours with her while I waited for Josie."

"I didn't hear that part of the story." Emily smiled at the thought of Jack hanging out at the farm with a little old lady.

"It was great. She showed me around the place and told me all about the kennels and what Josie had been doing."

"It sounds amazing. No wonder Josie's been in a bad mood. She must miss it."

"I think so. And there's the guy – Sam. He was there that day too. And Lizzie and Max. It was really awkward. They make me nervous, and then I crack stupid jokes and it gets more awkward."

"Josie's family can be a bit intimidating."

"Definitely." He started to say something else then stopped, looking unsure. "Was she seeing him while she was still with me?"

Emily shook her head quickly.

"Sorry," he said. "I shouldn't have asked."

"She wasn't. She wouldn't cheat on you."

"It was hardly a relationship at that stage, I'm not sure you could even class it as cheating. It doesn't matter. I just wondered about it."

"She definitely broke up with you before anything happened with him."

"Thanks," he said with an uncertain smile. "So what's the plan? Are you going to talk to Josie or shall I?"

"Me. Definitely me. You can't say anything."

"Okay."

A slow smile spread across his face. "You know, I only took the stupid acting job again so I could see you."

"What?" She screwed her face up. "That's not true."

"It is," he said. "I knew if I hung out with Josie I'd end up seeing you." He paused. "That sounds wrong. I like hanging out with Josie. But the night I stayed here was only because I wanted to see you."

She shuffled along the couch, and he put his arm around her as she snuggled into his chest.

"I'll have to go soon," he murmured into her hair.

After a slight panic about whether he was expecting to stay the night, she was suddenly dreading him leaving.

"Okay," she said, entwining her fingers with his.

Summer at the Old Boathouse

Chapter 40

They ended up watching a film snuggled up on the couch. When Jack fell asleep, Emily didn't have the heart to wake him and send him away. She was going to go to bed and leave him to sleep on the couch, but after a few minutes of watching him sleep, she settled beside him and rested her head on his chest. It was way better than her pillow.

In the morning, she kept panicking about Josie arriving back so Jack didn't stay long. He was working at the Boathouse in the afternoon anyway. Emily told him she'd speak to Josie as soon as she got back.

Unfortunately, Josie didn't arrive back until after midnight on Sunday, and by that time Emily was already in bed and fast asleep. Then they spent the first half of the week on opposite work schedules and didn't see each other at all.

It was Thursday evening when they were finally at home together.

"I'm making a cup of tea," Emily called from the kitchen when she heard Josie come in from a shift at the café. "Do you want one?" She felt like she needed something more than tea to get through the conversation, but there was nothing stronger.

"Please," she said, flopping onto the couch. "How

are you?"

"Fine. How are you? How was the weekend in Devon?" They'd already exchanged a few messages but Josie had been fairly vague.

She blew out a long breath. "Awful."

"You saw Sam?"

"Yeah. It was weird. He acted like we were old friends."

"That is weird."

As Emily put the tea on the table, Josie pulled her laptop onto her knees and opened it up. "I need to look something up quickly." She handed the TV remote to Emily. "See if there's anything good to watch …"

Josie must have hit the power button because the TV came on blaring. Emily muted it. "I wanted to talk to you actually. Something's been bothering me …"

Josie's head shot up. "I know. The apartment's too small for two. I am looking for somewhere else, but it's difficult finding somewhere on a budget."

"It's not that," she said quickly. "It's fine, you being here."

"Oh, thank God." She turned her attention back to the computer. "I thought you were going to kick me out. As if things couldn't get any worse in my life."

"Of course I wouldn't kick you out. That's not what I wanted to talk about. It's a bit awkward." She paused for a moment and her voice was feeble when she did speak again. "There's a guy. I really like him but …"

Josie squinted at her laptop screen. "Did you know you can do courses in dog training?"

Emily was utterly confused as she automatically

flicked to the next channel on the TV. "I can't say it's something I ever thought about much. But I suppose that makes sense. Why?"

"It just never occurred to me that you could train in this kind of thing. I always thought it was something you were either good at or you weren't." Her eyes scanned the laptop screen as she chewed her thumbnail. "There are courses in dog grooming, dog nutrition, health and well-being. All sorts of stuff."

"Okay," Emily mumbled. "Ignore me, let's talk about you as always."

Josie stared at her computer, completely oblivious to Emily. After a moment, Josie's phone vibrated around the coffee table and she leaned forwards to look at it.

"It's Sam," she said anxiously. "He keeps calling me. I think he wants to get back together. It's stressing me out."

"I thought you wanted him to call."

"I did, but I'm angry it took him so long. I don't know what to do. I feel like my whole life is a mess. I'm going to quit the acting job. I hate it. I feel like I'm going to have a nervous breakdown."

"I'm sure everything will work out," Emily said.

"Sorry. What did you want to talk about?"

"I can't even remember. Nothing important." She tossed the TV remote in Josie's direction. "What do you want to watch? There's not much on."

In the end, Emily took her tea into the bedroom and sat on her bed to message Jack, telling him she might have to wait a little while to talk to Josie. She promised she'd try again in a few days when Josie wasn't so fed up.

By the weekend, she still hadn't found the time to talk to Josie. Jack kept offering to talk to her, but she told him firmly not to.

A few days later she was lazing on her couch with her feet up when Jack called. It was early afternoon, which was an odd time of day for him to be calling.

"Is everything okay?" she asked.

"Yes." He sounded strange. Overly cheerful. "I'm round the corner from your apartment."

"What? Why?"

"I just want to see you for a minute. Make an excuse to Josie and come down. Go to the crossroads and turn left. I'll wait here."

"Josie's not here," she said, confused. "She's working all day."

"No. She quit."

"She was going to quit," Emily corrected him. "But they finally made it a speaking part so she's going to stick at it."

"No." He laughed. "She quit. Tell her you need to nip to the shop and come and meet me."

"She's not here," she said adamantly. "What is going on with you?"

Her head shot up as the door opened and Josie walked in.

"I'll wait for you," Jack said into the phone.

She put the phone down and stared at Josie. "What are you doing home?"

Josie's shoulders shook as she giggled. "You won't believe my day!"

"I thought you wouldn't be home until late. They gave you lines to say, didn't they?"

"I got fired," Josie said as she dropped heavily

onto the couch. She put her hand over her face as the laughter took over her. After a moment she hiccupped and took a deep breath in an attempt to calm down.

"Are you drunk?" Emily asked.

"Only a bit," she said with a grin. "It's Jack's fault!"

"Why is it Jack's fault? What happened?"

"Jack turned up at work and we were drinking shots of sambuca on set so we got fired."

"Why would he do that?"

"He was doing me a favour," Josie said. "He knew how much I hated it. We ended up in the pub for a drink. I tried to get him to come back here. I thought we could all hang out together, but he said he had to get back." She grinned at Emily. "I haven't had so much fun in a long time."

"That's lovely," Emily said. "Except you're drunk at one o'clock in the afternoon. I'll make you a coffee to sober you up."

In the kitchen, she discreetly tipped half a bottle of milk down the sink then went back to the living room. "We're out of milk. I'll run and get some."

"I'll have it black," Josie said.

"But I want milk in mine." She picked up her phone and purse. "I'll be back in a few minutes."

She walked quickly to the traffic lights and turned left. Jack was loitering outside a fruit and veg shop.

"What on earth is going on?" Emily asked. She was annoyed until his eyes lit up at the sight of her. It was difficult to be angry with him when he smiled at her so adorably.

"What did you tell Josie?" he asked.

"I said I was getting milk." She shook her head.

"Are you drunk?"

"Only a tiny bit," he said sheepishly.

"Josie said you got her fired?"

"She was going to quit anyway. I just made it fun." He stepped closer and put a hand on her hip.

She pushed him away. "I don't want to do this. I hate sneaking around."

"It's not for long," he said. "Josie's finally quit her job. It seems like she's going to sort things out with Sam. I'm fairly sure she's going to end up working back at the farm. And once she's back in Devon, we'll hardly have to sneak around at all – I can come over every weekend and she'll never know."

She was all set to shout at him when she caught the teasing in his eye. "I'm not in the mood for jokes," she complained.

"Sorry." He reached for her hand. "But as soon as everything works out for Josie and she's happy, I really think she's going to be okay with this."

"I hope so." Emily couldn't resist any longer and leaned in to gently kiss his lips. "I have to go," she said when she pulled back.

"Em!" he shouted when she was almost at the corner.

"Yeah?"

"Don't forget the milk."

Chapter 41

Jack was right about Josie: two weeks later she packed up her things and moved back to Devon. She'd sorted things out with Sam and was excited about working at the kennels again. After she left the acting job, the change in her was incredible. It was as though a weight had been lifted. She threw all her energy into getting her career on track. A completely different career but one that seemed to make her far happier. Sam was the icing on the cake.

As soon as Josie had left, Jack had called wanting to meet. Emily refused. She missed him and wanted to see him so badly, but she hated the sneaking around. Josie was going to be in Oxford the following weekend – collecting some things from her parents' house – and Emily was going to meet her and get everything out in the open once and for all.

She'd arranged to see Josie on Saturday afternoon, but Emily had the entire weekend off from the restaurant and agreed to go and see Jack on Friday evening.

"I missed you," he said, wrapping his arms around her when she walked into his flat.

"I missed you too." Butterflies fluttered in her stomach when he kissed her. "I can't stay long," she said automatically when they moved apart.

"Don't worry. Josie's going to be fine. She's all loved up, and she'll be happy you are too."

"I really hope so." They sat together on the couch and she reached for his hand, stroking his fingers before entwining them with her own. He moved closer and kissed her again.

It was an effort to pull away, but she was determined not to get carried away. Tomorrow, she'd talk to Josie and then things could move forwards with her and Jack without the need for secrecy.

"I really can't stay long," she said again.

He chuckled. "You mentioned that. I might have to get a jigsaw puzzle out just to get you to stay longer."

She beamed at the memory. "That was a good day."

"It was," he agreed. "Although I was pretty embarrassed."

"Why?"

He gave her a look as though it should be obvious. "Because I didn't want you to leave so I panicked and asked you about the puzzle. I was mortified that the only way I could think of to get you to stay longer was doing a bloody puzzle."

"I knew you hated it," she said giving him a playful shove.

"I enjoyed it. You were right about it being addictive. I lost sleep finishing that thing."

She beamed. "Don't pretend you finished it."

"I did."

"I have no idea if you're being serious." He looked serious, but she found it very hard to believe.

Slowly, he stood up and then pulled her up too.

"Where are we going?"

He led her to his bedroom and pointed to a picture on the far wall. It was a familiar scene. A lake and a castle. It took her a moment to register what she was looking at. She moved for a closer look.

"You really did finish it."

"I didn't have the heart to break it up after I finished it. I glued it and framed it." He smiled. "Which wasn't as easy as it sounds."

For a moment, she couldn't take her eyes off the stunning picture. Finally, she turned to Jack. "I can't believe you did that."

"I just hope you're not going to ask for it back. I'm quite attached to it."

Moving closer, she circled her arms around his shoulders and trailed her fingers up and down the back of his neck. "I think it's perfect where it is," she said quietly. "But I might have to come and look at it sometimes."

"You're very welcome to," he said with a boyish smile. "Anytime."

She kissed him then and her stomach turned wonderfully fluttery. Her eyes closed and her whole body tingled. As she lifted onto her toes, the kiss deepened, and when she finally pulled back she was breathing hard. Quickly, she pulled her T-shirt over her head and then did the same with Jack's.

She caught the surprise in his features as their bare skin pushed together. When she pulled him onto the bed, he stopped kissing her for a moment and looked deeply into her eyes. His breathing was loud and irregular. Mischief flashed on his features.

"I thought you weren't staying long."

She ran a hand down his toned torso. "I might have changed my mind.

**

When she woke late the next morning she was on cloud nine. The smile hit her lips as she turned in Jack's arms. He was already awake and grinned lazily.

He dotted kisses along her neck, making her giggle and squirm. "Good morning."

"Good morning," she replied. And it really was a good morning. The very best of mornings. For the first time in a long time she felt positive. "Josie will be happy for us, won't she?" It was more of a statement than a question. Suddenly, she felt she'd been worrying about nothing. When Emily was so ecstatic it seemed impossible that Josie would be anything but happy for her.

"Yes," Jack said, kissing the palm of her hand. "We'll be on a double date with her and Sam before you know it."

"That would be good," she mused happily.

"When are you meeting her?"

"Not until this afternoon. She's driving up from Devon this morning and said she had a few things to do first."

"It's almost afternoon now," Jack said, showing her his watch.

"Wow." She was surprised by the time. Although, it had been the early hours of the morning before they'd finally fallen asleep. Sitting up, she scanned the floor beside the bed where their clothes lay discarded. She reached for Jack's T-shirt and pulled it over her head. "I'll get coffee and see if I can rustle up some breakfast, or lunch I suppose."

Jack snaked an arm around her waist and pulled her back to him. "You stay here. I'll get breakfast."

"No." She straddled him, pinning him down. "You're getting breakfast in bed. I want to do something nice for you."

He raised an eyebrow. "As I recall you already did a few nice things for me last night. There's no way I'm letting you make breakfast."

"Will you do as you're told for once?" she said firmly. "Stay there." Hopping off the bed, she headed for the kitchen. She'd just put a mug under the coffee machine when he followed her in, dressed only in a pair of snug boxer shorts.

"I told you to stay in bed!"

"And I said there's no way you're making breakfast." He planted a kiss on her cheek and pressed a button on the coffee machine. "We can do it together."

She stopped short at the sound of three loud bangs at the front door.

"Your building must be like mine," she said. "People leave the front door open. It drives me mad. Are you expecting someone?"

"It'll be my neighbour. She comes round asking me random questions all the time. She'll go away again."

But the knocking returned. Followed by the sound of a key in the lock.

"Who's got a key?" Emily asked in a loud whisper, horribly aware of the fact that she was only wearing Jack's T-shirt.

Panic washed over Jack's face, and Emily realised who would have a key.

"Jack?" Josie's voice rang around the flat. They stayed completely still in the kitchen. Emily hardly dared breathe. "Jack?" Josie shouted again. "I'm finally returning your spare key." There was a jangle of keys and the sound of them clattering onto the table. Surely if she thought Jack wasn't in, she'd leave the keys and go again.

The coffee machine chose that moment to whir to life, spluttering out coffee into the waiting mug. Emily closed her eyes, as though if she couldn't see it, none of this would actually be happening.

Josie's voice was amazingly cheerful. Surprised and cheerful. "Hi!"

"Hi," Jack said flatly.

Emily opened her eyes in time to see Josie register the scene. She opened her mouth and then closed it again. She looked questioningly at Jack and when her gaze landed on Emily she bit her lip. Somehow she managed a fake smile.

"I left your keys on the table," Josie said to Jack. Then she turned and walked away.

Jack went after her. He put a hand on the front door to stop her leaving. She didn't say anything but batted at his hand and then turned and roughly shoved at his chest.

"Wait," he said, holding his ground. "Don't run off."

Josie pulled on the door handle in vain.

"I was going to talk to you." Emily's words sounded feeble and Josie didn't even seem to hear. "I can explain. Stay and I'll explain …"

Finally, Josie turned. Tears streamed down her face and her chest heaved as she fought for breath. Emily had never seen Josie look so upset. The hurt and pain stared her in the face, and she knew that she had inflicted it all on her best friend.

"Let her go," Emily said when Josie turned frantically back to the door. "Jack, move."

When he stepped aside, Josie flung the door open and took off at a run. Emily shot to the bedroom and pulled her jeans on before running after her. She took the stairs two at a time and was surprised she didn't end up in a heap at the bottom she was going so fast.

Josie was leaning against her car, sobbing.

"How long?" she spluttered angrily. "How long have you been seeing him?"

"Not long."

"When I was with him?"

"No," she said firmly. "I promise."

Josie looked right at her, blinking through tears. "I don't even know what to think."

"I was going to tell you today," Emily said. "I was going to explain everything."

Jack arrived beside Emily. "Why don't you come back in and we can talk about this properly."

When she looked at Jack the hurt in her eyes morphed to anger. "I've got nothing to say to you."

"Is it really so bad?" he asked. "*You're* seeing someone else."

She laughed, a horrible humourless laugh. "I am seeing someone else. But not your best friend. How would you feel if you walked into Lee's place and found me and him half naked?" She spat the words out.

"It's not the same."

"It's exactly the same," she said with wide eyes. As she opened the car door she turned back to them sadly. "You were supposed to be my best friends."

Emily's heart hammered as she watched Josie drive away. She was only aware of Jack when he put a hand on her elbow. Drawing quickly away from him, she went back inside. She grabbed her bag from beside the couch and then went to the bedroom and collected up the remainder of her clothes, shoving them into her bag so she could leave as quickly as possible.

"She'll be okay when she calms down," Jack said, following her around the flat. "It was a shock, but we'll talk to her and it will be fine." He followed her to the door. "Where are you going?"

"Home," she said. "I'm going to get changed and then go and find Josie." She needed to find her and sit down with her for a proper chat.

"Everything will be okay," he said. He moved to kiss her and she stepped back.

"I can't be with you if it means losing my best friend."

His eyes narrowed. "So what happens if she asks you to choose between me and her?"

As she stared at him, she realised she had no idea what she'd do if she had to choose. "I just need to talk to her," she said, moving quickly out of the door.

She couldn't think any further than that.

Chapter 42

When she arrived home, her mum poked her head out of the kitchen. She scrutinised Emily as she walked into the hallway.

"What are you wearing?" she asked, puzzled. "And where have you been? Are you okay? What's happened? Sorry, that's a lot of questions."

"Jack's T-shirt." Emily tugged on it as she addressed the first question. "Jack's place." The second question was pretty straightforward too. Was she okay? She had no idea so she skipped to question four. "Josie knows." Simple answers to simple questions. It would have been far easier if her mum hadn't been home.

"She caught you with Jack?"

Another easy question. She nodded in reply.

"Oh, Emily …"

"I know. I don't have time for you to tell me I'm an idiot. I need to get changed and go and find Josie." She hurried up the stairs and jumped in the shower. All she could think about was talking to Josie and sorting out the mess she'd made

***

Unsurprisingly, Josie didn't answer the phone to

Emily but she found her at her parents' house. Mrs Beaumont answered the door. She was polite and cheerful, so Emily assumed she had no clue what had happened. When Josie didn't respond to her mum shouting up the stairs, she sent Emily up to her. Their house was like a show home. Everything was perfectly in place, and everything screamed money. It was quite a contrast to the cosy little house Emily had grown up in with her mum.

Pushing the door to Josie's childhood bedroom, Emily asked if she could come in. Josie was lying on the bed, staring at the ceiling. She didn't reply so Emily crept in and sat gently on the edge of the bed. The room had been turned into a guest room and didn't feel lived in.

"I'm sorry," she said. "I didn't want you to find out like that."

Josie's voice took her by surprise. "I can't get things straight in my head. I used to think it was so sweet that Jack always asked about you. I liked that he took an interest in my best friend." She paused. "If I'd have known how much of an interest he had …"

"It's not like that," Emily said firmly.

"What about the time I had an argument with him and you told me to split up with him?" She continued to stare overhead and her words were full of bitterness. "Was that so you could have him for yourself?"

"No." Emily rubbed her temple. "No. I thought you were unhappy with him. But I should never have told you to split up with him."

"So you did like him then?"

"Yes."

"I feel like you've been lying to me all this time."

"I couldn't tell you how I felt," Emily said as tears dripped down her face. "I didn't know what to do so I moved to London. I avoided him and thought I'd forget about him if I didn't see him."

Josie sniffed and wiped at tears. "I never understood what happened with Stuart but I guess that explains it. It's like I'm replaying the last year in my head and everything is different to what I thought."

"Neither of us wanted to hurt you. And I swear nothing happened until the last few weeks. I was trying to find a time to talk to you."

"Jack's been lying to me." Josie spoke as though she wasn't even hearing Emily. "I thought it was so great that we could stay friends after we broke up, but it was only so he could get to you."

"Jack will always be your friend," Emily said. "He cares about you so much."

"He won't always be my friend," Josie said, sitting up abruptly and swinging her legs off the side of the bed. "I don't need friends like him." She finally looked at Emily. "Or you."

"Don't say that," Emily pleaded. More tears appeared as she spoke. "I understand you're upset but I'm still your friend. You can be angry with me, but we'll always be friends."

"I'll be angry with you today," she said coolly. "Angry and hurt and upset. Then tomorrow, I'll go back to Oakbrook and get on with my life. I'll pretend that you and Jack never existed."

Josie was always prone to drama, but Emily was worried that she meant it.

"Just go," she added. "There's nothing you can

say to fix this. Go back to Jack and have a nice life."

"Josie …" Emily didn't even know what to say, but she couldn't leave things as they were.

"You've made me feel stupid," Josie spluttered. "I trusted you. I can't believe you and Jack would sneak around behind my back. I keep imagining you talking about me. About how stupid I am, not noticing you carrying on right under my nose."

"We weren't …"

"Please just go." Josie was crying harder and Emily hated it. She'd do anything to make her feel better, but she also knew there was nothing she could do at that moment.

With a heavy heart, she walked away.

***

The next week was agony. Emily called work and told them she had flu. Then she acted like she had flu, lying in bed and staying in her pyjamas. She was miserable, and she hated herself for how badly she'd hurt Josie. Jack called her multiple times a day. Sometimes she answered, sometimes she didn't. He kept telling her that everything would work out fine, but she couldn't quite see how when she wasn't sure her best friend would ever speak to her again. To his annoyance, she refused to see him until she'd sorted things out with Josie.

Unfortunately, Josie was ignoring her calls, so fixing the friendship wasn't an easy task. The thought crossed her mind to drive down and see her in person. She threatened it on Josie's voicemail on Thursday. On Friday, she finally answered the phone. Emily had become so used to listening to the ringtone that the sound of Josie's voice was a surprise. She was speechless for a moment.

"I feel terrible," she said. "I'm so sorry. I wish I could fix everything."

"You can't," Josie said.

"I'd do anything for you. I can't believe I put Jack before our friendship," she blurted through tears. "Just tell me we're still friends. You can't pretend I don't exist."

"I only said that because I was angry. I'm so confused. I didn't think you'd ever do anything to hurt me."

"I know. And I'm so sorry. I didn't mean to."

"I don't think I can see you for a while. Please don't turn up here. Give me some space."

Space was okay. She could give her space.

"But we're still friends?"

"I don't know." Her voice was ragged and angry. "I'm not sure we can still be friends when you're sleeping with my ex."

"Josie. I made a mistake and I'm sorry."

"But you're seeing Jack! Things will never be normal between us again."

"I don't know what to say …"

"Maybe say you'll never see him again! That it was a stupid mistake and it's over."

Emily sobbed and wiped tears from her cheeks.

"You say you didn't want to hurt me," Josie snapped. "But you knew it would hurt me and you did it anyway. He's obviously more important to you than I am."

Emily's heart rate shot up. She had to clear her

throat to get her voice to work. "I'll break it off with him," she said with a croaky voice.

There was a brief pause. "Good. He'd only hurt you in the end anyway. One way or another."

"He never meant to hurt you."

"You can't make excuses for him," Josie snapped. "If you want to be friends you can't make excuses for him. In fact, don't even talk to me about him. I'm not sure I'll ever forgive him. I don't even want to hear his name."

"Okay."

Emily lay back on her bed when Josie ended the call.

For a week she'd convinced herself that if she could be friends with Josie again, nothing else would matter. But she'd never really thought Josie would want her to give Jack up.

Chapter 43

When she arrived at Jack's place that evening he looked so happy to see her it made her heart ache. She wondered if she could actually keep her promise to Josie.

"You spoke to her then?" He leaned to kiss her but she moved so he only caught her cheek.

She took a seat on the couch. "Yeah."

"I knew she wouldn't ignore you forever. She was upset and overreacting."

"But she has every right to be upset. She thinks her two best friends were sneaking around and keeping secrets from her."

"We can talk to her again and explain—"

"Explain what?" she snapped. "We *were* sneaking around. We *were* keeping secrets. We were terrible friends."

He reached for her hand. "She'll forgive us eventually and everything will go back to normal."

"Nothing will be normal between the three of us." She pulled her hand gently from his. "And I don't even know if she'll really be friends with me."

"Emily ..." There was an edge of panic to his voice as though he was figuring out where the conversation was going.

"I'm sorry," she said, finally looking at him and

using all her willpower not to cry.

"Don't do this," he said. "All I want is to be with you. It doesn't matter to me if Josie has a problem with it."

"It matters to me. I won't be able to live with myself if I don't do everything I can to fix my friendship with Josie."

"So you're choosing her over me?"

She nodded and stood up. If she didn't get away from him soon, she'd change her mind. "I'm sorry."

"You're upset," he said, following her to the door. "You're not thinking rationally."

When she looked in his eyes, she knew she wouldn't get rid of him that easily. He'd hound her until she finally gave in. And she would give in. She needed a clean break.

"We'd never work anyway." Her tone was icy. "As soon as the novelty wears off, we'd both get bored."

"What?" he asked, stunned. "What are you talking about?"

"We're completely unsuited. When I think about my future I don't see how you fit in. I have ambitions and dreams. I want to travel and develop my writing career. We have nothing in common. You play football, and you go to the pub and you work in a shop. And that's fine if that's all you want from life. But I want so much more."

He stared at her, saying nothing.

Emily kept talking. "If I really saw a future for us, there's no way I'd think of giving up on it. But when I spend my time wondering if it's even worth it, the conclusion I come to is that it's probably not. I don't think you can make me happy, and if I have doubts already I don't see how it's going to work."

Without a word, he went back to the couch and dropped his head into his hands. It broke Emily's heart to see him so defeated. He should have argued. She wished he'd argued because she was completely wrong. Of course he'd make her happy.

She hated how easy it was to convince him otherwise

***

The thought of going back to London was unappealing, and Emily took a few more days off work to wallow in self-pity. She didn't really want to leave her mum's house at all. It was good to have her mum's company and cooking, and she was dreading going back to her empty apartment.

On Monday, her mum came up to her bedroom after work and hovered in the doorway. "Are you okay?" she asked.

Emily was staring at the ceiling, contemplating the mess she'd made of her life. It seemed to be her new hobby.

"Yeah," she muttered.

"I'll make some dinner then." Her mum walked away with an audible sigh. Then she appeared in the doorway again.

"What?" Emily asked fiercely.

She walked away again. "Nothing," she snapped.

"Mum!" She came back again when Emily called. "If you've got something to say just say it."

"Okay then. I think you're being pathetic. I don't

agree with your life choices. Most of the time I feel like shaking you. You're wasting your life."

"I'll be back to London soon so you'll be rid of me." Emily sounded like a moody teenager, but she didn't really care.

"Why are you going back to London?"

"Because that's where I live." She rolled her eyes. "That's where my job is."

"But you can write anywhere. You don't need to be in London."

"I meant my waitress job. I'm not even writing any more."

"I've noticed." Her voice was angry. "But why not?"

"I finished the last book, now I'm having a break."

"So you're going to live in London and work as a waitress?"

"What's wrong with that?"

"You used to love your job at the castle."

"Mum. I worked in the shop. Waitressing is hardly a huge step down."

"But when people asked you what you did, they'd get the full history of the castle. You were passionate about it. Now you're just floating along."

"I can't live in Oxford after everything with Jack."

"Of course you can! If that's what you want. The trouble is you make all your decisions based on Jack and Josie. You don't do anything for yourself."

"So you think I shouldn't have split up with Jack just because Josie doesn't want me to see him?"

"I don't care about Josie or Jack. I care about you.

All I want is for you to do something to make yourself happy and stop worrying about what everyone else thinks."

"I don't know what I want," she said feebly.

"Then figure it out."

Her mum left Emily alone and she dragged herself up from her bed. After a shower, she got dressed for the first time in a couple of days. Her mum's words floated round her head. She *was* being pathetic, she couldn't deny that.

"I have no idea what I want to do," she said to her mum in the kitchen. "But I know I don't want to live in London. And I don't want to be a waitress."

Her mum chopped tomatoes and slung them in the salad bowl. "Well, that's a good start."

"Not really. I can't not have a job."

"Move back here for a while. Take a bit of time off. Do some writing and figure out what you want to do."

By the time Emily finished dinner, she'd decided that was exactly what she was going to do. She may have lost Jack, and Josie might never forgive her, but at least she could sort out the rest of her life. It felt good to have something positive to focus on.

***

It was easy to find someone to take over her apartment at short notice, and three weeks later, Emily handed over the keys and moved her stuff back to her mum's. She was determined not to see it as a step backwards. Going to London had been her running away from things, and now she was taking control of her life. It was definitely positive.

The lack of a job made her uncomfortable. After a month of being out of work, she started to get antsy. She searched the job sites but couldn't find anything that inspired her. Whenever she thought about getting a job, she came back to her mum's comment about how much she loved it at the castle. It had been an ideal job for her.

If she went and asked for her job back, was that a step backwards? She was supposed to be moving forwards and was worried she was going to end up in exactly the same situation she was in a year ago. In the end, she decided it wouldn't hurt to go and say hello to her old colleagues.

Doug was chatting to an unfamiliar waitress in the doorway of the café. He grinned widely when he saw Emily walking across the courtyard. Memories came flooding back, not only of her time working there but of her knowledge of the place. All the facts and stories. She hadn't thought about any of it for so long.

She embraced Doug in a big hug and only then realised how much she'd missed his smiling face.

"You look well," he told her. "How's life in London?"

"I've moved back to Oxford." She decided to be upfront. Now that she was back there, she was sure she wanted her old job back, and she was desperate to know if it was a possibility. "I was actually wondering if you might have a job for me." She bit her lip as she waited for a reply.

Her heart plummeted when he frowned. "I'd love to have you back but the shop's fully staffed. I could offer you a couple of shifts a week in the café but that's about it I'm afraid."

The café might be okay. She'd still be able to talk to people about the castle. Putting all her knowledge to use would be nice. She was mulling it over when she saw another familiar face. "Bernie!" she called automatically. Her favourite tour guide was on his way to meet a group but veered over to her. His beard covered his mouth, but his frown was evident in the wrinkles of his brow.

"It's Bernard," he bellowed as he got near her. "And how many times do I have to tell you not to distract me when I'm in character?" His features softened and he grinned at Emily. "How are you?" he asked as he wrapped her in a tight hug.

"I'm good," she said, realising that it wasn't even a lie. It felt great to be back at the castle. "You smell musty."

"So would you if you were a prisoner in the castle in 1902."

She laughed. He was so wonderfully eccentric.

"I have to go," he said. "But hang around and I'll have a coffee with you after my tour."

"Okay," she said. "I will. Break a leg!"

She watched as he theatrically introduced himself to the tour group. Then she turned back to Doug with a nervous smile. "I don't suppose you need any more guides?"

He searched her face, obviously not sure if she was serious. "You want to be a guide?"

"Yes." She scrunched her face up, realising it was exactly what she wanted, and if Doug said no she'd probably start crying.

"I thought you hated speaking in front of

strangers?"

"I did." She thought about how terrified she'd been the time she'd shown the school group around the castle. And how her nerves had vanished after the first few minutes. Then there was her writing group in London. She'd been so scared to join, but after the first week it was absolutely fine.

"I'm challenging myself," she said to Doug. "I know I can overcome the nerves. I'd be a great guide, I promise …"

"I'm sure you would." He chuckled, then looked at her seriously. "It wouldn't be a full-time gig … and it's not well paid. Mainly just tips—"

She flung her arms around him and squealed with delight.

Chapter 44

Becoming a tour guide at the castle felt like the best decision Emily had ever made. She was right about the nerves: they disappeared quickly, and the more tours she took, the more she found herself excited about them rather than anxious. It didn't feel like work at all, and she loved every minute of it.

She only wished she could take more tours. Three or four a week was all they could give her to start with, but Doug said that could increase over time. In the meantime she volunteered to cover any extra shifts in the café or gift shop, and even offered to help with admin work in the office. Being around the castle lifted her spirits.

It was the end of October when Emily decided to take advantage of the mild weather and eat her lunch on the castle mound after showing a group around. There was a chill in the breeze, but the autumn sun provided a little warmth. The sunlight glowed down on the beautiful city as she looked out over it from her high vantage point. She loved that spot. Suddenly she remembered the day Jack and Josie had visited her at work and they had had a picnic together in the very spot she was sitting.

She missed them both. Things still weren't right between her and Josie, and it niggled at her constantly. Emily called her at least once a week, and though Josie was pleasant enough, she never really had time for a proper chat. She was always busy or on her way somewhere. Emily had mentioned meeting up a couple of times, but Josie insisted she was snowed under with work and college courses.

It was hard for Emily to believe that she really couldn't make time. She even offered to go down to Devon and see Josie, but there was always some excuse why she shouldn't.

As always, she brushed thoughts of Josie and Jack aside. She'd been working so hard to get her life on track, and she'd only set herself back if she let herself dwell.

Instead, she thought about the tour she'd just given and the twelve-year-old girl who'd stayed by her side the whole time, firing questions at her and being completely absorbed by the place and the stories. It amazed her that she'd found a job that combined her two favourite things: history and telling stories. At the castle, it was so easy to make up stories based on the facts she knew about the prisoners. She really did love it.

It was a while since she'd done any writing, but she still carried a notebook with her everywhere out of habit. She reached into her backpack for it as an idea came to her. The pen moved quickly over the paper, and another idea came to her as she wrote. Then another and another.

When her fingers started to go numb, she headed back down the hill to the warmth of the castle café.

"I thought you'd gone home," Doug said. He was loitering at the counter, chatting to Joyce, one of the waitresses.

"I was up on the hill," Emily said. "And I had an idea for a book." She plonked herself at a table and continued scribbling in her notebook. "Ideas are going off like fireworks in my head," she told Doug. "I need to write them down before I forget."

The notebook was almost full of hastily scribbled notes when Emily left the café. She would have stayed longer but they were closing. Her mum arrived home from work just after she got in.

"I had such a crazy day," Emily said excitedly. "I had an idea for a new book. It's a bit different and I've no idea if the publishers will be interested in it, but I'm going to ask. It doesn't even matter about the publishers. I'll write it anyway. I can always publish it myself."

Her mum laughed. "Calm down! Come and tell me about it."

"I can't calm down. I'm too excited! I don't know why I didn't think of this before. A historical romance. Set in Oxford Castle. I just want to get on and write it." She headed for the stairs. "I'm going to get some more done before dinner. Shall we order pizza?"

Her mum agreed and Emily shot up to her bedroom and opened a new document on her laptop. She was completely exhilarated as the ideas flooded from her mind to the computer. Her fingers could hardly keep up. In the end, her mum brought the pizza up to her room and Emily typed with one hand as she ate.

She finally collapsed into bed in the early hours of the morning. Her eyes wouldn't focus on the screen any more so she decided it was time to stop.

At the crack of dawn she was back to it with renewed vigour. It felt fantastic to have ideas again, not to mention actually having the time to write. Working at the castle definitely hadn't been a step backwards for her.

The writing had to be paused while she took a group around the castle that afternoon. It was so amazing. Walking around the setting for her next book was inspiring, and even more new ideas hit her as she showed the group of American tourists around.

Her enthusiasm for the project filled her with positivity, and on the way home late in the afternoon, she was suddenly desperate to share it with Josie.

She answered the phone after a few rings. Emily had become used to her unenthusiastic greetings and tried not to dwell on it.

"I've had a new idea for a book," she told her quickly. "I'm actually writing again. I honestly thought I'd never come up with another idea for a book, but it just came to me."

"That's great," Josie said flatly.

"I'm so happy." Emily refused to let Josie dampen her excitement. It was hurtful that she was so frosty with her. Things would probably be better once they saw each other, but any time Emily suggested it, Josie had an excuse.

"Are you coming up to Oxford any time soon? You could tag along on one of my tours and see me in action."

"I don't seem to have a minute free," Josie said. "Never mind enough time for a trip to Oxford."

"Okay." She was disappointed but couldn't really

argue. "You'll be back at Christmas, won't you?"

"I'm not sure yet. We'll probably spend Christmas at Annette's place, on the farm. I wouldn't leave her alone. Lizzie and Max will come there, I guess. They'll have the babies by then so they're not planning too much. Anyway, my parents will probably come down to Devon too so there's not much reason for me to get back to Oxford."

Tears stung Emily's eyes. She was fairly sure Josie had no idea how hurtful her comment was. She forced herself to sound casual. "Don't forget you were going to tell me when you had a weekend free so I could visit you."

"I've not forgotten. I've just been so busy. Weekends are the busiest time."

"Of course," Emily said.

"I'm sorry. I was actually in the middle of something when you called. I'm going to have to go, but we'll talk again soon and I'll let you know when things calm down a bit here so you can visit."

The line went dead before Emily even had chance to say goodbye.

Over dinner, she relayed the conversation to her mum.

"If she doesn't want to be friends with you any more you can't force her. I don't get it – she makes you jump through hoops to stay friends with her, and then she treats you like dirt anyway."

"Things will be fine eventually." At least that's what Emily kept telling herself.

"Aren't you tempted to call him?"

They didn't often talk about Jack, but when they did they rarely said his name. Her mum generally avoided the subject completely. Probably because she was scared Emily would slip back into staying-in-bed-in-pyjamas mode.

Emily wondered how to answer the question. Of course she was tempted to call him. All the time. Late at night was the worst time; her mind would always drift to him and when she was tired she could usually convince herself that it was a good idea. She resisted, knowing that nothing good would come from it.

"Not really," she finally said. Her mum must know that was a lie.

"But if Josie's not going to be friends with you anyway why did she tell you not to be with him? Is she trying to torture you?"

"I think she's just stressed with the new job and everything. She's got a lot going on."

Emily wasn't sure why she was defending Josie. She clung to the hope that eventually things would get back to normal between them. In the meantime, she had to try not to dwell on Jack. If she stopped and thought about how much she missed him, she'd surely break her resolve and call him. Not that he'd talk to her after the awful things she said.

At least the writing was taking her mind off things. Between working at the castle and writing her next book, she was pretty busy. There was also a bit of excitement in November when the paperback of her first book was launched in WHSmith's. She went to investigate with her mum and was excited to see it prominently displayed. But her mum was far more excited than Emily was. All Emily could think of was Jack joking about dragging her around the shops to sign copies. It was a bittersweet day.

It was also the same day she got a message from Josie to say Lizzie had given birth to the twins. Two little girls: Maya and Phoebe. They were a month early but everyone was fit and healthy.

In the middle of December, Emily was roped into working a full week in the castle gift shop to cover sickness. It was an enjoyable enough week, but she was frustrated at not having so much time to work on the book.

She hated winter; getting the bus home in the dark after work was depressing. And the buses were so unreliable in winter. One day in December she waited so long for a bus that she finally gave up and set off in search of a taxi. There didn't seem to be many taxis around, and to keep warm, she kept moving. It was only when she arrived at Folly Bridge that she registered where she was.

She knew there was a taxi rank nearby – that's why she'd gone that way. It was a part of town she generally avoided. Without giving it much thought, she walked to the bridge, stopping at the halfway point to look down the river. It was such a different scene in the winter; the trees were bare and everything looked dull and bleak.

The boathouse wasn't visible from the bridge, but it felt strange to be so close to it. How many times had she happily wandered from the bridge along the footpath to spend an afternoon with Josie and Jack? Looking back, those days seemed so carefree. She'd taken them for granted at the time. Now all she wanted was to go back to that wonderful summer at the Old Boathouse.

Reminiscing wasn't doing her any good. If she

didn't leave soon, she'd dissolve into a blubbering wreck. Plus she was freezing. Quickly, she headed back towards the taxis. A group of people walked out of the pub as she passed. The Head of the River held lots of memories for her too. In future, she'd stick to avoiding that part of town.

One of the group hung back. Emily had her head down against the wind, but he was blocking the path and she finally looked up, wondering why he wasn't moving out of the way.

"Hi." The familiar voice took her by surprise.

"Hi," she said, taken aback by the sight of Stuart.

"Long time no see," he said with a smile. "How are you?"

"I'm fine, thanks." She shivered. "Freezing but fine!"

"Are you still living in London?"

"No. I'm back here now. Working at the castle again."

"That's great." There was an awkward silence, and she hopped from foot to foot in an attempt to get warm. His eyes sparkled when he laughed at her. "I don't suppose you've got time for a drink?" He pointed at the pub. "It'd be nice to catch up properly. And I'm worried you're about to freeze!"

"I think I am." She blew into her hands. "A drink would be good. I was waiting forever for a bus home. I'd just given up and was looking for a taxi."

"It helps if you look where you're going," he said as they walked into the pub. "I thought you were going to walk right into me."

She shivered again and then sighed as the warmth of the pub enveloped her. A log fire burned in a hearth near the entranceway.

At the bar, she was surprised when the man next to her cheerfully said hello. She beamed when she saw it was Clive, Jack's uncle. Automatically, she gave him a big hug. What a weird day. How many more people would she bump into? Panic hit her then and her eyes darted around, checking out the pub over Clive's shoulder.

"Are you with Jack?" she asked, worried she was about to have a heart attack at the thought of seeing him.

"No. I'm on my own. I was about to leave, but let me buy you a drink first."

"No, you don't need to do that." She remembered Stuart and turned his way. "This is Clive," she said. "He owns the Boathouse. Clive, this is my friend, Stuart."

"It's a great café you've got," Stuart said as they shook hands.

"Thanks. It's nice in the summer, not so pretty at this time of year. It's all closed up for the winter, but I've just been down to check on the place."

It was probably only a couple of seconds of silence, but to Emily it seemed to stretch on. She wanted to ask about Jack. That would be the natural direction of conversation. It was too hard, though. Everything felt so raw still. She couldn't have a normal chat about him. No way. She'd probably burst into tears.

Clive checked his watch. "I've got to get home or I'll be in bother."

"It was really good to see you," Emily said, suddenly wishing she'd asked about Jack. Part of her was dying to hear about him – how he was, and what was new with him.

"Have a lovely evening!" Clive called as he left them.

"He's related to your friend, isn't he?" Stuart asked.

"Yeah. Jack's uncle."

"Do you still hang out with him and ..." He looked thoughtful.

"Josie," she said. "No. We don't hang out much." A lot had happened since she last saw Stuart, and there wasn't much of the past year that she was keen to talk about. "They split up. I still talk to Josie but I'm not in touch with Jack at all."

"That's weird ..." He paused to order drinks as the barmaid arrived.

She could have left it at that and moved the conversation on, but she was intrigued as to why he thought it was weird.

"What's weird?" she asked as they moved to a table.

"That you don't all hang out. I guess it makes sense if they split up. I could never really figure the three of you out. You were so close. It annoyed me how much you talked about them. Maybe it's because I don't have any friends like that. The three of you seemed more like family."

"They felt like family," she said sadly. "We've just drifted apart. Josie lives in Devon now," she said, keen to move the conversation away from Jack. "She works at a dog kennels."

"That sounds interesting." He chuckled. "And you're back at the castle?"

"Yes. I'm a tour guide now," she said proudly.

His eyes widened. "I always said you were a great tour guide. That's brilliant news."

"The writing's going well too. I've just started something new. Historical romance. I think it's going to end up being a series."

Stuart was impressed by her recent career choices, and the conversation flowed easily. Strangely, it was Emily who did most of the talking. She realised she didn't socialise very much any more, and it was a refreshing change to spend the evening chatting and sipping wine.

It was a couple of hours later when she finally got in a taxi and headed home. She wasn't even home when her phone beeped with a message from Stuart, saying it had been great to catch up and it would be lovely to go out again sometime.

It made her feel utterly miserable. Because she knew if she agreed to go out with him again it would be a date. And even though she'd enjoyed chatting to Stuart, the only person in the world she wanted to go on a date with was Jack.

Chapter 45

Emily threw herself into her writing. Getting lost in an imaginary world suited her perfectly. Christmas drifted by, and the new year arrived without fanfare. Eventually her enthusiasm for her new job at the castle and for her writing started to wane. She still enjoyed it, but increasingly she found it hard not to think about Jack. Surely, she'd stop missing him soon. Things were supposed to get easier. But every day she felt a little bit worse.

Towards the end of January she seemed to hit rock bottom. She decided to organise to go down to visit Josie. A change of scene would be good for her, and if she could spend some time with Josie and focus on their friendship, she might convince herself that she'd done the best thing as far as Jack was concerned. It might help her move on.

The problem was, Josie wasn't answering her phone. Emily sent her a couple of messages and got a reply to say she was crazy busy but would be in touch soon.

"I'm so annoyed," Emily grumbled to her mum. "She finally answered the phone but all she did was say she's too busy to talk. How can she possibly have no free time? I know she works long hours, but she must have five minutes at the end of the day when she could call."

Her mum started to say something, but Emily paced the kitchen and continued her rant. "I think you might have been right. This is her revenge. She made me break things off with Jack, but never had any intention of being friends with me. She's evil. I actually think she's evil." She dropped into a chair at the kitchen table.

"Maybe—"

She cut her mum off again. "I don't know why I was so upset about what an awful friend I was. She's being way worse. At least I didn't do it intentionally. I might just give up on her. I've had enough of chasing her."

"Can I speak yet?" her mum asked, pulling a casserole from the oven.

"Okay," Emily said with a small smile.

"Stop worrying about Josie. Get on with your own life. You seemed really happy at work and with the new book."

"You're right," she said reluctantly. "I should focus on the positives. I only wish things had worked out differently." She chewed her lip as she fought off tears. "Maybe I should find a writing group in Oxford," she said finally. Her mum put chicken casserole in front of her. "I'll probably feel better if I have more of a social life. I kind of enjoyed my writing group in London. In a weird way."

"That sounds like a good plan," her mum agreed.

But Emily didn't actually do anything about it. Life just plodded on until finally she hit breaking point.

It was Valentine's Day and she'd taken two tour

groups around the castle. She was in a phenomenally bad mood and directed her pent-up emotions at her mum as soon as she got home from work.

"Doug gave me a Valentine's card," she said angrily, throwing the offending item onto the coffee table as she walked into the living room. "A sympathy card basically, because he knows no one else will send me one. And some crazy old man at the bus stop came up and gave me a kiss on the cheek and wished me Happy Valentine's Day. What is wrong with people?" Her mum looked thoroughly amused. Emily dropped onto the couch. "And all the way home, all I can see is hearts – heart balloons, heart decorations, bloody hearts everywhere. And flowers! Half the men in Oxford are carrying flowers ..."

Her chin twitched then and she put a hand over her face as tears flooded her eyes. "Everyone's going on dates and I'm on my own." She sobbed and her shoulders shook. Her mum moved to her side and pulled her in for a hug. "I miss Jack," Emily spluttered. "I miss him all the time, every day."

"Then call him," her mum said.

"I can't."

"You can't really still think Josie cares what you do?"

"Not because of Josie," she said. "I was horrible to him. He won't want to know me."

"Tell him you're sorry and you didn't mean it."

"He's probably seeing someone else. It's Valentine's Day. He'll have a date."

"You don't know that. He might be missing you as much as you're missing him."

"If he missed me, he'd have called."

"And he might be thinking the same about you. At least if you call him, you'll know for sure."

"I'll think about it." She wiped the tears from her cheeks, embarrassed by her outburst.

"Fancy a glass of wine?" her mum asked.

"I thought you were going out with the girls. Your Valentine's tradition."

"I can stay in with you instead."

"Go out," Emily insisted. "I'm fine. The meltdown's over."

"Okay. But you should chill out for the evening. Have a break from the writing. It'll do you good."

Emily did as she was told and settled on the couch with a glass of white wine. The wine was probably a bad idea. She knew that after a few sips. Alcohol always affected her easily, and when she was an emotional wreck to start with, it just intensified everything.

It also made her do things she wouldn't normally do.

She'd just drained the glass when she reached for her phone.

Chapter 46

She didn't really expect Josie to answer. She hadn't the last few times she'd called.

"I'm sorry." Josie's voice came loud and manic down the phone. "Sam's taking me out for dinner and I'm in a rush to get ready. Can I call you back tomorrow?"

"No," Emily said firmly. "I'm not doing this any more." She wanted to be strong and firm, but the tears flowed freely and her voice was choked with emotion. "I understand that you're angry, but I don't think I deserve it and I'm sick of waiting for you to be my friend again."

"What?" Josie's attempt to sound confused was almost convincing. But Emily knew her too well. The acting lessons had obviously done some good. "I've just been busy with the kennels and my classes," she said. "I barely have time for anyone …"

"Well, you don't have to worry about making time for *me* any more," Emily said bitterly. "I'll save you the trouble of making excuses for why I shouldn't visit you or why you don't want to meet up."

"They weren't excuses—"

"They were! It's all excuses. You're selfish and stubborn and I'm sick of being the one that tries to fix our friendship when you're clearly not interested."

"Of course I'm interested. You're my best friend."

"Best friends don't treat each other the way you've treated me. I might have done some stupid things, but I apologised. I never wanted to hurt you. But I think you want to hurt me."

"Please, just calm down and we can talk about it properly …"

"I can't calm down," Emily shouted. "I hurt Jack. I did it on purpose and he'll probably never speak to me again. But you don't even care."

Josie was silent for a moment and when she spoke her voice was quiet and confused. "I don't understand …"

"You and Jack were my best friends." Emily choked through a sob. "And I lost you both."

"That's not true," Josie said desperately. "Of course we're still friends."

"No," Emily snapped. "We're not. I won't call you again. I don't want anything to do with you."

She ended the call and fell back on the couch, emotionally exhausted. Josie called her back five minutes later but she ignored it. Dragging herself off the couch, she went up and changed into her pyjamas. Snuggled up in bed she scrolled through her phone, hitting ignore on another call that came from Josie. A message popped up from her too, but Emily didn't even read it. Instead she went into Facebook and searched for Jack's profile. It was something she hadn't allowed herself before. But now she was desperate to glean any snippet of info about what he'd been doing since she last saw him.

She braced herself for the possibility that he was

seeing someone else and Emily would find photos of them all over his profile page. There was nothing, though. Nothing new. The last post was from six months ago and was some silly meme about football.

It occurred to her that he might have blocked her, but surely she wouldn't see anything then. She could still get into all his photos and scroll down through old posts. It was like he hadn't been online. So much for finding anything out. She was none the wiser.

She swiped away a notification about a message from Josie, and clicked on Jack's profile picture until his smiling face filled the screen. Then she lay down and stared at his photo.

She cried until she ran out of tears.

***

It was late morning when she finally crawled out of bed the next day. She forced herself to shower and get dressed.

Her mum was on the way out to her Pilates class when Emily wandered downstairs. She said goodbye and went to the kitchen in search of coffee and breakfast. It was hard to drum up any motivation to do anything. Unfortunately, she had nothing to do for the day. A distraction would do her the world of good. Quite often she had a few tour groups on Saturdays, but this weekend she was only scheduled in for Sunday afternoon.

She didn't think much of it when the doorbell rang, and then she was completely stunned to find herself holding the door open and staring at Josie.

"What are you doing here?"

"You didn't answer your phone."

"I didn't want to talk to you," she said and then hated how hurt Josie looked.

"I went to Jack's place."

Just hearing his name made Emily feel funny. "How is he?"

"I don't know. I was looking for you."

"At Jack's place?"

"Yes."

Emily scrunched her eyebrows. "I don't understand."

"I thought you'd be at Jack's place." Josie shifted her weight from foot to foot and her breath fogged in front of her face. "Can I come in?"

Emily stepped aside.

In the living room they stood looking at each other. Emily still didn't understand why she was there.

"I'm sorry," Josie said. "Everything's been so crazy with work and I'm doing these college courses too. I honestly wasn't ignoring you on purpose."

"I kept trying to be friends and you didn't want to know. Why are you even here?"

"Because you said you don't want anything to do with me." Josie's voice was a hoarse whisper and tears appeared in her eyes. "Then you wouldn't answer your phone. I woke up early and I couldn't stop thinking about what you said so I got in the car and drove here."

"I thought you were still angry with me," Emily said. "I thought you didn't want to be friends."

Josie shook her head. "What did you mean about not speaking to Jack again? Where is he? What happened?"

Emily narrowed her eyes. "I don't know," she said slowly. "I haven't seen him since the weekend you left."

Tears welled slowly in Josie's eyes and then spilled down her cheeks. "Why?"

"Because you told me not to see him again. You said we could still be friends if I didn't have anything to do with him."

"No." Josie's lips quivered and she covered her mouth as she let out a sob. She dropped onto the couch. "I didn't say that … or I didn't mean it. I was angry and rambling. I didn't think you'd actually end it with him." She looked stricken. "I thought you were together. All this time I thought you and him were together."

Emily paced the room, shaking her head. "You knew. I told you I was breaking things off with him."

"I didn't expect you actually would. I thought you were in love with him."

She stopped dead. "I was."

"But you ended it so you could stay friends with me?"

Emily looked at her pitifully. "You really thought me and Jack were still together?"

"Yes. It annoyed me that you'd never even mention his name."

"You told me not to," Emily reminded her fiercely. They looked at each other blankly for a moment as they tried to untangle the crossed wires. "Is that why you always made excuses not to talk to me? Because you were angry I was still with him?"

"No." Josie's face crumpled. "I wasn't angry,"

she said. "I was jealous."

"Of me and Jack?" Emily stared in confusion. "But you've got Sam. I thought you were happy."

"I am. I love Sam. It wasn't jealousy in that way. I was jealous that you two were still friends. I felt like you'd pushed me aside. I thought you were together, happily getting on with your lives without me." Tears sprang to her eyes. "I spoke to Jack once, right after I found you together. We had a huge row and then he didn't call me again and you never mentioned him so I thought he didn't want to know me."

Emily sat down beside Josie. "I missed you."

"I missed you too," Josie said, sniffling. "I'm so sorry."

"Me too," Emily said as they embraced.

Josie wiped her tears on the sleeve of her jumper and looked seriously at Emily. "We need to find Jack."

"I don't think he'll speak to me," Emily said. "I said some things to him …"

"He'll speak to you," Josie said confidently. "He loves you."

Emily had missed that about Josie. Her unwavering optimism.

"He wasn't at home."

"He'll be at work," Emily said, glancing at her watch. Were they actually going to find him? Was she finally going to see him again? She felt anxious at the thought.

"I went to the phone shop before I came here," Josie said. "Apparently he doesn't work there any more. They told me he left abruptly almost six months ago. That's all they knew."

Whenever Emily had thought about Jack, she'd imagined him in his old routines. But all this time he hadn't been working in the phone shop. She needed to know where he was and check he was okay.

"Can you call him?" she said to Josie.

She pulled her phone from her pocket and tapped on the buttons. "He never answers," she said, holding it to her ear. After a minute she shrugged and put the phone away again. "You can try. He might answer if he sees it's you calling."

Emily hurried upstairs to get her phone but had already decided she wouldn't call him by the time she was back in the living room.

"I won't know what to say on the phone," she said to Josie. "We should go to his place again and see if he's there. It'll be better to talk in person."

Josie drove them over to his place but refused to go in when they got there. "It'll be better if you talk to him alone. You sort things out with him, and then we'll see if he'll ever be friends with me again."

"He might not even talk to me." Emily peered out of the car window and craned her neck to look up at his building. She might be about to see him, and she had no idea how she felt about it. Excited, but that was wrapped up with a lot of fear and nerves. "What if he's seeing someone else?"

"No," Josie said. "No way. Just go. I'll wait until you get in the building. And if you need me to pick you up later just call. I'll go and see my mum and dad."

"Okay." Emily undid her seatbelt and reached over to hug Josie.

"Tell him I'm sorry," Josie said quietly.

Emily promised she would as she stepped out of the car. She was a nervous wreck as she walked to the door and pressed the button beside his name. Her heart was going crazy. Then she heard his voice on the intercom, and she had to put a hand on the wall to steady herself.

"It's Emily," she said. "Can I come up? I need to talk to you."

There was a pause before the door buzzed and she pushed it quickly open. Up at his door, she'd just raised her arm to knock when it slowly opened.

"Hi," he said.

She took a step back. It was so strange seeing him again. He looked so good, and she got the faintest whiff of his familiar scent. All she wanted to do was grab hold of him and hug him to her. There was just the issue of the door between them. He'd only opened it a crack. She realised he was waiting for her to say something, and now that she was in front of him she had no idea where to start.

"Have you got time to talk?" She nodded behind him, hoping he'd invite her in.

His hand gripped the door by his head and he looked nervous, as though he was searching for an excuse to get rid of her.

"It's not really the best time."

"Okay." When she glanced behind him, he moved his head, blocking her view. He was hiding something. Or someone. Emily felt like she'd been punched in the gut just thinking about him with someone else.

"The place is a mess," he said.

"I don't care." Why wouldn't he let her in? At

least let her apologise. Her eyes filled with tears and she blinked them away. "I wanted to say I'm sorry."

His features softened and his arm relaxed. The door opened a fraction wider. She automatically looked behind him into the living room. When she took a step closer, he blocked the way again.

"We could go out somewhere," he said quickly. "I'll get my jacket …"

"It's not a mess," she said, pushing the door open and stepping around him. Her breath caught in her throat as she crossed the living room.

Beside the couch she stared down at a pile of books. The pretty pink and white cover was all too familiar. They were stacked in a column like an overgrown Jenga tower. A circular white tray lay on top of them. There was a matching tower of books at the other end of the couch.

"You made side tables from my books?" she whispered.

It was rare that he was ever lost for words, but it took him a moment to speak.

"I might have a bit of a problem," he said lightly. "I can't seem to walk past a bookshop without checking to see if they have your book. And if I find one I have to buy it."

"You bought my books," she whispered, bending down for a better look at the unique construction.

A smile flashed onto his lips and he shoved his hands into his pockets. "They love me at WHSmith's. Roll on the fifth of March so I can get some diversity around this place."

She ran a hand along the spines of her books and fought off tears. "You know when my next book is coming out." She straightened up and stared at him in disbelief. "I thought you hated me."

"No." He moved away from her and paced around the back of the couch. "That would be cheaper."

She fought for something to say, unable to take it in. She thought he'd moved on with his life. But he'd been thinking about her all this time?

"I thought you'd forgotten about me."

"No." He looked at her like she'd said something completely idiotic. "Of course not."

"But I was so awful to you last time I was here. I assumed you hated me."

"No, I never hated you. You were right. I wasn't good enough for you. I didn't deserve you."

"Jack." Her shoulders drooped as she sighed. "That's not true. I only said it to hurt you. So you'd be so angry you wouldn't want to be with me anyway."

"It was true. I was just sailing through life with no real direction."

"But I didn't care what you did for a living. I only cared about you."

He didn't look at her, but stopped pacing and gripped the back of the couch. "I changed jobs. I thought if I sorted my life out that maybe—"

She moved beside him and clamped her hand over his. The warmth of his skin against hers sent her heart rate skyrocketing. "I didn't care about your job. I just felt so guilty about Josie. That's the only reason I said it. I'm so sorry, Jack."

Pulling his hand gently from hers, he stepped away, moving to sit on the edge of the couch. "I heard you got back together with Stuart."

"No." She shook her head. Why did he think that?

Her mind raced back to the last time she'd seen Stuart, and she remembered seeing Clive that night too. Tears blurred her vision and she blinked them away. "I bumped into him once. The same day I bumped into Clive. He told you …" She trailed off. "I'm not with Stuart," she said firmly.

Jack's forehead creased as he frowned. He'd lost weight, Emily noticed. He looked well for it.

"I was going to call you," he said. "Once I sorted myself out. But then I heard you were with Stuart. I thought you'd moved on."

"No." She sat beside him, placed a hand on his cheek. "I missed you every day."

"I missed you too." He didn't move, just looked at her in disbelief.

"And you forgive me?" Tears rolled down her cheeks and she touched her forehead to his. "Please forgive me."

He pulled away from her, looking at her in confusion.

"Please," she whispered.

Finally, he brought his hands to her face and wiped her damp cheeks with his thumbs. "There's nothing to forgive," he said.

Then he pulled her face to his and gently kissed her lips. "Just promise you won't leave me again."

"Never." She trailed her hands through his hair and laughed through her tears.

There was no way in the world she'd ever let him go again.

Chapter 47

"Shall I wear a shirt, or is a T-shirt fine?" It was a week later and Emily sat on Jack's bed watching him get dressed, fresh from the shower. "Do you think Sam will be wearing a shirt?"

"We're only going to the pub. I don't think it matters what you wear."

"But you're all dressed up." His gaze roamed over her grey jersey dress. She had thick tights on and a pair of knee-high boots. A new outfit she'd treated herself to.

"I'll wear a shirt," he said decisively.

"Are you nervous?" Emily asked with a smirk.

"No." He pushed his arms into a crisp blue shirt.

"I think you are." She moved to stand in front of him as he buttoned the shirt.

"I'm not," he insisted. "But we're going out with my ex-girlfriend and her new boyfriend. I need to make sure I look better than him."

She laughed and pulled on his collar to kiss him. "I'm certain you will."

"So my shirt looks all right?" He took a step back.

"Well, you looked better without it," she said cheekily. "But yes, it looks good."

He grinned as he pulled her closer again. "Did I tell you how much I missed you?"

"I think you mentioned it. Did I tell you I missed you more?"

"Once or twice," he replied with a grin.

They'd spent the past week arguing about who'd missed who the most. It had been such an amazing week. Whenever they weren't working, they were together. He'd even been over to her place to have dinner with her and her mum. The three of them had had a wonderful evening together.

Everything was falling into place, and they were finally going on the double date that they'd talked about all those months ago.

"Are you sure it's not going to be awkward with you and Josie?"

"I spoke to her on the phone," Jack said. "Everything's fine. Stop worrying. Weren't you complaining that she hasn't made any effort to see you in the last six months? She's finally coming to visit and you're worrying about it."

"I just want everything to be like it used to be between the three of us."

"That would be weird," he said, smirking.

She poked him in the ribs. "You know what I mean."

"Come on. Let's go or we'll be late."

***

Josie had chosen to meet at The Head of the River. She'd said she wanted to take Sam down to the river and show him where the three of them used to hang out. They only had a weekend in Oxford, and she wanted to show him all her favourite places.

Emily had been a little anxious about the three of them meeting up. It felt like so long since they'd been together, and she was nervous that with everything they'd been through it might be uncomfortable. She hoped it wasn't a bad idea. It was only drinks, though. Josie and Sam were having dinner with Josie's parents so they couldn't stay long.

When she saw Josie standing next to the bar, beaming at them, Emily relaxed immediately. They hugged tightly, while Jack and Sam shook hands.

Emily broke away from Josie and turned to Sam. "It's so lovely to finally meet you."

"You too," he said. "I've heard all about you."

She liked him immediately, because she knew that wasn't entirely true. At least he hadn't heard much about Emily until a week ago. Josie had told her that's what had made her realise how bad things had got: when Sam didn't even know who Emily was. Josie had kept everything that happened to herself, not wanting to talk to anyone about it. Unfortunately, that meant she'd hardly mentioned her to Sam.

There was an atmosphere between Jack and Josie that made Emily glad they were only meeting for a drink. They didn't hug when they saw each other, just exchanged a strained greeting before Jack ordered drinks at the bar.

"We'll grab a table," Josie said. They took their drinks to sit beside a window overlooking the river.

"I thought you said it would be fine with you and Josie?"

"I only said that to make you feel better."

"That was really awkward."

"Yep." He paid the barman then handed Emily a

glass of wine. "At least they have dinner plans. They'll probably only stay for one drink."

"I wanted us all to be friends again," Emily complained.

Jack took a sip of his beer. "I'm still annoyed with her."

"Well get over it," Emily said fiercely. "And quick. I don't want things to be weird."

He raised his eyebrows, then planted a kiss on her cheek. "Yes, boss." As they walked across the pub, Jack leaned to whisper in her ear. "I look better than Sam, don't I?"

"Hmm?" She pursed her lips together as though deep in thought. He gave her a discreet nudge and she let out a laugh that drew Josie's attention.

"What's so funny?"

"Nothing," she said, making the atmosphere tense again.

"Josie was saying you recently changed jobs?" Sam said to Jack when he took a seat opposite him.

"Yeah. I work on the non-emergency ambulances. Driving patients to and from their hospital appointments."

"I'll bet that's an interesting job."

Jack nodded. "I'm enjoying it. When I was younger I wanted to be a paramedic. I actually started the foundation course at university, but I dropped out before I finished it. It's good to be on the right track again."

"Can you progress to paramedic eventually then?" Sam asked

"It's a possibility. If I could get on as student paramedic and study while I work then I'd probably go for it. I'm enjoying what I do at the moment so I'll just wait and see what comes up."

"I never knew you wanted to be a paramedic," Josie said, propping herself up with an elbow on the table. "Why did you drop out of the course?"

"My dad died and money was tight. I needed an income. The phone shop was the first thing I found." He shrugged as if it was no big deal, but Emily knew differently from the conversation she'd had with him about it earlier in the week. He'd told her all about his dad and how close they were. She suspected even mentioning that difficult time around his dad's death was a big deal for Jack. Under the table, she found his hand and gave it a squeeze.

"How's *your* job?" Emily asked Josie, sure that Jack would appreciate the subject change.

"It's great," Josie said, smiling dreamily. "But it's hard work."

"That's because you've taken on about a million different things at once," Sam said with a raised eyebrow. "She never stops."

"Because I love it," Josie said. "I've been trying to expand the business. I took a course in dog grooming." She glanced at Sam and smiled. "It's not as easy as you'd think," she told them. "I thought it would be like being a hairdresser for dogs, but I didn't really think about the fact that dogs won't always sit still."

Sam grinned. "Tell them about the time you accidentally gave a poodle a Mohawk."

Josie struggled to swallow a mouthful of wine before she started giggling. "My clippers broke while I was in the middle of grooming him. So I'd cut off all his fur apart from one streak down his back!" She laughed again and they all joined in.

Sam took over the story. "She turned up at my place with the poor dog and finished him off with my shaver!"

"I didn't have much choice," Josie said. "The owners were about to come and pick him up." She immediately launched in to another story and then another, keeping them all amused and the atmosphere light.

Emily barely noticed time going by. They got another round of drinks and when they finished those they discussed whether anyone wanted another.

"I'll have a soft drink," Emily said. "But I can't have any more alcohol on an empty stomach."

"What are you guys doing for dinner?" Josie asked. "Eating here?"

"Probably." Jack looked to Emily who nodded her approval.

Josie turned to Sam. "Shall we eat here too?"

"I thought you had plans with your parents?" Emily said.

"No." Josie grinned cheekily. "Sam just wanted to have an excuse to leave in case it was awkward. It's fine, isn't it?" she asked him.

"It was until you told them that!"

She leaned her head on his shoulder. "But they're my best friends. I tell them everything."

"I'll get another round," Jack said, chuckling as he stood. "And find some menus."

"I'll give you a hand," Sam offered.

"Just get me an orange juice," Emily said to Jack.

"Don't worry. I've seen you drunk," he said

lightly. "I'm not risking that again."

She glared at him and he moved away quickly with a silly smile.

"Sounds like there's a story there," Sam said, then followed Jack to the bar.

"When were you drunk?" Josie asked.

"Ages ago," Emily said. "I swore Jack to secrecy."

Josie frowned. "While we were still together?"

"Yes." Emily sighed. Things had been going so well, and she had the feeling this conversation might just ruin the evening. "But it wasn't like that. I was out on a date and Jack happened to be in the same bar."

"Tell me the story," Josie said softly. "I hate us having secrets. That's what upset me most when I found out about you and Jack. I hated that the two of you had secrets from me."

Emily bit her lip and then told Josie all about the night she went on a date and got horribly drunk. They ended up laughing about it, and Emily was pleased that things were finally getting back to normal between them.

"Aww." Emily smiled as she glanced at the bar. "They're bonding!"

The drinks were lined up on the bar, but Jack and Sam were deep in conversation and seemed to have forgotten about Josie and Emily.

"What do you think of Sam?" Josie asked.

"I think he's great." Emily grinned at her. "Perfect for you." It was true. Josie was so relaxed around him. She wasn't quite as manic as usual, as though his calm nature balanced her out a little.

"I love him," Josie said. "So much."

Emily reached over and squeezed her hand, just as the men headed back with their drinks.

"I've got a bone to pick with you," Josie said, glaring up at Jack. "You let me believe you'd cleaned the apartment that day when it was actually Emily who'd done it!"

"You told her that story?" Jack said accusingly to Emily.

"It was you who brought it up," Emily reminded him.

"True." He shuffled his chair closer to hers when he sat down. "I'd forgotten that bit. I was only thinking about pulling you out of a taxi and carrying you up three flights of stairs!"

Her hand shot to her mouth. "Did you?" She'd had no idea about that.

"The lift was out of order," he said, shaking his head. "Good job you're a skinny little thing!"

She punched his arm lightly at his mocking tone.

"Let's order food," he said, passing out menus. "I'm starving."

***

There was only the last shred of daylight remaining when they left the pub early in the evening, but Josie suggested they walk a little way down the river so she could show Sam the Boathouse.

Emily had her arm through Jack's, gripping him tightly for warmth. After the heat of the pub it was a shock to be outside in the frosty air.

"It's a bit different in the summer," Josie told

Sam when they reached the dark, unoccupied building. It was hardly recognisable.

"I'll be honest," Sam said, zipping his coat all the way up and raising his shoulders. "It's hard to imagine."

"It's all green and lush," Josie said. "And there are geese and ducks everywhere. It's really lovely."

"Just bring me back in the summer," Sam said, shifting his weight from foot to foot.

"We can all come in the summer," Josie said, looking to Emily and Jack who nodded their agreement. "We better head back," she continued. "We've got a busy day tomorrow. Are you working, Emily? I thought we might sneak onto one of your tours."

"I'm not working," she said. "But I can take you on a private tour if you want?"

"Will you wear the costume like it's a real tour?" Josie asked excitedly.

"No," Emily said with a laugh. "Definitely not!"

"Spoilsport. It'll be fun anyway. I'll message you in the morning to arrange a time." Josie gave her a big squeeze and then Emily hugged Sam goodbye, telling him how nice it was to meet him. When she let go, Josie and Jack were locked in a tight embrace.

She smiled as she watched them, realising that it was the first time she'd seen them be affectionate with each other without her being hit by a sledgehammer of jealousy.

Jack kissed the side of Josie's head before he released her. They shouted goodbye as Josie and Sam made their way back towards the road.

"We should go too," Emily said. "It's freezing."

Jack put an arm around her shoulder, and she didn't comment when he continued walking away from the road. They stopped at the bench a little further along, and she leaned close to him when they sat down.

"That was really lovely, wasn't it?" Emily said.

"Way better than I expected," Jack agreed. "It's good to see Josie so settled."

"Definitely." Emily blew into her hands. "Can we go now? I'm freezing."

"I wanted to ask you something …"

"Ask me quick then before I turn to ice!"

He looked at her seriously. "Will you move in with me?"

She laughed. "Jack!"

"What? I want to live with you? Why is that so funny?"

"Because we've only been dating a week. Of course I won't move in with you." She shook her head. "Have you gone crazy?"

"Maybe." He turned to face her and his features were tense. "I know that technically we've only been together for a week. But I also know how I feel about you. I want to be with you forever. Moving in together doesn't seem crazy to me … it seems natural."

She squeezed his hand. "Moving in together feels natural to me as well. I just think it's too soon. Why rush it?"

He opened his mouth to say something but she cut him off.

"I don't want to miss out on anything with you. I want to go on proper dates with you, and to date you for at least a few months before we move in together. I want moving in together to be an exciting next step, not something we rush into. I'm not Josie – I don't want to move in with you because it's convenient."

He looked at her seriously. "Can we try not to bring Josie into every conversation?"

"Sorry," she muttered. It also wasn't a habit she wanted to get into.

He sighed. "I'm not saying move in with me because it's convenient. I'm saying move in with me because I love you ... And I know I'm probably ruining your schedule by saying that too soon but I do love you so—"

She cut him off with a kiss. "I love you too," she said while her lips still brushed against his.

"You're still not going to move in with me are you?" he asked.

"Three months," she said happily. "Date me for three months and then I'll move in with you."

"Are you allowed to stay at my place during this dating phase?"

She nodded eagerly. "But maximum three nights a week otherwise it's like we're living together anyway."

"You really do like to plan, don't you?"

She smiled and turned to look out over the darkening water. "It's a good plan."

"Okay, but if you change your mind next week, I'm still going to make you wait three months."

"I'm not going to change my mind," she said lightly. "I like to stick to my plans."

They slipped into an easy silence, and she nestled into his chest when he put an arm around her and pulled her closer.

"Just so I get the timeframe right," Jack said, breaking the silence. "How long do I have to wait to ask you to marry me? I'd hate for you to say no because I ask too soon or on the wrong day of the week or something."

She looked up at him, surprised by the lack of teasing in his eyes. He bit his lip. "I love you so much, I'd ask you right now. But the fact that you said no to moving in together seems like a bad indicator." His mouth twitched to a lazy smile then.

Emily couldn't hold his gaze. She watched the ripples on the water as her eyes filled with tears. She loved him too. So much. And if he asked her to marry him now, she'd say yes. But she didn't want him to ask yet.

His hand gently rubbed her back. "Sorry," he whispered. "I didn't mean to make you uncomfortable."

She turned back to him. "One year." The tears fell down her face as she spoke. "Ask me one year from today."

His features softened. "You don't like surprises, do you?"

She laughed through her tears. "Not at all."

"In that case I may as well tell you, I'm going to ask you right here on this bench."

Her grin was wide and she swiped the tears from her cheeks. "Do *you* like surprises?"

He shook his head. "I'm not a big fan."

"In that case, you may as well know that one year from today, on this bench, I'm going to say yes." She beamed at him. "And I'm going to be the happiest person in the world."

"I hate to ruin your plans ..." He leaned over and gently brushed his lips against hers. "But it'll be me who's the happiest person in the world."

THE END

Coming February 2019!

Whispers at the Bluebell Inn
(Hope Cove book 4)

Rumours travel fast in a village...

Josie loves her new life in the country with **Sam**. But she has a secret that she doesn't want anyone to know. Unfortunately, it's hard to keep anything to yourself in a tiny village.

Lizzie is adjusting to motherhood, and finding it more demanding than she ever expected. Life has become a haze of sleep deprivation and dirty nappies, and it's taking its toll on her relationship with **Max**.

Emily finally has the man of her dreams. However, life with **Jack** isn't as straightforward as she expected. A certain ex-girlfriend and money worries wreak havoc on their relationship.

As the three couples reunite in the peaceful Devon scenery, what better place to catch up than the local pub? There are laughs, tears and rumours aplenty.

But one thing soon becomes clear: you shouldn't believe everything you hear at the Bluebell Inn...

Other books by Hannah Ellis

The Cottage at Hope Cove (Hope Cove book 1)
Escape to Oakbrook Farm (Hope Cove book 2)
Whispers at the Bluebell Inn (Hope Cove 4)
Always With You
Friends Like These
Christmas with Friends (Friends Like These book 2)
My Kind of Perfect (Friends Like These book 3)
Beyond the Lens (Lucy Mitchell Book 1)
Beneath These Stars (Lucy Mitchell Book 2)

Acknowledgements

Many thanks to the people who read and gave feedback at the various stages: Anthea Kirk, Nikkita Blake, Sarah-Jane Fraser, Michele Morgan Salls, Sarah Walker, Sue Oxley, Kathy Robinson, Hazel Baxter, Dua Roberts and Stephen Ellis.

Thanks to Katherine Trail for another great editing job. It's a pleasure working with you.

Massive thanks to my Mario for everything you do.

Last but not least, a big thank you to my wonderful readers.

Printed in Great Britain
by Amazon

43272471R00232